The Last Death of the Year

ALSO BY SOPHIE HANNAH

Little Face
Hurting Distance
The Point of Rescue
The Other Half Lives
A Room Swept White
Lasting Damage
Kind of Cruel
The Carrier
The Orphan Choir
The Telling Error
Pictures Or It Didn't Happen
A Game for All the Family
The Narrow Bed
Did You See Melody?
Haven't They Grown
The Couple at the Table
No One Would Do What the Lamberts Have Done

HERCULE POIROT MYSTERIES

The Monogram Murders
Closed Casket
The Mystery of Three Quarters
The Killings at Kingfisher Hill
Hercule Poirot's Silent Night

NON-FICTION

How to Hold a Grudge
Happiness: A Mystery—and 66 Attempts to Solve It
The Double Best Method

The Last Death of the Year

THE NEW HERCULE POIROT MYSTERY

Sophie Hannah

WILLIAM MORROW
An Imprint of HarperCollinsPublishers

Without limiting the exclusive rights of any author, contributor or the publisher of this publication, any unauthorized use of this publication to train generative artificial intelligence (AI) technologies is expressly prohibited. HarperCollins also exercise their rights under Article 4(3) of the Digital Single Market Directive 2019/790 and expressly reserve this publication from the text and data mining exception.

This is a work of fiction. Names, characters, places, and incidents are products of the author's imagination or are used fictitiously and are not to be construed as real. Any resemblance to actual events, locales, organizations, or persons, living or dead, is entirely coincidental.

AGATHA CHRISTIE, POIROT, the Agatha Christie Signature and the AC monogram Logo are registered trademarks of Agatha Christie Limited in the UK and elsewhere.

www.agathachristie.com

THE LAST DEATH OF THE YEAR. Copyright © 2025 by Agatha Christie Limited. All rights reserved. Printed in the United States of America. No part of this book may be used or reproduced in any manner whatsoever without written permission except in the case of brief quotations embodied in critical articles and reviews. For information, address HarperCollins Publishers, 195 Broadway, New York, NY 10007. In Europe, HarperCollins Publishers, Macken House, 39/40 Mayor Street Upper, Dublin 1, D01 C9W8, Ireland.

HarperCollins books may be purchased for educational, business, or sales promotional use. For information, please email the Special Markets Department at SPsales@harpercollins.com.

harpercollins.com

FIRST EDITION

Designed by Michele Cameron

Library of Congress Cataloging-in-Publication Data has been applied for.

ISBN 978-0-06-342451-7
ISBN 978-0-06-346679-1 (international edition)

25 26 27 28 29 LBC 5 4 3 2 1

For Alex Michaelides, my wonderful friend and fellow Agatha superfan, whose eager anticipation of my Poirot novels and enjoyment of them once they appear is one of my favorite reasons for writing them.

The Last Death of the Year

PROLOGUE

New Year's Resolutions

Before I properly knew any of the inhabitants of the house with three names, I knew what each of their New Year's resolutions was for 1933. Let me tell you, it is as good a way as any to get to know a person. If deeper or accelerated acquaintance is what you're after, then December 31 is the perfect day on which to meet somebody for the first time, for you will hear all about which habit they wish to abandon or introduce as soon as January rolls around.

I expect you would not believe me if I told you it is possible to solve a murder simply by reading a list of all the suspects' New Year's resolutions, while knowing no more about any of them.

Unlikely as it sounds, it is the truth. Though I do not intend to imply any comprehension of motive or anything like that. What I mean to say is that if one sought merely to separate the guilty from the innocent, let me assure you that on the small Greek island of Lamperos, as the hour staggered toward the summit of the final day of December, it was entirely possible to work out who had committed murder and who had not if one only read with sufficient care the list of resolutions I have provided below—and, indeed, that is why I plan to share that list with you before I tell you anything else, though I admit it is an unconventional way to begin a story.

Naturally, I have Poirot's approval. "*Mon ami,* why not let your readers meet our cast of suspects *précisément* as you yourself met them?" he said, eyes glowing green and bright. "The resolutions they wrote down were the first significant morsels of information we had about them, *n'est-ce pas*? The words they each dropped into the bowl?"

Since Poirot and I were part of the assembled company at Liakada Bay that night, I shall include us on the list for completeness' sake—and also to give you two reliable examples of what one might write on such an occasion if one were not planning to commit murder.

Here, then, are the collected New Year's resolutions of the people present that night, December 31, 1932, at Liakada Bay:

1. Edward Catchpool (your narrator: Inspector Edward Catchpool of Scotland Yard, since I neglected to introduce myself at the start)—to swim in the sea every single day, without exception and irrespective of temperature or weather.

2. Hercule Poirot—to discontinue the practice of proceeding directly from one event or appointment to another. Instead, to reserve time, in between bouts of activity, in which to do nothing at all, or for spontaneous, unplanned outings.

3. Nash Athanasiou (real name Nathaniel, our host on Lamperos and leader of the group at what he called "The House of Perpetual Welcome," what the Liakada Bay locals called *Spíti Athanasiou,* and what the exclusively English and American residents of the house all called The Spitty)—to complete ten practical assignments, to be devised for him

by Austin Lanyon and Matthew Fair, (his two closest friends and chief advisors at the house), designed to turn him into a better living example of the fruits of the spirit: Love, Joy, Peace, Long-suffering, Gentleness, Goodness, Meekness, Temperance, Faith and the most important one: Forgiveness. (One assignment for each "fruit', he specified, and the challenges should be maximally taxing.)

4. Austin Lanyon—to read and attempt to write poetry every day.

5. Matthew Fair—to be tidier, less forgetful and more punctual.

6. Olive Haslop—to be open, always, to learning new things and being proven wrong, and never to allow closed-mindedness to afflict her.

7. Rhoda Haslop—to write a formal essay on the topic of the greatest of all the fruits of the spirit, Forgiveness, in order to understand it more thoroughly and practice it more effectively.

8. Charles Counsell—to say nothing in someone's absence, to a third party, that he would not be equally willing to say in their presence.

9. Thirza Davis—to create a better and fairer world by never giving up on sound reason or justice.

10. Betlinde (called "Belty" by everybody) Ricks—to wake earlier and not waste the start of any glorious day in this beautiful Greek paradise.

11. Pearl St. Germain—to have said "yes" to a proposal of marriage from the man she loves by this time next year, having first persuaded him *his* resolution should be to make that proposal without further delay.

That was without doubt the hardest list I have ever had to type, and not only because the words "a proposal of marriage from the man she loves" in relation to the romance-addled Pearl St. Germain made me wince as my fingers tapped them into existence on the page. No, what made a particular agony of the task was my ability to see so clearly now what I did not perceive at the time. Today, the wickedness and the guilt positively leap from the page, but they did nothing of the sort last New Year's Eve, nor in the days that followed. Poirot didn't spot it either, though he is the shrewdest, most keen-eyed man I know. He, of course, was the one who pointed it out eventually—though not, sadly, in time to save the lives that were lost.

All of which is to say: while it is and always was *possible* to work out from the above list who was planning to commit murder, not all possibilities are realized, and that one, fatally, was not. Furthermore, when Poirot finally worked out the truth, the list played no part in leading him to the correct conclusion.

Why? That is easy to answer: because, like me, he was comprehensively distracted by the twelfth resolution—the one I have not included in the above list, which contained not merely the word "murder" and the prospective victim's name, but also the clearly stated intention to commit that crime.

CHAPTER I

Arrival on Lamperos

The island of Lamperos, positioned in the Aegean Sea between the larger islands of Skiathos and Skopelos, was quite the most beautiful place I had ever visited—and the wonder of it started before one even arrived. As our boat sailed closer on the last day of the year of 1932, I could scarcely believe the vivid colors that sprang forth to greet us. Living in England, one imagines that Mother Nature is a more cautious, understated sort. It turns out that she is far more flamboyant off the coast of Greece: positively riotous when it comes to the brightness of every color. If it were not for the chill in the air, I should not have believed this was winter.

"Look, Poirot!" were the only words I could manage as I gazed at the azure sea and sands so blond they were almost white. "It is perfect." We had almost reached the shore, and the port of Lamperos Town. I could see tiny figures in the distance—between ten and twenty people, no doubt waiting for the boat to take them back out to mainland Greece: the reverse of the journey Poirot and I had just undertaken.

"Yes, perfect—if one enjoys a large amount of sand and cold, salty water," my Belgian friend replied. The green that normally confined itself to his eyes had spread to the rest of his face, I noticed, though I had asked him twice if he was feeling seasick and he had denied it. "Also, roads too rocky and uneven for motorcars," he grumbled. "Do you know, Catchpool, that the only dependable means of getting around Lamperos are by foot, by bicycle or on a horse? There is only one short road—one!—along which motor vehicles would be able to drive. They do not, for there is nowhere for them to go at either end. Then why build such a road in the first place? It is madness, Catchpool."

It all sounded wonderful to me. An island this small with a circumference made up almost entirely of beaches and bays—it was my idea of heaven on earth. In the approach to Christmas last year, Poirot and I had spent some time on the Norfolk coast. Ever since, I had been unable to banish from my mind the knowledge that some people—ordinary folk like me, not only the especially wealthy—lived their entire lives within easy strolling distance of the sea. My new awareness of this inconvenient fact was becoming rather a problem, since my job as a police inspector was at the undeniably landlocked Scotland Yard, and my favorite of all my friends, Hercule Poirot, was also very happily resident in London.

Determined to warn me in even more detail, he went on, "Do you know, also, that the horses here are particularly small? They have the special little native breed—the Lamperos Ponies, they call them. Less than four feet in height."

"Sounds ingenious to me," I said merrily. "One wouldn't want huge beasts lumbering about on a tiny island."

"And have I told you—no, I do not believe I have—that when we arrive at the port, we will nevertheless not yet have arrived? Even after all of these buses and boats we have already endured?"

He had a point there. I had never before undertaken a journey requiring quite so many transportation changes in such

The Last Death of the Year

a short space of time. Before the gloriousness of Lamperos at close range had perked me up, I had been feeling quite exhausted, having engaged in what felt like a year's worth of damp and inelegant clambering into and out of various moving contraptions.

"At the port of Lamperos Town, our friend Monsieur Nash will meet us with a smaller boat, to take us around the island to his home, Spíti Athanasiou," said Poirot. "It is the most straightforward way to get there, I am told—but why, Catchpool, can we not be taken straight to Liakada Bay in *this* boat? That is what I would like to know."

"Tell me more about the island," I said, preparing to approve of every aspect and characteristic of the place. "And stop encouraging me to resent our destination in advance. It was very kind of you to invite me to tag along, and I'm afraid you won't succeed in spoiling it for me, no matter how grumpy you are. I've been looking forward to this holiday."

I knew I did not need to remind Poirot that this was my hard-earned, post-Christmas break after a cheerless week spent in my childhood home with my parents, who seemed lately to dislike each other every bit as much as they disapproved of me. Had he not invited me to join him on his New Year's holiday on a Greek island precisely to cheer me up after that very ordeal?

He had been far more enthusiastic then: "*Mon ami,*" he had said, gripping my arm. "You will love the tiny island of Lamperos. We will be staying in the most beautiful place there, Liakada Bay. It has sunshine all day long, even throughout the winter, and the house that will accommodate us is said to be the most extraordinary architectural creation. There are large stone terraces extending out from most of the rooms, on many different levels. Our host will be a young monsieur by the name of Nathaniel Athanasiou, known as Nash. He has told me he wishes for my friend Catchpool to be the very good friend of him also. Others live in the house too—all of whom wish to be our very good friends even before they have met us. Does that not sound appealing?"

I should probably have questioned him more extensively before agreeing to come to Lamperos, but I did not, largely because of the proximity of the sea to the house he had described. I had learned something about myself in the past year: days when I swim amid foaming waves and get to plunge my feet into the sand of the seabed and smell that tang of salt in the air are better days for me than when I do not, by a considerable order of magnitude. I had swum daily while Poirot and I were in Norfolk last December, but the house we had stayed in was atop a cliff, and getting all the way down and up again was a somewhat hazardous enterprise. Poirot, as a result, had known exactly what to tell me about the prospective Greek holiday: "At Liakada Bay, the sea is an easy walk from the house, I am told. Mere footsteps away. And remember, unlike Norfolk, Lamperos has the sunshine every day."

This struck me as a little implausible, but Poirot insisted: "It is rumored to be Greece's sunniest island. Also, you will not be bothered by the jellyfish in winter. They only come in the summer."

He seemed inordinately keen for me to accompany him, which should have made me suspicious, but did not.

"I do not know a great deal about Lamperos," Poirot said now in response to my request to hear more about the island. "All I know is . . ." I smiled at his definition of "not knowing a great deal," as he settled into his narration: Lamperos was prone to earthquakes, so we would need to watch out for them, though it was extremely unlikely that one would coincide with our visit. Equally unlikely was that we would suffer the same fate as whichever daughter of a Greek god it was who had first been turned into a wolf, then kidnapped and brought to Lamperos, only to be kidnapped back again; I could not remember all the details, as I hadn't given the tale my full attention.

Much more recently, the famous English war poet, James Gresham-Graham, author of "If, for a better day . . .", died in 1915 at the age of 18 on a French hospital ship that was moored off the island's coast. He was buried on Lamperos, just a short walk from Liakada Bay. "Then more death came to these shores," Poirot said sadly. "In 1918, nearly half of the island's inhabitants died of the Spanish Flu. The population of two thousand was reduced to only one thousand."

Some of those, I imagined, lived in the little white houses I could see dotted all over what Poirot had described as "the famous Lamperos Mountain" and the surrounding hills.

No sooner had we disembarked from the boat than we were met by our host, Nathaniel Athanasiou, a tall, thin man with hair and eyes so dark they looked black. He wore a blue suit that might once have been smart but was now shabby, and had a slightly nervous manner when he insisted that Poirot and I call him Nash; it had been his nickname since childhood, he told us in a justificatory tone, as if afraid of our ridicule. "At least until we get to The Spitty," he added. "That is what we all call the house. *Spíti* is 'house' in Greek. Once we arrive there, I am *Próti Foní*."

I frowned to myself as he and Poirot walked on ahead, wondering what these words meant. Surely not that we would be required to start calling him something different once we arrived at his home . . .

"This is Rasmus, and that is his beloved *Pelagia*." Nash pointed to a man with tanned skin who might have been anywhere between fifty and seventy, and who had neither hair nor eyebrows. He was standing about twenty feet away, leaning against a dilapidated mess of splintering wood that seemed to be trying to pass itself off as a boat. I heard a sharp intake of breath from Poirot, by my side.

Having looked around for Rasmus's female companion and spotted nobody at all—he seemed to have placed himself where he was in order to avoid proximity to all other people—I worked out that *Pelagia* must be the name of his boat. This proved an accurate guess.

"Shall we hop on board?" Nash suggested. As the three of us approached, Rasmus nodded and climbed back onto his craft without looking at any of us or uttering a single word. "He speaks no English," Nash explained, "but he somehow understands everything. I have been told he is from Estonia, but also that he was born in Norway. I don't suppose it matters. The wonderful thing about Rasmus is that he is always ready to take one back and forth between Liakada Bay and Lamperos Town, and to any of the island's other bays and coves. He really is a marvel. I cannot tell you what language he speaks, however. He does not tend to say much in any tongue and seems only to understand direct instructions to him. He won't understand any of what I am saying now, for instance. It's only when he is required to assist us that our words seem to make sense to him."

As he placed his first foot into the *Pelagia*, leaning on my arm, Poirot murmured, "*Que Dieu nous protège.*" His skin looked suddenly quite green again as the frothing waves started to rock us back and forth.

"Do not worry, the boat is quite safe," Nash assured him, looking and sounding worried himself. It felt almost as if he intended to imply that the boat was perhaps the only safe thing . . . but I told myself not to be so fanciful. Surely, on a beautiful island like Lamperos, there could be no cause for alarm, especially when one was off, as Poirot and I were, to spend some time in the company of those so keen to befriend us.

Nash's comportment became no more relaxed as we set off out to sea, however. He started to recite a number of facts, sounding as if he had rehearsed them in advance: first Poirot and I would have the chance to unpack, then to rest. After that there would be dinner on the terrace with everybody, followed by New Year's Eve festivities and games . . .

All I could think about was diving into the glorious bluegreen waves. If anybody thought I would be dining or partaking in any games before I had my first swim, they would soon discover how wrong they were.

Once he had finished describing exactly what the rest of our day would contain, Nash moved on to his next list: all the people Poirot and I were about to encounter at the house. "They will be delighted to make your acquaintance, I am sure. Monsieur Poirot, I have told them all about you. I must say: you are exactly as I imagined you would be. I had heard about your famous moustache, and . . . may I say? It is quite spectacular."

"*Merci mille fois.*" Poirot smiled proudly.

"Now, your bedroom and your friend Inspector Catchpool's are in a slightly different part of the house from where the rest of us have our quarters," said Nash. "I hope that is acceptable. You will have to walk through Manos's kitchen to get to your rooms, which is a bit inconvenient, I know, but it's really not far at all. It's a slightly odd route, is the only thing. I should say: Manos is our wonderful cook. Really, we would be lost without him."

Evidently, he wished to put us at our ease, yet he was not in easeful spirits himself. He spoke emphatically and at great speed, as if under pressure. I was starting to find his nervous energy tiring. And why had he given the impression of meeting

Poirot today for the first time? I thought back, in case I had misremembered . . . No, Poirot had definitely said "a very good friend" when describing Nash. It was a puzzle.

"Manos has expressly forbidden the rest of us from entering his kitchen, but you are both allowed to walk through it whenever you need to," said Nash. "Which is lucky." He attempted a smile. "It isn't, strictly speaking, the only way to reach your rooms, but the other way is inconvenient and takes three times as long. Speaking of inconveniences . . ." He cast his eyes downward. "I'm afraid that building our community has taken so much time and energy—making the people side of things work, I mean—that we have rather neglected the building itself, the furnishings . . . everything else, in fact. There are no locks on any of the bedroom doors, so we have to trust each other not to intrude, you know. And I'm afraid our chairs and beds are rather rickety—uncushioned wood in most cases—so I hope you're both the hard-wearing sort." I nearly laughed at the look on Poirot's face in response to having this description of himself offered to him.

As Nash described the others we would meet at The Spitty, it became clear that they were permanent residents: "Matthew—that's Matthew Fair—came out here with me a few years ago, helped me set everything up. For a year it was just the two of us. That was the happiest year I can recall, from my whole life so far. Not that the years since have been bad. I am still happy, of course," he assured us, looking anything but. "I always intended for the community to grow, for others to come and join us in our work."

"Community" felt like an unusual word for a group of friends living together, and it made me wonder what precisely it was that Nash sought to "grow" here on Lamperos. What was the nature of the work? Had the friends first met via their profession, whatever it was?

"Matthew is just the nicest fellow you could hope to find," Nash went on. "Entirely selfless, the biggest heart of anyone I have ever known. Boundless enthusiasm for all life has to offer! He and I were at Oxford together, and thick as thieves from the moment we met. When he heard about my plans for The Spitty, Matthew said to count him in, as I had known he would. Then a short while later, Rhoda Haslop and her older sister, Olive, joined us out here. Matthew and I knew Rhoda from our Oxford days. She worked in a tailor's shop and Matthew was always putting huge rips in the only smart clothes he possessed." Nash smiled at the memory, which somehow made him look sadder. "And good old Rhoda has always been such a devoted supporter of my . . . thoughts. She knew she wanted to be part of it, as soon as she heard about what I hoped to do out here."

As if he had spotted something potentially alarming in the distance, Nash narrowed his eyes and said, "She and Matthew were meant to be getting married, but . . . well, it hasn't quite worked out that way. Not yet, at any rate. I have not given up hope, however." He sighed in the manner of one who had done just that. "When a community like ours expands, it brings with it certain . . . complications. Rhoda and Olive were easy to accommodate, and so was Austin—oh, I forgot to mention Austin. He's American, and a real force of nature. He arrived a few months before Rhoda and Olive, having heard about what I was trying to do here from a cousin of my mother's. I have an English mother and a Greek father, but both now live in America. Separately," Nash said emphatically. Clearly he had strong feelings about his parents no longer living together, though I could not tell if these were positive or negative. "Both with more money than they could ever spend in five hundred lifetimes," Nash added with undisguised disapproval. "Which is how I come to have The Spitty, one of their many houses, all to myself, and all the money I need in order to make the community of Very Good Friends function effectively, and to fund my work on Lamperos and beyond. I am grateful to Mother and Father naturally, though I wish they . . ." He broke off, evidently deciding he would prefer to keep his wish to himself.

I was about to make a polite enquiry as to the nature of his work "on Lamperos and beyond" when my green-faced Belgian friend, clutching tightly at the edges of our little boat with both hands, said, "So at the house in Liakada Bay there is an American, Monsieur Austin Lanyon, and there is you and Monsieur Matthew Fair, and *les soeurs* Rhoda and Olive Haslop. Who else lives there?" His tone surprised me, being familiar from the various times he and I had worked together to solve murders. I knew the difference between Poirot in crime-solving mode and Poirot at leisure, and his voice had clearly signaled the former state. He had sounded as if he were listing possible suspects, which made no sense, given that we were supposed to be here on holiday. Perhaps it was simply his antipathy toward the rolling waves that had made him sound unduly severe. As Nash started to answer, Poirot's eyes darted back and forth from the water, as if he didn't trust it not to do something life-threatening if not watched carefully.

"Just this year, new people started to beat a path to The Spitty's door in the very way I had hoped would happen," Nash was saying. "Word had obviously spread, in England, in America. Belty—that's Betlinde Ricks, a native of Henderson, Nevada—arrived first, in February. She is American through and through, though she had not lived there for some time, I believe, and travelled here from London. There was a little argument about whether she should be allowed to stay, but I made it clear I wanted her here." He frowned, perhaps wondering if he should say more.

The Last Death of the Year

I waited. Poirot did not seem curious. He aimed yet another warning look at the sea as a droplet of saltwater landed on his coat.

"The proper name of The Spitty is 'The House of Perpetual Welcome,'" Nash went on. "That is deliberate. I chose it for a sound reason: we extend our welcome to all. Anyone who arrives here is our very good friend, no matter what they have done."

"I see," I said, feeling more confused than ever. What a strange name for a house. Most people plumped for something more pastoral, like The Willows or Mill Stream Cottage. And was he suggesting that this Belty character had done something wrong, or even criminal? I would have felt impertinent if I had asked. Was there something afoot here that Poirot had not told me about? I tried to catch his eye, but he was still concentrating on the water all around us.

"Then this last April, Charles Counsell arrived with his fiancée, Thirza Davis," said Nash. "Charles is a thoroughly reliable sort. Very conscientious chap, and quick-witted too, though too serious and critical of himself for his own good. As for Thirza, she is . . . well, rather hard to get the measure of. She is fascinating, and spirited, and sometimes fierce . . . but then at other times she appears to lose all interest in everyone around her. She can disappear into her own mind for hours. I sometimes worry she does not truly belong, or aspire to belong, in the way the others do. She is a riddle I have yet to solve, shall we say." Again, Nash attempted a reassuring smile and succeeded only in looking rather desperate. "And then in June we were joined by our latest arrival: Pearl St. Germain."

His voice had dulled and flattened out as he spoke this last name, leaving me with the sense that, by his reckoning, Pearl St. Germain represented all manner of trouble.

"Ah, look—here is Liakada Bay," he said as we came closer to a crescent-shaped beach. There was no white-gold sand here, only small gray pebbles, but all the same, it was a beautiful sight to behold. At the farthest end of the bay stood a building that looked almost derelict: a two-story structure with a sort of outdoor café terrace extending from its ground floor out onto the pebbly beach. A navy-blue awning protruded from its middle, ready to shield the few tables from the sun. "That's the Liakada Bay Hotel," said Nash, pointing. "The owners are a local married couple, Yannis Grafas and his wife Irida."

"An hotel." Poirot gave a very small shake of his head, and I knew he was pitying anyone who might have had to stay there. From the outside, the establishment looked as rickety as Rasmus's boat—which, in all fairness—had shepherded us quite safely to our destination.

At the nearest end of the bay stood a much sturdier building—tall, wide and made of honey-colored stone, into which windows and doors appeared to have been placed almost at random: dotted about everywhere. "That is The Spitty," Nash said. "Our House of Perpetual Welcome."

Despite its bizarre design, it was impressive to look at and did indeed project a welcoming air. (And yes, I would have thought so even if I had not known its formal name.) A dozen or so paved terraces, some with low walls around them, erupted from its lower half as if to say, "You might want to come in or look out at the sea here . . . or here . . . or here." Clearly, whoever had built the house had intended for it to endure for at least five hundred years. It looked as if it was minded to sit there solidly forever.

As Rasmus steered us into shore, two people appeared on the nearest terrace above our heads and waved down at us. "The one with the beard is Manos," said Nash. "He is our talented culinary artist, as he likes to be known. He does not live here—his own little house is along the road down there, but it is the kitchen at The Spitty, he always says, that truly feels like home to him. He is beside himself with joy on account of tonight's New Year's Eve feast that he has been preparing for so long. Now, do beware, though: he will lecture you in great detail about everything you must promise not to do when in his kitchen—it is his private kingdom and you will need to agree to behave according to his rules whenever you pass through it."

"Hi there!" the tall man with sandy hair and no beard called out, waving enthusiastically. "Welcome, welcome to our two new very good friends!"

"Who is that?" I asked, liking the look of him straight away. I soon worked out what it was about him that had elicited my instant approval: he was wearing bathing attire and had a towel tucked under one arm. This was a man who clearly intended to go swimming, and it was all I could do to stop myself from yelling back at him, "I want to swim too! Wait for me!"

"That is my wonderful friend who is better than any brother. That is Matthew. Matthew Fair." For the first time since I had met him, Nash Athanasiou smiled and looked happy at the same time.

CHAPTER 2

The House of Perpetual Welcome

It was Poirot who spoke up on my behalf and said to Nash, "I imagine that Catchpool here will want to swim before he does anything else, *n'est-ce pas, mon ami*? Even before taking a little rest."

"Oh? You are partial to the freezing sea, then, Inspector?" Nash shivered. "So is Matthew. I do not understand that particular predilection myself. He will be thrilled to have you accompany him, I am sure—a fellow icy-water enthusiast to entertain. He must be thoroughly tired of hearing me call him a lunatic. I would rather poke out my own eyes than immerse myself in the nearly frozen waters of Liakada Bay in December."

The next thing I knew, I was off to the pebbled beach with Matthew Fair, leaving poor Poirot in charge of my suitcase, once I had whipped out my bathing suit and towel, and obliged to listen to the many stipulations of Manos the cook about which items in his kitchen kingdom must on no account be moved or touched.

The sea was perfect: calm and still, but with a strong breeze blowing in from the east that created a constant rippling effect on the water's surface. Matthew and I swam vigorously back and forth for a very happy ten minutes. He kept calling out, "Isn't it heavenly? Heavenly!" and occasionally made loud exclamations that were not words: "Hayeeee!" and "Woooplahee!" All round he was a far jollier companion than Nash Athanasiou, and, as we dried ourselves on the chilly pebbles and threw on our clothes, he professed himself to be as devoted to Nash as Nash was to him.

"It is an honor to be *Défteri Foní* to his *Próti Foní*," he said. "I take it Nash translated for you, yes? Second Voice, that's me, and he's the First Voice. A bit like being Headmaster and Deputy Headmaster, heheh! Though I do keep saying to Nash: he really ought to give my title and responsibilities to Austin, who is far more suited to being in charge of important things than I am."

"When you say 'title and responsibilities' . . . ?"

"Yes," Matthew said firmly, as if we had just agreed upon something. "Do you know, Catchpool, I am not fond of having to be in charge of *myself* most of the time."

"I often feel the same way," I admitted, for I found myself liking this jovial, loud-voiced, apparently guileless man rather a lot.

"Oh, good. I'm glad I am not the only one." Matthew grinned. "Life would be much easier if someone else were always on hand to tell us what to do, don't you think? I made such a hash of things with Rhoda—the whole Pearl business." He half groaned. "I imagine Nash has told you?"

"No, I—"

"If only someone had taken me to task when Pearl first came to The Spitty, I would not now be in this ghastly mess I cannot find a way out of." He shook his head. "Though I'm being unfair. Nash *did* try to speak to me, but it was as if I had succumbed to a mysterious fever and could not hear him or think coherently. Proves what I'm saying." He chuckled.

"I should not be in charge, or even deputy-in-charge, of anything. Except, perhaps, guidance as to how best to approach swimming in a cold sea. On that subject, I am supremely confident. If I see someone shilly-shallying about, tiptoeing in up to their knees, then running away shrieking, then tiptoeing back in up to their waist, then retreating again—"

"Oh, that's the very worst way to do it," I agreed. "One must get neck-deep as soon as possible. No back and forth."

"Exactly." He slapped me on the back. "Isn't it funny that no one realizes? It is not even a question of not prolonging the agony, because there *is* no agony if you plunge straight in."

"Who are those two? Are they staying at the hotel?" I pointed to the far end of the beach, where a man and woman sat side by side in chairs that were too small for them. Both looked about forty years old. She had long, unkempt hair, swirls of black with lots of silver threaded through it that brought to mind ocean waves at midnight. His hair was glossy and lighter brown, ending in curls at the top of his neck. Both were staring at the sea and completely ignoring each other.

"They own and run the place," said Matthew. "Yannis and Irida. I am sure you will meet them. Yannis is a good friend of Manos, our spectacular cook. I often see him emerging from the cave—that is how I think of Manos's kitchen. One can easily imagine getting trapped in there if a sudden tide of new utensils flooded in, ha! Just wait until you taste some of Manos's creations. The man's a genius. I never tasted food like it until I came here. Still . . ."

Matthew broke off with a sigh. A second or two later, he said, "How *is* England?" as if enquiring about an ailing relative. "I miss it rather desperately at times. I always secretly hoped Nash would end up doing his House of Perpetual Welcome venture in the West Country, near Barnstaple—that was where it was going to be at first, but then his mother decided a cousin of hers needed to be allocated the Devon house, and so the only one available to Nash was this one. He is so wonderfully generous. Do you know—Nash was probably too modest to tell you—that it costs none of us anything at all to live here? Nothing! He stumps up for all of it. Well, I mean, it's his parents' money, so I suppose it's the whole family that is generous."

"The Spitty is certainly an interesting building," I said as the two of us set off back there, wet towels over our shoulders. "I can't work out the windows. They seem to be dotted about in no particular order. And all the terraces at different levels. Surely the house does not have"—I counted as we got closer "seven floors?"

"No." Matthew laughed. "Not unless you count as separate floors the various little landing spaces that spill over where you would least expect it. The architect must have been a whimsical sort who enjoyed defying convention. One might argue that The Spitty's layout makes no sense, conventionally speaking, but I have to say, I find it immensely comforting, the strange jumble of it all. Never could stomach those perfectly square houses that are four perfectly square rooms of exactly the same size, top and bottom—two on either side of a hall or a landing, slavishly symmetrical. Our lovely house really is the most wonderful, welcoming place, Catchpool. I do hope you and Monsieur Poirot enjoy your time here!"

Once I had said goodbye to Matthew, I explored a little. The staircase, immediately in front of the main door in the wide, stone-floored entrance hall, was indeed substantial—imperious, though in a rustic sort of way. It made me think more of an old castle than, for instance, a manor house. I was not sure Greek islands had manor houses, come to think of it.

On the ground floor, off the main hall, there was a small kitchen, a long, narrow dining room, a library, a very large sitting room and a music room with a grand piano and a large harp inside it as well as some chairs, all of which looked either painfully hard, half-broken or lumpy.

The little kitchen seemed to be almost empty, and was covered by a thin layer of dust. This could not be Manos's private kingdom, I decided—not least because it had only one door, the one that led to the entrance hall. Manos's kitchen, I deduced, must have a door at either end if it was the route to my bedroom and Poirot's.

Next, I examined the top two floors of the house, I found bedrooms, lots of them, and two more surprisingly positioned terraces, sprouting from those little landings Matthew had described. Each wooden bedroom door had a name painted on it in a different color, which should have looked ghastly but somehow did not. (Nash's name was in yellow, Matthew's in pale blue.)

I headed downstairs and outside, in search of Manos's den of culinary creativity. Following my nose (the aromas were sublime), I soon found it, at the bottom of a steep flight of stone steps on the side of the building that did not face Liakada Bay.

As I walked into what struck me immediately as an emporium of chaos, I heard the crackle of something roasting. Smells competed for my attention: burning meat versus burning wood. I zigzagged the only possible path through the long, crowded room full of teetering towers of objects—some recognizable, others less so—and imagined Poirot having done the same a little earlier. How he would have resented being made to traverse such disordered territory! There was not only food and cooking equipment in here, but also blankets, towels, cushions, boxes of a dozen different types, three pairs of large rubber boots, a cloth bag filled with what looked like stones . . .

"I cook for you the delicious dinner, Inspector Catchpool!" Manos's voice sounded faint and distant to me as I stepped over an upturned wooden crate on which were balanced two bruised-looking bananas. I looked around but could not see him anywhere; he must have been concealed behind one of the colorful heaps of paraphernalia on the long table, or crouched down behind that big brown glass jar.

"I am looking forward to it very much," I called out.

I made it to the end of his kitchen and out the other side and found myself on a small terrace. Apart from the door that belonged to the kitchen, there were two others. One was ajar, and I assumed it was mine. Sure enough, I entered and was soon reunited with my suitcase. In one corner was a chair with a seat that looked scratchy as well as hard, as if designed to shred garments and skin. I decided I would do better to sit down on the bed instead and was about to do so when I heard voices, which I soon identified: Poirot and Nash.

I could hear them as clearly as if they were in the room with me, which made sense when I looked at the wall to my left and saw that it was not in fact a wall; it was thick white cloth that had been stretched and pinned. The word "tent" entered my mind, and I sighed. My Belgian friend had better not snore too loudly, I thought; I would need to keep an eye on his consumption of *les sirops*.

"We will not have time until tomorrow at the earliest," Nash was saying. "New Year's Eve traditions make it more complicated. There are several preparations I need to make before dinner and Austin insisted we eat early in order to make room for whatever dramatics he has planned."

"We cannot delay too long," was Poirot's response. "My work here is more important than this game, yes?"

His work? This was all the evidence I needed that the true reason for our visit to Lamperos had been hidden from me. I cannot say I was terribly surprised.

"Yes, yes, of course." Nash sounded apologetic. "Forgive me, Monsieur Poirot. I am not thinking straight. This threat has been hanging over The Spitty for an intolerable length of time, and I have been fearing the worst for what feels like an eternity. No doubt I have sent myself half mad. I had no one to talk to about my concerns until you arrived. The last thing I wish to do is frighten anybody. Normally I tell Matthew everything, but he does not thrive when confronted with upsetting realities. Needless to say, I thank you with my whole heart for coming. We shall make time to discuss your . . . business here, one way or another, and as soon as is possible."

Well, well, I said to myself. *How very intriguing.*

As soon as I heard Nash excuse himself and leave, I made my way outside and knocked on Poirot's door, already proud of how measured and polite my rebuke to him would be.

"Catchpool," he looked happy to see me. "I trust you enjoyed your swim? The sea here is satisfactory?"

Was he deliberately trying to distract me? "Why are we here, Poirot?" I said. "The true reason, please—for this is not a holiday, is it? Who are all these people, and why do they live together? What exactly is this community? That's how Nash described it. Do they have special . . . beliefs or practices or something like that? Nash Athanasiou is the leader and Matthew is the deputy—I know that much. It all seems most peculiar."

Poirot opened his mouth to answer but was interrupted by the arrival of a new person who dropped down, apparently from the top of the wall behind me, onto the terrace, making me wonder if he had been hiding up a tree. There was one with the fattest trunk I had ever seen, standing in a corner, only a few feet away.

"Welcome, welcome and thrice welcome!" said the newcomer, a tall, broad-shouldered, athletic man of about my age, with intelligent green eyes that were lighter and a rarer shade than Poirot's; it was almost the green of sun-bleached grass. This chap had unruly red-brown hair that was wavy at the front, and a look on his face that told me he thought he knew better than anybody else about every conceivable topic. (I tend to be quick off the mark when it comes to identifying know-better types.) He had an American accent and proceeded as if we were all taking part in a show of which he was both the director and the main star. "I am Austin Lanyon Esquire," he said. "You may call me Austin. It's a pleasure to make your acquaintance. Welcome to The House of Perpetual Welcome. Now, tell me: do you like that name? Or would Eternal Welcome or Unconditional Welcome be better? Do not confer, please. I wish to know your individual opinions. Nash and I have got a bit of an argument brewing on that score, you see. He has already decided, I should say—the house has been named, officially—but I do think I might prefer 'Unconditional'. That word gets to the heart of everything we represent with devastating accuracy. Don't you gentlemen agree?"

I had no idea what he was talking about.

"We welcome people to our home here without attaching any conditions, no matter what they have done," Austin barreled on. "Sounds like unconditional is the very word you'd want, if that's what you mean to convey. Still, Nash is the First Voice, which means Big Boss where I come from." He looked at me. "And your swimming companion, Matthew? He's the Second Voice, which means *I don't got no voice at all.*" Austin did a little dance as he said these last few words. His short laugh left a bitter trace hanging in the air.

Did I imagine it, or had he looked at me rather accusingly while saying "no matter what they have done"? Had he meant to imply that I had done something inexcusable? I categorically had not. On the contrary, I had spent most of my life acutely aware of all the terrible things I might do if I didn't watch myself, and had made sure to do none of them, so I did not at all appreciate the implication.

Austin Lanyon seemed to be enjoying my discomfort. "Would you ever open your home in the way we have, Inspector Catchpool, and be willing to befriend, unconditionally, whoever presented themselves?" Then he leaned in and said something odd—almost whispered it in my ear: "'Ask me how I know sin's self-defeating. Oh, my friend! I was flawed. I was brave.'"

"Is that a quote from something?" I asked.

"It is." Austin beamed. "From a poem called "Ask Me How I Know,", by one of this island's wisest men. Lamperos is a very poetic island. Nash must have told you that the famous war poet, James Gresham-Graham, is buried here?"

"He did yes," said Poirot. "I already knew, of course."

"You should try to visit his grave while you are here," said Austin. "To answer the question you asked when you didn't know I was out here listening, Inspector Catchpool . . . We are a religious community here at The Spitty—and no, I am not embarrassed to use that word. We plan to do nothing less than save the world. That's right." He raised his voice ostentatiously, as if addressing a large crowd, and yelled, "The whole world! And no, that's not too big an ambition, nor is it unrealistic in the slightest. Offer people something with no downside, they're going to lap it up like cats at a bowl of buttermilk. Let me tell you, gentlemen: if I could be saved—and I was, in spite of everything—then anyone can. Boy, did I used to be a sinner. I was the worst sinner of everyone I knew. I was a gambler, a liar, a cheat, and as for the way I treated the ladies . . . Rarely was I seen without a loose woman on my arm—"

He was interrupted by a scuffing sound. The door of Manos's kitchen opened and it felt as if Austin's narration had conjured a young lady into being. "Oh!" she said, staring at me and Poirot, looking stumped for a moment. Then she giggled and produced a flirtatious smile. "We have company, then. This must be Monsieur Hercule Poirot and . . . well, I can only assume that *you* are Inspector Edward Catchpool? Of Scotland Yard?"

"I am," I confirmed.

"Delighted to meet you. I'm Pearl St. Germain." She had a tiny waist and large hips, and wore a pale mauve dress that was shaped and styled to draw attention to both. Her eyes seemed huge, thanks to some skillful paintwork, and her long, thin mouth—a little too long for her face—moved sideways and downwards as she spoke, creating the impression that the words were pulling it that way as they exited. "Don't let Austin tease and torment you." She fluttered her eyelids at me.

"You're the tease and tormentor around here, Pearly," Austin said without enthusiasm. "Not me. Anyways . . ." He turned his back on her. "I came here with an important message, gentlemen. I don't know if you are in the habit of making New Year's resolutions, but you're going to need one each this evening. You too, Pearly," he added grudgingly, with a brief glance at her over his shoulder. "We're going to be playing a game we have never played before—and I can say that with confidence, because I only just invented it a couple of days ago. You're going to love it, all of you. I decided we needed to inject some energy and innovation into our mission and practices here if we're going to thrive as a community—don't you think so, Poirot? Inspector? That's why we welcome newcomers—that, and we have no choice, with Nash's rules and all." Again, I heard bitterness in his laugh. "You never know: maybe you'll like it so much here, you'll want to stay," he said, looking directly at me.

"Well, I do love the sea," I replied with a polite smile. The truth was that I never wanted to stay anywhere for very long. There were only two places in the world where I felt truly comfortable: Poirot's rooms at Whitehaven Mansions in London, and the lodging house where I had lived for some years now. The latter was Mrs. Blanche Unsworth's home, not mine (I merely rented space there), but I had come to realize that nothing made me feel as if I belonged more than fitting in, quietly, with someone else's domestic regime.

"Well, we'll have to see if you pass our very exacting entrance test." Austin folded his arms and straightened his back. "Not everyone does. You failed, didn't you, Pearly?"

"Whatever do you mean?" she said haughtily, scowling at him before turning to beam in apparent delight at me. "I have never failed at anything I have set my mind to, as far as I can recall."

"I had better get washed and dressed," I said, eager to rid myself of the burden of prolonged awkward conversation with these two strangers. For how long, I wondered, might I be able to sleep, before dinner and this blasted game got underway? And why was it that, wherever I went, I seemed to encounter someone determined to invent a board game, or a parlor game, and compel me to play it with them? What had I done to deserve such a fate?

Still, I had to admit, I had perked up substantially when Austin had mentioned the New Year's resolution requirement.

I had one all ready: to cease working for Scotland Yard and find a different occupation that would allow me to live beside the sea.

I looked forward to seeing Poirot's response, for I had not yet told him that this was my plan.

CHAPTER 3

The Rules of the Game

Dinner on the largest of the outdoor terraces was truly something to behold. Every time I decided that Manos must surely by now have brought out the last dish, he surprised me by darting back to the kitchen and then reappearing with another two or three. Each one was introduced to all of us by name, as if these were his beloved relatives and not simply edible items he had prepared.

Arranged around the table were six large stone basins in which fires were burning, their flames leaping up in the air. I had feared we might all freeze out here, but it was quite warm enough, and the blaze had attracted some unexpected visitors, too: two tiny horses, one brown and one gray, two white goats, and Rasmus the boat man, who was stretched out on the flagstones under a tree, propped up on one elbow. He did not speak to anyone, and no one spoke to him.

How sensible of him to eschew the chairs around the dining table, which could have doubled as instruments of torture, I thought. My bones were already starting to feel a little sore from The Spitty's hard, uncomfortable furniture.

Poirot and I exchanged greetings with everyone we had met already and were introduced to the remaining members of the household. These were, in order of their arrival at the table:

Two sisters, Olive and Rhoda Haslop. "From Oxford," Rhoda said as I shook her hand. I guessed that she was around twenty-five. Olive was older by at least twenty years, I thought at first, though I adjusted that estimate downward when I looked carefully at her face. She listened patiently and with a neutral expression as her younger sister elaborated upon how wise and brilliant Nash was and how his work was one day going to save the world and everyone in it.

The resemblance between the Haslop sisters was strong; both had severe eyebrows, long chins that curved slightly inward and nostrils that flared when they spoke. Both had short hair: iron gray curls in Olive's case, and a smooth, straight light brown cap for Rhoda that made me think of a medieval monk. Both wore long, flowery, shapeless dresses that did not suit them in the slightest.

Next arrived a more stylishly dressed woman of around forty with sculpted golden hair, wearing dark red lipstick and a black dress that rustled as she walked—though walking didn't feel like an accurate description in her case. She seemed instead to glide very slowly, like a glamorous snail in no hurry. Like Austin Lanyon's, her accent was immediately identifiable as American. Nash, following close behind, introduced her as Miss Betlinde Ricks.

"But you gotta call me Belty, both of you," she told Poirot and me. Shaking Poirot's hand, she said, "I wish it could be as nice for you to meet me as it is for me to meet you, Detective Poirot."

"I am not a detective, madame," he told her. "Well, of course, I am, but I do not hold the rank of—"

"Ranks be damned," said Belty with a smile. "I have no official title, but I know who and what I am: the worst and least forgivable sinner here. And you're the greatest detective in the world."

She seemed to be waiting for Poirot to comment, but he and I were distracted by the next arrivals: the tiny-waisted Pearl St. Germain, with Austin Lanyon and Matthew Fair behind her. Pearl was certainly the youngest of the women at The Spitty. She looked almost like a girl, but I supposed she was twenty at least. She started to wave at me frantically, as if trying to attract my attention from a thousand miles away. *Oh, dear,* I thought, alarmed by the pitch of her enthusiasm. I made a point of looking away, and thanked my stars that the two seats on either side of me were taken by Nash and Olive Haslop respectively.

Next to arrive was a third goat, a gray one this time. Manos, who walked past at that moment carrying a wooden crate, stroked its head and spoke to it in, presumably, Greek. Then he placed the crate in front of Rasmus, to whom he addressed a remark. The boatman showed no sign of having noticed or heard, and I will never know why Manos thought that fellow needed or wanted a wooden box set down in front of him. Within ten minutes of this mysterious occurrence, Rasmus got up and strolled away in any case, followed by one little horse and one white goat.

A man and woman, both tall and thin with long necks, arrived on the terrace next, holding hands and looking rather strained—like two tense swans plucked out of the water against their will. These two, the last of our party, were introduced as Charles Counsell and Thirza Davis. Both looked thirty or thereabouts. "Charles and Thirza are engaged to be married," said Nash, and I noticed—it was impossible not to—that both grimaced when their impending nuptials were mentioned.

Charles Counsell asked both Poirot and me a sequence of courteous questions: had our journey been pleasant? From where in England had we travelled? "Oh, London? Which part of London?" He had been happy to leave that city, he told us, after seeing the historic Hotel Cecil pulled down. Belty Ricks, who must have overheard, leaned over Austin Lanyon to say, "As long as they don't touch the Savoy. If they touch a hair on that building's head, I swear I'll make them regret it. I'm there at least three times a week."

Thirza Davis pointedly turned her back when Belty spoke. Unlike her fiancé, who had said hello to everyone, Thirza was more selective about whose presence she was willing to acknowledge. Olive Haslop, Matthew Fair and Nash had received warm "Hellos," but she had completely ignored Belty Ricks, Pearl St. Germain and Austin Lanyon as each of them attempted to greet her. She had stopped beside a chair that was next to Rhoda Haslop's, touched it as if to pull it back and sit down, then changed her mind and walked around to sit next to the older sister, Olive.

"That must be difficult from Lamperos, Belty," Austin teased her.

"Hmm?" she said lazily, her smile forming before she understood what he meant.

"Getting to the Hotel Savoy three times a week when you live out here—that is no mean feat."

"Oh, silly Austie! You know what I mean." Her smile widened.

Once Manos had endorsed every element of our meal with his personal recommendation, Rhoda Haslop asked Nash's permission to say grace, which he granted.

She opened her mouth to begin, but before she had the chance, Matthew Fair said loudly, "Darling Rhoda. I do so love your graces."

Rhoda let out a ragged gasp, as if he had spoken harshly to her. Then she composed herself and began to speak in a language I did not understand. Once again, I assumed it was Greek.

The food was truly extraordinary—so good that it made me want to say grace all over again, in a language I could actually speak. Once the noise of everyone eating and chattering had started up all around us, Olive whispered to me, "My sister is a little sensitive. It causes her to behave unusually from time to time. You must excuse her."

"Of course," I said.

"You are very attuned to the feelings and moods of other people, I believe, Inspector Catchpool?" Olive put it to me as a question.

"I suppose I am, yes."

"I am too," she said. "Rhoda and Matthew were engaged to be married for some months. Then Pearl arrived at The Spitty and Matthew was rendered quite feeble-minded with lust. We could all see that Pearl would tire of him within the week, and sure enough . . . Well, actually it took a little longer than that. Their romance lasted twenty days from start to finish—I counted each and every one. It was the most appalling ordeal for poor Rhoda. And, by extension, for me. She is more like a daughter to me than a sister, really. We lost our parents at a young age, you see. And I am considerably older than her: forty-nine to her thirty-two. Tell me, Inspector Catchpool . . ."

"Please, call me Edward."

"Edward, then. What would you do if you were me, and in the parental role?"

"Do about what?"

"Matthew would have us believe he now loves Rhoda more than ever, having realized Pearl was nothing more than a foolish distraction," said Olive. "And of course she has forgiven him—that is the duty of all of us here, to forgive without question or qualification—" She stopped and laughed. "Not you or Monsieur Poirot, obviously," she said. "I am referring to our way of living here, to what it means to be a member of our community of Very Good Friends . . ."

I knew instantly that I did not wish to join and wondered if this meant I wasn't as good a Christian as I believed myself to be, if the thought of forgiveness without question scared me away so easily.

"Rhoda has forgiven Matthew, but should she consider marrying him, after his head was so easily turned by Pearl?" Olive went on. "I tend to think she should *not*, yet it makes her even more miserable to have to keep refusing him. Part of me wishes he would stop asking. Really, it sometimes seems as if he is determined to torture her. Though, bless his heart, Matthew is the kindest man in the world . . . but I don't think he quite understands the complexity of Rhoda's emotional . . . machinery, shall we say?"

"It sounds difficult," I said.

"And what if they married and were very happy together?" said Olive. "Rhoda certainly is not happy now. Watch her face, though do not make it too obvious. Every five seconds or so her eyes dart toward Matthew. He smiles back lovingly at her, and she looks utterly bereft. It is no fun for anybody. It must be *stopped*, somehow."

"Not a happy state of affairs," I acknowledged.

Olive gave her head a hearty shake, as if coming out of a reverie and back to reality. "I must apologize for being so frank, Edward, having only just met you. I don't really do polite dinner party chitter-chatter. It's a waste of breath."

"I agree," I said, then realized that wasn't true at all. There was something comforting and quite pleasurable about discussing trivialities with others who valued the maintenance of a safe, polite distance. It enabled one to concentrate on the food, for one thing.

"I am *so* relieved never to have been disturbed by the romantic love agonies that ruin so many young people's lives," said Olive. "I have never fallen in love, nor been fallen in love with. Thankfully, I am not the sort of woman to whom any of that happens. Give me thinking in preference to feeling any day of the week. Thinking is a habit that has served me well throughout my life. The problem, for all the romantic love people, is that they are never *free*. Their heads are stuffed with nonsense most of the time."

"I quite agree," I murmured. This time I meant it.

Austin Lanyon had risen to his feet and started to talk about his New Year's Resolutions game. He was explaining the rules, which unfortunately I could not hear, since Olive was still dropping confidences into my ear: "It was my head that brought me out here to Lamperos, not my heart. Rhoda was so enthused about Nash's great masterplan, which, I must admit, struck me as lunacy at the time. Having said that, I've always been a fan of experimentation. Though I did say to Rhoda that this particular experiment of Nash's was highly unlikely to succeed. Saving the whole world is hardly a small undertaking—even if one has a few friends in tow to help out. What no one understands, Edward, and certainly my sister does not, is that the joy is in the trying, not in the succeeding."

The passion in her voice seemed to demand my full attention, so I stopped trying to hear what Austin was saying and turned back to face her. "To experiment bravely, even knowing you are almost bound to fail . . . why, that is the real prize, is it not?"

"Well . . ." I began.

She spoke over me: "I knew my dear friend Carl would approve, though he had died the previous year, of septicemia. When Rhoda and I lived in Oxford, I worked for many years as assistant to Professor Carl Yaxley—are you familiar with his work? He was a scientist. Worked on the photoelectric effect."

I nodded as if I understood what that was.

"Carl had the most impressive brain of anyone I have ever known. He might even have given Hercule Poirot a run for his money." She smiled. "He often said to me, 'Olive, all of my most successful experiments were your idea.' It was quite true, even if I say so myself. And, no, before you ask, I was not secretly in love with him, nor he with me. He had a face like a doorstep—but I loved him dearly as a friend and teacher."

Eventually, Olive left me to my own devices and struck up a conversation with Belty Ricks, which gave me the chance to be a silent observer for a while. There were a lot of wistful glances and sighs travelling between Matthew Fair and Rhoda Haslop, with the latter looking more tearfully heartbroken as the meal progressed. Matthew mouthed the words "Darling Rhoda" at her more than once.

Thirza Davis seemed to be doing her best to divert his attention away from Rhoda and in her direction instead. I wondered if she was trying to make her fiancé, Charles, angry. If so, it was working; he was positively glowering at her.

Nash, at the head of the table, sat with his shoulders hunched and apparently lost in thought. I wondered if he was worrying about whatever had caused him to invite Poirot to Liakada Bay in the first place.

"Shhh!" Belty Ricks said when Thirza said something loudly to Matthew in a flirtatious tone. "Poor Austin is trying to tell us the rules of the Resolutions Game."

"Yes, everyone, stop chattering," said Pearl. "I'm terrible

at games that have rules, where I cannot simply do whatever takes my fancy. It's always so hard to remember what is permitted and what is not."

Thirza ignored both women, and continued to talk to Matthew, though she fell silent at once when Austin—sounding angry, and twice as American as he had previously—said, "Can everyone quit chattering and let me say what I need to say?"

I looked over at Pearl St. Germain and caught her watching me, which I found most irritating. Fixing my eyes on Austin, I listened intently as he started from the beginning and explained the rules of the game he wanted us all to play. They were straightforward: everyone was to write down their New Year's Resolution for 1933 and place it in a wire bowl. One by one, these would be pulled out and read aloud, and the objective was to guess the writer of each resolution. *Excellent*, I thought. Poirot would know at once which was mine, and we could discuss it later when we had time; what an enjoyable and surprising way for him to find out, I thought.

Then Austin said, "Except you, Catchpool. We need someone to act as master of ceremonies and present the resolutions—so, no need to write one of your own."

"I will be the ceremonial master," said Poirot. "I cannot think of any resolution I wish to make, having perfected my life already."

"No, Poirot, you must join in," Austin decreed. "You are our star guest! Everyone will feel deprived if one of the papers in the bowl is not yours. So, Catchpool . . . once we've finished with the food, we're going to need that wire bowl, some pencils and paper." He had apparently mistaken me for someone who took orders from him.

"I have pencils and paper in my room," said Olive, standing up. "I'll go and get them now."

"Catchpool, could you bring the bowl?" said Nash, who

also seemed to think I was someone for him to boss around. "It's on the table in the sitting room—black, and made of wire, funny looking old thing. Be a sport and fetch it for us?"

I was livid. Deciding that the best way to disguise this from the others was to remove myself, I obeyed the order, thinking, *How dare he?* What right had Austin Lanyon to exclude my New Year's resolution from the game? Did he imagine I was his pet dog?

I made my way to the sitting room where I soon spotted the ugly object I was after. I picked it up and was about to turn on my heel and return to the terrace when I noticed what looked like a framed poem on the wall, next to a tiny square window. I recognized the title at once: Austin Lanyon had quoted it at me, and told me it was written by one of the wisest men on the island of Lamperos. I started to read.

Ask Me How I Know

It was cheating that made me hate cheating.
It was gambling that taught me to save.
Ask me how I know sin's self-defeating.
Oh, my friends! I was flawed. I was brave.

It was lying that made me hate lying.
When I faked my own death in my youth,
It was failure that led me to trying
A more prosperous tactic: the truth.

When you say "Never stray. It won't serve you,"
And advise me that sin leaves a scar
On the skin of the soul, I unnerve you
With "You're right—but you can't know
     you are."

> "Well, of course that's your view. How
>   convenient,"
> You reply. Friend, but what if it's true?
> Facts are neither reproving nor lenient.
> I know more about goodness than you.

Not a bad poem, I thought to myself—quite thought-provoking. Then I noticed the smaller letters at the bottom, which read: "Austin Lanyon, September 19, 1931."

An exclamation of disgust escaped from my mouth. So, he had been talking about himself when he had described the wisest man on the island, the pompous oaf! I was debating whether I could get away with hurling the wire bowl at the framed poem without breaking the glass when Poirot walked into the room.

CHAPTER 4

Secrets, Surprises and Lies

"Catchpool." Poirot wore a concerned expression. "You must not allow Austin Lanyon to goad you into irritability."

"It's a little late for that," I told him.

"I have the solution: imagine that nothing frustrating has happened to you, and as a consequence you feel no resentment at all."

I did as instructed. This invented version of myself was thrilled to be in sunny Greece and determined to make the most of his stay at Liakada Bay. I'd have swapped places without a moment's hesitation. Indeed, I would have given a lot, at that moment, to bring that more serene creature into being. Unfortunately, however, I knew it was impossible. The fact was, I was cross—and with my dear Belgian friend as much as with Austin Lanyon.

"Why didn't you tell me the truth, Poirot?" I said. "There was no need to pretend this was a holiday with your friends. You must have known I'd leap at the chance to feel the sun on my face in December, visit a country I'd never seen before, swim every day from a beautiful bay no more than forty easy footsteps from my bedroom. You also know by now, I hope, that assisting you with your investigations is quite the most rewarding—"

"Catchpool, please allow me to explain—"

"—work I ever get to do. And the thing is, people like to have a modicum of control over their own choices. Even unassuming coves like me prefer not to be tricked into—"

"*Mais tu as tout à l'envers*!" Poirot erupted. "The upside-down way of wrong around, Catchpool. It was not supposed to be a *trick*." He looked crestfallen. "*C'était prévu comme un cadeau*. A gift—that is what I planned. Evidently, I miscalculated. Forgive me."

"A . . . a gift?" My heart plummeted to the floor of my stomach. I expected to feel thoroughly ashamed of myself in no time at all; indeed, that emotional state was already bedding in around the edges.

"I told you a large portion of the truth," Poirot declared with pride. "The stone house overlooking the bay, with the many terraces laid out liked the petticoats of a dancing lady, each one a different shape—you do not remember me saying any of this?"

"Of course I do, but—"

"And did I not tell you that a group of very good friends resided here at Liakada Bay?"

"You led me to believe they were *your* close friends, and keen to be mine too," I said. "In fact, you had never clapped eyes on any of them until today!"

"That is correct. Our purpose here is not merely *le divertissement* but also to get to the bottom of a problem that plagues Monsieur Nash's House of Perpetual Welcome. That element of surprise, the intriguing revelation that a mystery awaited us at Liakada Bay, was going to be my Christmas present to you, Catchpool. The cake of the cherry! I thought you would be delighted to discover that we have another conundrum to solve together—and to *discover* it, rather than be told by me."

"I see. Well . . ." I hesitated. "I suppose that might have been an excellent surprise had I been in a different frame of mind. Perhaps Christmas with Mother and the bullying manner of that horrible Austin fellow have combined to put me in a bad temper."

"Imagine, Catchpool, that you are in the highest and most jovial of spirits."

"That makes me feel worse," I told him.

"Ah. Then you are not doing it in the right way. When I say, 'Imagine it,' I do not mean as if from a great distance. Inhabit the fantasy *as if it were the reality*. It is New Year's Eve, *mon ami*. You are in the seaside, your favorite place. We have just eaten a most magnificent feast!"

"I can imagine cheering up in the relatively near future," I told him. "Will that do?"

He nodded. "Let us return to the others—and I will solve for you the problem of the Resolutions Game. Of course you must join in." He turned and started to make his way toward the door.

"Wait," I said. "Can you tell me a little more about these people we're staying with? Austin Lanyon said they were a religious community."

"Soon, my friend. All in good time."

With that, he was gone.

Alone in the room again, I reread Austin Lanyon's poem twice in order to confirm my dislike of it. He had laid on the rhyme and meter with a trowel, and the message was an endorsement of moral corruption as far as I could make out. *Despicable*.

I was about to step out into the night when something slammed into me. I cried out in alarm, for this creature was on the prowl and far from inanimate. It turned out to be Pearl St. Germain. "Oh, Edward, do forgive me," she said breathlessly.

"No harm done," I said curtly, stepping aside so that she could pass. "Please, go ahead."

"Oh..." She peered past me into The Spitty's sitting room then evidently changed her mind. "No, don't worry. I...I see you have the bowl. I was just coming to get it, that's all. Shall we return to the terrace together?"

I nodded.

"Topping!" She linked her arm through mine. "I shall protect you from any Greek goat that happens to pass by. They're terrible pests, you know, and they're simply everywhere on Lamperos. One nearly sent me hurtling to my death a few weeks ago. It came out onto the terrace that adjoins my bedroom and did its best to shove me off. I would have been smashed to bits on the rocks beneath if it had succeeded."

"Golly," I said. "I did not realize that succeeding was a thing goats did."

Pearl howled with laughter and clutched my arm a little more tightly. Then I pretended to inspect the wire bowl closely, to give myself something to focus on that wasn't how much I disliked being grabbed hold of by anybody, but especially by her.

In addition to being irksome, she was also a liar. No one could have been in any doubt that I had gone to The Spitty to get the wretched bowl, so why on earth would she come to the house to perform the exact same task? No, whatever she had intended to do, she was not prepared to tell me, or to have me witness it.

I wondered what it was—though not for too long, since there are more things one might wish to do inside a house in which nine people live than it is possible to list. I decided to give the question no further thought.

CHAPTER 5

The First Mention of Murder

Pearl and I arrived back at the dining terrace to find Olive Haslop handing out paper and pencils, and Poirot addressing the rest of the group on my behalf: "There is no reason why Catchpool should not add his own New Year's resolution to the bowl," he said. "He has seen the handwriting of nobody here and will therefore be in the same position as everyone else: able to make a fair guess at the authorship of each entry that is not his own."

A general murmur of agreement followed.

"You are quite right, Monsieur Poirot," said Pearl. "Besides, I'm not sure I want to play if we aren't going to hear Edward's New Year's resolution. I for one cannot wait to be inspired by it." She smiled at me as if some kind of secret pact existed between us.

"Of course." Rhoda Haslop sounded flustered, looking at me apologetically as if all the blame for the oversight were hers. "I should have thought of that. No one should have to miss out on such an important ritual anyway. Turning it into a game is all very well, but the setting of resolutions for a new year is an exercise that ought to be approached mainly with serious intent. As Pearl says, each one shared might act as a source of spiritual instruction for another person."

"Goodness me, Rhoda!" Pearl laughed. "Not everything has to be about instruction or improvement."

"Especially not when you're around, eh, Pearly?" Austin Lanyon quipped.

"Rather than be offended, I shall assume you mean there is no possibility of improvement in my case," Pearl pouted flirtatiously, her eyes still glued to me as if she was daring me to agree or disagree.

No one raised any objection to Poirot's proposal. Soon, those smoking cigarettes were extinguishing them, and everyone had taken their seats either at the long wooden table or in one of the differently shaped but equally hard and uncomfortable deck chairs nearby. I sat on the wall at the far end of the terrace in order to be as close as possible to the fresh, salty scent of the lapping waves.

Once we were all settled, Austin Lanyon reminded us, unnecessarily, of the rules he had already recited twice:

- Everyone must write down their true resolution for the year to come—the one change they most desire and that would make the most difference to their life, not something false and wildly out of character, designed to hinder other players' ability to make accurate guesses.

- No one may write more than one resolution.

- Write in block capital letters only, for ease of reading.

- Once you have written your resolution and nothing else (especially not your name) on the piece of paper, fold it so that the words aren't visible, and place it in the bowl.

- As Catchpool reads each resolution aloud (including his own) with a number attached to it (1 to 11), each participant must write down their best guess as to who authored it.

- Catchpool will then read them all again, a maximum of twice more, to give everyone a chance to change their minds and amend their answers.

- Catchpool will next read them all out, one by one, in order for them to be claimed by whoever wrote them, at which point players will award themselves two points for any correct guess and no points for an erroneous answer.

- For every person who guesses your resolution is yours, you lose a point. (Some players might, accordingly, end up with scores in minus points.)

- The winner—surprisingly—is *not* the person with the most points at the end. Or rather, one can view that person as having triumphed if one is determined to adhere to an especially pedestrian slant of mind, but the true winner will be the person Austin Lanyon deems to have come up with the most impressive resolution. (I assumed, incorrectly, that he was joking.)

Once the rules had been established, twenty minutes or so of silence followed as we all tore strips from sheets of paper, wrote on them, folded them and put them in the wire bowl.

Soon I was holding the bowl in my hand and ready to start. "All right," I said. "Number 1: 'To write a formal essay on the topic of the greatest of all the fruits of the spirit, Forgiveness, in order to understand it more thoroughly and practice it more effectively.'"

"Oh, that's a tricky one." Thirza Davis's mouth twisted as she tried to work it out. "There are only two people it could be, but which one was it?"

"Let me quickly add an extra rule," said Austin. "Absolutely no commentary or discussion should take place at this stage of the game, in case we inadvertently say too much and—"

"Nothing I said gave anything away," Thirza said in a cold voice.

"Didn't say it had." Austin grinned at her. "But the next person who opens their trap might not be so judicious. And you're overestimating your own discretion. There could be those now wondering which two names you have in mind who weren't before, and coming to conclusions."

"Some are in no position to wonder any such thing," Charles Counsell said. "M. Poirot and Inspector Catchpool don't know any of us. They are at an unfair disadvantage."

"I wouldn't be so sure," said Thirza. "It's possible to get the measure of most people in less than an hour if your senses are finely attuned." She wasn't looking at her husband as she addressed him; her eyes were fixed on Austin Lanyon, and the look she was aiming at him disinclined me to criticize her about anything at all, ever, if I could help it.

Austin appeared entirely unperturbed. "All right," he said. "Has everyone written down their guess for the writer of Number 1?"

When they had, I read out Number 2: "'My resolution is to read and attempt to write poetry every day.'"

"Oh, that's too easy!" trilled Pearl St. Germain. "It's obviously Austin. He's the only poet among us."

The Last Death of the Year

"Pearl, really." Nash Athanasiou sighed.

"She has given nothing away—though she's a featherheaded fool," said Austin. "Remember, it's the New Year's *Resolutions* Game: what we want to *start* doing. I already write and read poetry. Why would I resolve to do something that's an established habit? When you think about it carefully, it makes more sense if the person who wrote Number 2 is not me but an admirer, inspired by my example."

"Well, that's all of us, naturally," said Matthew Fair. "You're a thoroughly inspiring chap, Austin."

"You do not write or read poetry every day, though, do you?" asked Nash. "Not every single day?"

"What has become of the 'no commentary or discussion' rule, Austin?" Thirza's voice was leaden. "You were happy to apply it to me, but it's acceptable for you, Nash and Matthew to comment as much as you like—is that it?"

"Call me fussy, but . . . I kinda feel games should be more fun than this one has been so far?" Belty Ricks said with a chuckle.

"Belty's right," said Olive Haslop. "Let us stop if it's going to be nothing but wrangling from start to finish."

"Better still, let's change the way we're approaching the game in order to prevent it from falling apart." Nash stood up. "Since when do we give up, when improvement is a choice we could make just as easily? Forgiveness—our central creed—is not merely a notion to be applied to ourselves and other people. It is as vital to forgive an occasion, or an activity in progress, if it's not going the way we want it to." He turned back and forth as he spoke, making sure to look at each of us. "Instead of abandoning our enterprise, we must forgive it for not unfolding, thus far, in the way we hoped."

"What a marvelous notion." Rhoda's eyes shone. "Quite

correct. I should have thought of it myself." Then she said two words I did not quite catch. They sounded a little like "pretty funny."

Rhoda must have noticed my confusion, because she said, "It's a Greek phrase: *Próti Foní*. It means 'First Voice' in Greek. That's Nash's role here in our community." I remembered that Matthew had explained as much while we were swimming. Rhoda repeated the title again as if it were a prayer, then asked Nash, "If we were to forgive the Resolutions Game for its . . . inopportune start, what would we do next?"

Nash frowned and said nothing.

Austin turned to Matthew and said, "*Défteri Foní?*" *Second Voice.*

"Oh, gosh." Matthew looked somewhat overawed. He blinked a few times. "Um . . . lawks a mercy . . ."

Rhoda stood up and cleared her throat. "We would start again, after unanimously agreeing to a no-commentary-and-no-discussion rule," she said. "Then Inspector Catchpool would start again from Resolution Number 1."

"Excellent idea!" said Matthew Fair. "You would make a wonderful *Défteri Foní*, Rhoda. It really ought to be you, not me."

"What else?" asked Nash. "Apart from starting again with that agreement in place?" He looked from face to face.

"Hold no grudge and harbor no grievance about what has transpired so far," suggested Charles Counsell.

"That, definitely. But what else?"

"How about: laugh till our sides split," suggested Austin.

"Laugh?" said Rhoda. "At what?"

"Why, at ourselves," he said. "Here we are, all intelligent people—well, for the most part—yet we can't play the simplest of games without growing querulous and quarrelsome and spoiling any fun we might have had. And that's not just us, here, tonight—it's how the whole damn world carries on, the whole damn time."

"I am sure we will have more fun once we start again," said Olive briskly. "Please do continue, Edward. I'm tired and looking forward to going to bed as soon as we have seen in the New Year. I certainly don't want to be still up and guessing which resolution is whose at two in the morning. And there's no need to say the first two resolutions again—I'm sure we all remember them: writing a spiritual essay, and reading and writing poetry every day."

"Yes, what fun it will be this time round," Austin muttered, shaking his head. "Why don't you read out the rest, make them all sound like minutes of a dry committee meeting?"

"Edward is reading out the resolutions," Olive replied firmly. "Go on, Edward. If Nash agrees, that is."

The "First Voice" of the house gave a small nod.

I reached for another folded piece of paper, guessing that the chances of my being able to read out Numbers 3 to 11 without heckling or disruption was close to nought. As for what happened instead . . . well, I would have said there was a less than zero chance of that occurring—so please do not imagine I am claiming an unqualified flair when it comes to predicting the future.

I ended up putting paid to the smooth progression of the Resolutions Game myself. Unfolding the piece of paper in my hand, I saw that it was not in block capitals as instructed. Instead, this was joined-up writing of an excessively loopy kind. The next few seconds were something of a blur. I had not been prepared, you see, to read these particular words. A siren of intense alarm started to sound inside me, blotting out everything else. I thought, "This must be a joke," and then "Surely this is linked to the reason why Poirot was invited here."

What I did, though I cannot remember deciding to do it, was spring to my feet, sending the wire bowl and all the bits of paper flying. "Oh dear," I mumbled. (Poirot told me much later that this was the perfect combination of verbal understatement and physical overreaction.)

Owing to my prior position—perched on the farthest wall, as close to the sea as possible—some of the folded pieces of paper had fluttered down, like tiny white birds in the night, to a different terrace below, and I hurried this way and that, ignoring Poirot's concerned questioning—"What is the matter, Catchpool? What have you read that has so alarmed you?"—in search of a flight of stone steps leading down to the lower level.

I found no such thing. Would you believe that not one of the external areas attached to The Spitty was connected, neither by external stairs, sloping paths nor by any other means, to any of the others? It was the most absurd thing: one needed to go back inside the house and find the relevant room, or stone platform by the side of a staircase, if one wanted to reach any of the house's other outdoor areas. And although Liakada Bay was almost within touching distance of the lowest three stone patios, it was not possible to get to it from any of them, not unless one wanted to hop over the wall. Only from this highest terrace with the dining table was it possible to exit The Spitty's grounds and walk directly down to the sea.

Urgent as I knew it was to retrieve those pieces of paper that had flown out of reach, any jump from where I was standing might have proved very hazardous indeed.

"Catchpool!" Poirot was standing in front of me. He took from my hand the piece of paper I had not realized I was still holding and read aloud the words that were written there so that all present could hear them. It was a little poem of sorts, though I hardly wished to dignify it with that name, for it was easily the most menacing quatrain I had ever clapped eyes on:

The Last Death of the Year

We are resolved to murder Matthew Fair.

I have a helper—staunch and sure is she;

Quite as intent am I. Then let this be

At once the last and first death of the year.

I understood every word—there could be no mystery about what was meant by "last" or "first." Yet at the same time and especially having met the amiable and obviously wholesome Matthew Fair, the poem made no sense to me at all.

CHAPTER 6

The Midnight Mistake

Poirot looked at each of the nine Spitty residents in turn, rather as Nash Athanasiou had minutes before. "Which of you wrote this? You must tell me at once. It is a joke, I hope."

I knew even then that it was nothing of the sort. I had held the resolution in my hand and felt evil intent pulsing between my fingers.

"No need to look so stern, Monsieur Poirot." Matthew Fair was smiling. "Someone's ribbing me, that's all. I am quite safe. There are no murderers here."

"Even if there were, Matthew is such a sweetie, and the very last of us that anyone would kill," Belty Ricks contributed. She seemed to be holding in laughter, her mouth trembling. Simultaneously, she was trying to catch the eye of Austin Lanyon.

I might have considered whether this was a prank cooked up by the two Americans (that country's sense of humor is, after all, quite different from our English sensibility) except that Austin looked appalled and not at all amused. He was staring down at the table, his large, open hands resembling two meaty claws ready to scratch someone's eyes out. Nash Athanasiou, by his side, looked shocked.

"Come on, you two." Matthew Fair addressed them. "Don't look so glum. It's no more than a tease. If I'm not taking it seriously then you shouldn't either."

"Who wrote it?" Nash repeated Poirot's question. "Speak up now, please. If Matthew is right and it was a joke, then the joke is over. The writer of this . . . alarming resolution must announce himself or herself now, without a moment's delay."

We waited in silence for a good ten seconds, but no one claimed the sinister little verse as their own.

I studied their faces and consolidated my initial impression: there really was a marked difference in responses among the group. Matthew and Belty were taking it lightly, and growing increasingly bewildered by the concerned demeanor of the others. Olive Haslop's face was grave and thoughtful. Her younger sister, Rhoda, looked horror-struck, as if in possession of terrible secret knowledge that was burning her up from the inside. Pearl St. Germain looked shifty and a little guilty. Charles Counsell's face hadn't changed, which is to say that he still looked as miserable as sin. Thirza's expression was one of mistrust and curiosity. She was looking from face to face, as I was, and if I'd had to guess at her thoughts I should have said they were along the lines of "Which one of you is a killer? I wouldn't put anything past any of you."

"No one wishes to own up," Poirot said quietly. "I see. It is not, then, the joke. We must treat it as a serious threat. Monsieur Athanasiou, I wonder, is this perhaps . . . ?"

"No," Nash said definitively. He shot Poirot an imploring look and his meaning was clear: *Please do not mention the thing that is in your mind. Not now. Let us keep that between ourselves.*

Poirot gave a small nod and looked away—willing, for now, for whatever it was to remain private between him and Nash Athanasiou.

"No, we must not treat it as a serious threat," insisted Matthew Fair. "This is a silly fuss over nothing. And, look, as the intended and intermittently willing victim, I ought to know. While I appreciate your solicitude on my behalf, Monsieur Poirot, there is really no need to sound so ominous. I shall still be knocking around the place tomorrow, you'll see—swimming in the sea with Catchpool here, right as rain. No one is going to kill me—you have my word on that. Neither before midnight nor just after it will I be removed against my will from this mortal coil." He chuckled at the idea.

"What if you're wrong, Matthew?" said Olive Haslop. "It cannot do any harm to take some precautions, surely."

"What do you mean by 'the intermittently willing victim,' Monsieur Fair?" enquired Poirot.

"Hmmph? I didn't say that, did I?"

"Yes, you did," I confirmed.

"Oh, well, you know . . . I don't suppose I meant anything, really, apart from . . ." He glanced around, as if hoping someone else would feed him his lines. When no one did, he said, "Look, everyone here knows I appreciate a good giggle. I'm just the sort of fellow who would say, 'Oh, do let me be the murder victim!' in any sort of . . . charade or dramatic production or . . . performance of that sort."

"And did you say that to somebody in relation to this game?" Poirot asked. "Before the resolutions were written and put into the bowl?"

"Heavens, no." Matthew snorted with amusement at the suggestion. Then he answered a question no one had asked: "I'm no poet. I don't know how other chaps make their verse come out as if it's the most natural thing in the world and just happened to roll off their tongue, or their pen, in exactly the right shape and with the right sounds at the ends of the lines."

"Might we hear the poem again, Monsieur Poirot?" said Austin Lanyon.

Poirot read the verse aloud once more in a brisk and toneless manner.

"Is it your joke, Austin?" Matthew asked with a grin. "You're the only poet among us, after all."

"That's precisely what whoever wrote those lines wants everyone to think," said Austin. "No, I didn't write them. I'm too talented, for one thing. There's no flow to the language at all. Each line is more cumbersome and wooden than the last. Monsieur Poirot, if you want proof I cannot have written it, go inside and look at the framed poem on the sitting room wall. I wrote it. It's called 'Ask Me How I Know.' You'll see at once the difference between poetic talent and the lack of it."

Thirza Davis rolled her eyes. "No one gives a damn about your literary prowess, Austin, for pity's sake. We are rather more concerned about whether someone is planning to strangle poor Matthew in the middle of the night."

"It is inconceivable that anyone should wish to harm Matthew," said Nash. "The rhyming resolution has to be some kind of . . . outrageous joke, not a credible threat of violence."

Pearl had stood up and walked around the table to where Poirot was standing. She looked over his shoulder at the piece of paper in his hand. "That is nothing like Austin's handwriting. In fact, it looks almost exactly like mine, though the letter *s* is wrong. My *s*'s are different."

"Let me see." Thirza was on her feet and soon by Pearl's side. "Goodness me, yes. It *does* look like your writing. Though I think the capital *F* of Matthew's last name is wrong. Your capital *F*'s veer off to the left at the bottom—like kite strings in the wind."

"They do not!" Pearl protested indignantly. "They look very like this one."

"Did you write this quatrain, mademoiselle?" Poirot asked her.

"No, I did not. I promise most sincerely, I did not. How funny." Pearl tittered. She darted over to where I stood in the middle of the terrace and leaned against me as if I were an unoccupied tree. "Isn't it funny, Edward? What a fathead the writer of the poem-resolution must be!"

"Why do you say that, mademoiselle?"

She blinked a few times, giving an impression of being absorbed in the most tumultuous mental activity. "I don't know if I can explain. Let me . . . Wait, yes, I've got it: if they are minded to imitate Austin, with all that rhyming, then why fake my handwriting? They could have written in block capitals, as we were told to. Why didn't they? And if they wanted me to get the blame for writing it, why have the murder threat presented as a poem that is so . . . correctly put together? It's perfectly possible to say you're going to kill someone using normal, everyday speech that doesn't rhyme."

"For pity's sake, Pearl!" Austin snapped. "You simply cannot be a stupid as you seem. Has it not occurred to you that someone might have tried to implicate both of us? The poem makes clear that the killer will have a helper, remember?"

"Pearl has a point, Austin," said Olive. "If the writer was attempting to replicate Pearl's handwriting, but wished to cast suspicion on you at the same time, why would they not have written 'I have a helper—staunch and sure is *he*,' instead of 'she'?"

"I don't know." Austin looked preoccupied. "I could take a guess."

"Perhaps because you are the writer of *les poèmes*,

monsieur," Poirot suggested. "If the poem was your creation and Pearl was your helper, you would say 'she.' It makes sense. Possibly we are supposed to believe you wrote the poem and read it aloud to Mademoiselle Pearl for her to write down."

Austin nodded. "That's what I was thinking. But you all saw what happened when the game began. I dictated no threatening verses to Pearl or to anyone else."

"You might have done it much earlier," said Poirot. "Prepared the folded piece of paper this morning. It was you who suggested playing The Resolution Game, was it not?"

"It sure was," Austin agreed. "And that means, and proves, nothing! I'll tell you what happened, Monsieur Poirot: a mischief-maker—a cunning wretch disguised as a friend—quietly penned those words with the aim of sowing discord in our until-now harmonious community."

"I fear that is correct." Rhoda Haslop had started to cry.

"Come now, Austin," Matthew Fair said forcefully. "You're upsetting our darling Rhoda, which you must not do. Monsieur Poirot, do please stop taking this so very seriously. You too, Nash. It's an audacious joke and nothing more. It must be—because everyone here is a thoroughly good egg, and I am too. See what I'm saying, old chap?" He looked hopefully at Poirot. "What we have here is an absolute dearth of plausible victims and plausible killers—conditions in which no murder could take place. That is not by accident. It is by design. Has Nash explained to you yet the beauty of this little paradise he has created?"

"No one has explained it to me," I said quietly.

"Not now, Catchpool," Poirot shushed me.

"This is my promise to you all, dear friends," Matthew continued to try and jolly us away from our concerns. "If any blackguard comes at me at midnight clutching a dagger or a poisonous snake, I shall knock him to the ground and cry for help immediately. Now, please, let us proceed with the game."

"I don't want to play games anymore," Rhoda said miserably, at the exact moment that Belty said, "Wait a second! The game . . . Couldn't we work out who wrote the verse by process of elimination? Once we know the authors of all the others, we'll be able to see who is left."

"You are assuming no one put more than one entry into the bowl, mademoiselle," said Poirot. "They could easily have done so—no one, I think, would have noticed. But you are right, we should pursue this avenue of investigation *néanmoins*. Catchpool, please retrieve as many of the papers as you can, including those that fell over the wall."

"We must stay close to Matthew and guard him," said Nash solemnly. "Keep him safe, until midnight at least, and probably thirty minutes after that, I should say."

Poirot turned slowly to face him, an expression of puzzlement on his face. "This midnight!" he said. "You are the second person to say it, Monsieur Athanasiou. Monsieur Fair referred to it twice. Please could somebody explain what is the significance of midnight?"

Several people exchanged baffled looks with those sitting nearby—wondering, no doubt, if the fabled little gray cells were failing. "Is it not obvious?" Austin said with a certain amount of belligerence.

"Midnight is when the current year ends and the new one begins," offered Olive Haslop, more cooperatively.

"And it's written in the threatening poem." Rhoda pointed at the piece of paper in Poirot's hand.

"It is not, mademoiselle," he corrected her.

"Why do you seek to waste time, Monsieur Poirot?" Thirza

Davis said impatiently. "Perhaps it is not written there in so many words—"

"It is one word, mademoiselle: midnight. I do not see it." Poirot made a performance of holding up the paper and examining it under the candlelight. "No, it is not here."

Rhoda said, "M. Poirot, we all know what the writer of the verse was trying to communicate, poetic flourishes notwithstanding: if Matthew's murder is to be the 'last and first death of the year,' then surely the plan is for it to happen at midnight?"

"The *stroke* of midnight—that's what I took it to mean," said Thirza. "Am I alone in thinking so?"

"No. I thought the very same thing," Olive told her. "The last death of 1932 and the first of 1933: midnight tonight, in other words. On the dot. What else could it mean? Though it's peculiar, because . . ."

"*Mais non*!" Poirot declared, making a flamboyant sweeping gesture with his arm. Nash looked taken aback. So did Rhoda Haslop. Belty Ricks folded her arms and raised her eyebrows. She alone of the group had the manner of someone at the theatre for a night's entertainment; nothing that happened could rile her, and the more entertaining and unexpected, the better.

"What were you about to say, Mademoiselle Haslop?" Poirot asked Olive. "I apologize for my interruption."

"Only that it's rather odd, and certainly counterproductive, to specify the time at which you plan to kill someone," Olive said. "We shall all be watching Matthew vigilantly as the clock strikes twelve."

Poirot gave a small nod. "You are right and, at the same time, wrong," he told her. "It would not serve the killer's interests to tell us when he plans to make his move—correct!

Or *her* move—for the resolution informs us that a woman is involved—or theirs if it is two people. *Eh bien*, our murderer would be delighted if we all made what I shall henceforth call 'The Midnight Mistake.' *Vous comprenez?*"

No one spoke.

After a few seconds, Poirot said, "We are *supposed* to leap to the wrong conclusion that midnight is the chosen time." He waved the piece of paper in the air. "That is why 'last' and 'first' have been arranged in this bizarre, back-to-front way, eh? The expected order would be 'first and last'—but not here, because the present year comes before the next one. *Eh bien*, the *last* death of 1932 must come before the *first* death of 1933."

"Well . . . exactly." Thirza Davis looked bewildered.

"There will be no murder at midnight," Austin said wearily. "What there might be as the clock strikes twelve is an *announcement*."

"Announcement?" I heard myself snap.

"Yes. I have a feeling that is when this mischievous resolution's author will reveal him or herself. I think we should play a new game and spend the time until then guessing who it is. My money's on you, Belty."

"Well, then we're the perfect pair, Austin, dear—because mine is on you. The poem's the clue. You say it's poorly written, but a good poet can write even terrible poetry better than a bad one."

"You have a point there, damn you," Austin said amiably.

"I do hope you're right, anyway," Belty said. "That it's all a game and we'll find out the answer at exactly midnight. That would be thrilling."

"You delude yourselves, *mes amis*," Poirot said gravely. "And I shall soon explain why. Catchpool, please. Why are you not doing as I asked?"

The Last Death of the Year

"What do you . . . ? Ah, yes, the resolutions," I said, remembering. It was I who had carelessly tossed them over the wall, and my responsibility to collect them. As I went off to begin my search of the lower terraces, I heard Matthew say something cheery-sounding about a joke with a midnight punch line and how clever and thrilling it all was, and I tried to force myself to believe he was right.

CHAPTER 7

Murder Takes Longer Than Death

Luckily, none of the folded pieces of paper had been swept away by the wind into the sea; I was able to find every last one. I returned to the dining terrace where, once I had caught my breath, I assembled and counted them. "Twelve in total, including the death threat," I said. "Since there are eleven of us, that means someone wrote two." I considered mentioning the cook, Manos, simply because he was a twelfth person and had been at The Spitty for the earlier part of the evening. But he couldn't be the culprit, I realized: his last appearance had been at least ten minutes before I had brought the empty wire bowl up to the dining terrace.

"Unfortunately, they are all written in gray pencil lead, so no clues there," I said.

"Read them aloud, all of them," said Poirot. "Mesdemoiselles et messieurs, please identify the one you wrote as soon as you hear it."

This next part proceeded efficiently. I picked out my own first of all and briskly informed the assembled company that I would be swimming in the sea every single day of 1933—and yes, I was disappointed when Poirot did not instantly furrow his brow and say, "But *mon ami*, you work in London, at Scotland

Yard. There is no seaside near there." Maybe he would invite me to explain this discrepancy later on, I thought.

I read out the remaining resolutions (my readers have seen them already, so I won't list them again here) and each was promptly claimed by its author. Pearl's—to persuade the man she loved to propose marriage to her, and then accept—made everybody laugh, and she looked crestfallen. "I am sorry you all consider love to be so risible," she said in a fired-up voice, her eyes welling with tears.

"Only yours, Pearly, only yours," quipped Austin. "I picture your affections as a kind of grasshopper—yes, a feverish, frenzied grasshopper, hopping from one poor fellow to another. I'd warn the next one if I knew who he was. You've run out, haven't you? Or perhaps you have found a stash of likely victims in the rooms over there." He gestured toward the Liakada Bay Hotel.

"You have no room to talk about that!" Pearl snapped at him. "You are as fickle as the day is long."

"I wonder . . ." Poirot had begun to perambulate around the terrace. I knew his slow-thinking walk well. "M. Fair, your New Year's resolution is to be more punctual, yes?"

"Yes," said Matthew. "What is the relevance of that?"

Pearl, who had sidled over and pushed herself into the small gap between me and Thirza Davis, turned to me and said, "I wondered that too, what your French friend just suggested."

"Belgian," I told her. "And he didn't suggest anything. He asked a question."

"I suppose so," she said. "Still, maybe 'last and first' in the wrong order is some sort of reference to what we call 'Matthew Time.'"

Thirza leaned over Pearl and said to me, "The funny thing is, Inspector Catchpool: Matthew often goes to bed at least two hours before the rest of us, don't you, Matthew, dear? You would think the man who is always late would be the last to go to bed, wouldn't you?"

"Why would anybody think that?" Charles Counsell snapped. "The one does not follow from the other." No doubt he objected to his fiancée speaking to another man in such a flirtatious tone.

"It's all the sea-swimming," Matthew said. "Tires me out."

"Catchpool." Poirot beckoned me over, and I moved toward him with some relief. That last little conversation had left an odd taste in my mouth; there had been tension in the air, and Charles and Thirza had been the source of it. Thirza had spoken much too emphatically about Matthew's early bedtimes, as if there was some hidden significance to them—almost as if she sought to convey a disguised message of some sort.

When I reached Poirot's side, he addressed not me but the whole group. "Ladies and gentlemen," he began. Everyone fell silent and stared at him. "Allow me to explain to you this most obvious thing you have failed to notice. A murder at midnight tonight—and, make no mistake, I shall personally ensure that nothing of the kind takes place, but still, let us imagine that in different circumstances it might. *Eh bien*, this killing, if it were to happen at midnight, would be a murder at the start of 1933. That is when the new year begins. A murder *at* midnight, or at any time *after* midnight would be a death belonging to 1933. Whereas a murder at fifty-nine minutes past the hour of eleven? This crime would be one that occurred at the very end of 1932."

"You are right, of course, in a technical sense," I said. "But the writer of the verse could easily have been a little less pedantic than you, and thought of midnight as the cusp of 1932 and 1933, and therefore belonging to both."

"I agree with Inspector Catchpool," said Charles Counsell.

"So do I," said Olive. "Midnight would be viewed by many

as the point at which two days, or two years, meet."

"Besides, there is nothing else that 'last and first death of the year' can mean," said Belty.

"Are you sure about that?" Austin asked her. His tone was teasing.

"Tell me more," she said.

"All right, then." He stood up. "A murder could take considerably longer than one second to commit, if you include both the action and the result. Imagine if I were to stab a fellow—Matthew, let us say"—the two men smiled at one another—"at fifty-five minutes past eleven. He might only die five minutes after midnight. I mean, why the deuce would anybody expect him to die punctually when he's hours late to everything else?"

Pearl, Matthew and Belty laughed. Thirza managed a thin smile.

"I would have commenced the process of murdering him in 1932, but my end would only be achieved in 1933," said Austin.

There was some merit to this argument, I thought, yet it seemed to infuriate Poirot: "The resolution says 'the last *death* of the year,' monsieur, not 'the last murder.' If it is pedantic to observe that these two words do not mean the same thing, then I am happy to be the pedant."

"Oh, come on." Belty snorted.

"Life ends in an instant, mademoiselle," said Poirot quietly. "Unlike murder, which starts with the intent—often years before a crime is committed. But death? One is alive, and then suddenly one is not."

"We are going round in pointless circles." Nash's voice vibrated with anxiety. "To me it seems clear that whoever wrote the resolution had midnight in mind, so we must make sure Matthew is safe at midnight."

"No such thing is clear," said Poirot. "Though I agree, it would be remiss not to take this precaution. If nobody objects, then I propose we all stay here until 12 o'clock. It is not too long to wait."

"It is forty minutes," said Austin. "How do you suggest we fill that time, Monsieur Poirot, now that you've insisted on spoiling the game I invented?"

"M. Fair," said Poirot, ignoring Austin, "can you think of a reason why anyone, anyone at all, might wish to kill you? Or does anybody else have any ideas?" Above his head, the moon looked like a spotlight that might have been placed there deliberately to shine light on the only one of us capable of untangling this mess.

There was a certain amount of shuffling in response to the question. Pearl, Thirza and Belty all said, "No," "Never" and "Of course not!" or words to that effect. Charles Counsell said nothing. He was staring down at his hands. Jealousy, I thought, would be his motive; might he have threatened Matthew's life as a way of warning him to stay away from Thirza? But Matthew had no interest of that sort in Thirza as far as I could tell, no matter how she might have felt about him; Rhoda Haslop was the focus of Matthew's romantic attention.

Nash said nothing, but kept shifting in his chair, as constantly on the move as it is possible for a seated person to be. He looked stricken. Austin's face had the closed off look of a shop that has pulled down its blinds in the hope of driving away customers. Did he have something to hide? Had I been a betting man, I would have placed a large wager on his knowing something about this whole unsavory business.

Rhoda and Olive Haslop both looked as if they were trying very hard not to say something. Olive's mouth was pinched and she had made fists of both her hands. Rhoda stared down at the table, wide-eyed and unblinking, shoulders hunched;

Belty continued to look amused and vague, as if something pleasant but mildly confusing was unfolding around her.

Come to think of it, Pearl, Thirza and Charles also looked uncomfortable in their skins as Poirot's question echoed in the air around them. Perhaps they could all think of motives for killing Matthew—their own or those belonging to others in the group.

"I see," Poirot murmured after a few seconds. "This is most fascinating. Each and every one of you could shed light on this mystery ... but you prefer not to do so. That, of course, is your prerogative. I shall warn the murderer only once more: abandon your plans to commit this evil act. You will regret it very bitterly. Monsieur Fair—you wish to say something?"

"I ... no, Monsieur Poirot. Goodness, this is awfully dramatic, what? I'm looking forward to it being over. Roll on 1933!" He laughed awkwardly, and I noticed he had a strange look about him, similar to the expression on Austin Lanyon's face and ... yes, now Nash Athanasiou's as well. All three men struck me, suddenly, as appearing ...

"Guilty" was the only word I could think of that fit the bill, which made less than no sense at all. Surely Matthew Fair could not have been plotting his own murder ...

Or could he?

CHAPTER 8

The First Death of the Year

Nothing remarkable happened at midnight. At fifty-nine minutes past eleven, the eleven of us were sitting in silence on the dining terrace, watching each other and waiting, wrapped in an atmosphere that was far from festive. That state of affairs took us smoothly through the changing of the year, and all the aforementioned conditions still applied in the first few minutes of January 1933.

I was surprised to find myself rather shocked by this, and realized I had expected a distinct Something. Naturally, I was relieved that Matthew Fair remained alive and well, but after such a stirring buildup, I think we were all rather hoping for a grand gesture, or at least a flurry of explanation, to burst forth from someone or other. I had wondered if Nash Athanasiou was behind it all and would solemnly announce that it was part of a spiritual lesson he wished to impart, for which all this subterfuge had been necessary.

Soon after midnight, Nash said, "Everyone is exhausted, Monsieur Poirot. Shall we perhaps—?"

"*Oui*," Poirot agreed before the question was complete. "After all the travelling of the day, and the seasickness, and tonight's threatened trouble, I have rarely felt so fatigued. To be so physically depleted has a deleterious effect upon the constitution that cannot always be reversed."

"But Monsieur Poirot, you said you don't believe the writer of the resolution meant to kill Matthew at midnight," Nash protested. "We must continue to—"

"True, true," Poirot agreed. "I am starting to believe that our menacing poet sought to create only psychological distress, not cause a death, but we must take no chances. Monsieur Fair, is it possible to lock the door of your bedroom?"

"None of the doors have locks," said Belty.

"M. Poirot, if it will make you and Nash happy, I shall push an item of heavy furniture in front of my bedroom door to make it unopenable," Matthew said. "But, really, as I have maintained from the start, nothing is going to happen. The drama is over. It was a joke, that's all. A malicious one perhaps . . ." For the first time, he frowned and looked unsettled by the events of the evening. "But serious murderers do not advertise their crimes in advance," he concluded with a somewhat forced grin.

A loud burst of laughter erupted from Belty Ricks. "I can hardly believe it—in all the panic, we have forgotten to say 'Happy New Year' to one another. And we didn't even notice! I think we must all have gone a little mad." She raised her empty right hand—miming holding a glass—and said, "Happy New Year, to all my very good friends—old and new."

"It does not feel happy at all," said Rhoda Haslop.

"You'll feel better in the morning, darling," Matthew Fair told her. Thirza gazed at him and sighed, and Charles Counsell's face set into a rigid mask as he no doubt realized that his fiancée's apparent attraction to another man had not been discarded among the tattered remnants of 1932. Olive, who had been leaning against a tree nearby, swayed suddenly and rather violently in Matthew's direction.

Violently? No, that was overstating the case; she had simply moved swiftly, while looking at him. Perhaps Belty Ricks was right, and a madness had descended upon us all. New Year's Eve is a night on which most people are prone to feeling out of sorts; no other calendar date is as effective at making one aware of both the preciousness of each individual moment and, simultaneously, the gargantuan insignificance of those same moments in the rolling sea of time.

Olive opened her mouth, then immediately closed it again. Whatever she had planned to say to Matthew Fair, she had decided against it.

"Yes, the outlook will be quite different tomorrow—much brighter," said Poirot, as if delivering the weather forecast. He rose from his chair, stretched his arms and said, "In the morning, when we have all had some rest and the feverish emotion of this evening's highest . . . what is the word? Ah, yes, jinx. When these highest jinx are behind us, perhaps the person responsible for writing the unpleasant resolution will explain to us his or her meaning."

"Not this evening," Austin corrected him. "All the 'feverish emotion' happened last night, even if we haven't had a night's sleep in between. I rather miss that feverish past," he said fondly. "I would choose it over this morning's stunned bleakness any day of the week."

We said a few more unconvincing Happy-New-Years, many goodnights and then went to our rooms, which is to say that everyone apart from Poirot and I entered The Spitty through its front door, for their bedrooms were all on the first and second landings: Nash, Matthew, Austin and Charles were along the corridor at the top of the first landing, and the ladies were above them: Thirza, Belty, Pearl—and Olive and Rhoda, who shared the largest room on the second floor.

Poirot and I walked through Manos's kitchen to reach our designated quarters. We passed messy heaps of knives and forks, and still-damp plates that had slipped off each other's backs. Saucepans were everywhere, all their handles pointing in different directions, some facing down, others facing upward—perhaps in case of a roof leak, I mused, though there didn't seem to be slightest threat of rain at Liakada Bay.

I wondered if Poirot might be too tired to express his disapproval, or remember there was no need, since he had already regaled me with his full grumbling routine.

No such luck. "It baffles me that such delicious food as we ate tonight can come from this . . . place of disaster and disarray," he said, slowing down to examine it more closely. "I am not sure I will be able to sleep in proximity to chaos of this magnitude."

To distract him, I asked, "What is the precise nature of this little encampment, Poirot? A spiritual community of some sort, I gather, with Nash as its leader—but what sort of jig is it?"

"Jig?" Poirot shook his head. "No, no, no. There is nothing lighthearted about it. Monsieur Nash is extremely serious about his little project here. Indeed, he intends for it to become much larger."

"But what is the project, exactly?" I asked him. "Also, I should dearly love to know why he invited you here in the first place. Did he fear for the safety of Matthew Fair even before the drama we've just witnessed?"

"All of this is a conversation for tomorrow," Poirot said with the authority of a parent who announces lights out and will brook no argument. "We have much to discuss, but now, Poirot must sleep. It can be postponed no longer. As you know, Catchpool, I do not make mistakes. Yet I made one tonight, and it happened as a result of physical and mental weariness. *Eh bien*, the revivification of the little gray cells must be delayed no further."

"What mistake?" I asked him. We had come out through the door at the other end of the kitchen onto the little trapezium-shaped terrace that faced toward the hills behind the house. From all the terraces attached to The Spitty, ours was the only one from which the bay could not be seen. Poirot would have laughed if I'd admitted this annoyed me, just as I could not understand how some randomly distributed saucepans and forks in a nearby room could disturb a person's sleep. Other people's minds are always such a mystery.

"I was wrong to think the writer of the resolution-in-verse had in mind the clever misdirection," said my friend, in answer to my question. "Of course they did not fashion a clue of such sophistication as to confound the finest mind."

I knew which mind he meant, of course, but he pointed at his forehead to clarify the matter.

"They wanted nothing more than to spoil somebody's, or perhaps everybody's, New Year's Eve fun. Yet for a short while I felt certain that they hoped we would all assume midnight was the time to which they were alluding, and fail to work out whatever they truly meant by 'the last and first death of the year.' Ah well . . ." Poirot sighed. "Sometimes, Catchpool, one imagines—because one wishes for—an adversary who is truly deserving of one's fullest attention, the ideal instructor for one's investigative sensibility."

"Surely all that matters is that Matthew Fair is still in one piece," I said.

"That is welcome, indeed," said Poirot. "It is not, however, all that matters. Other things matter."

We said our goodnights and retired to our rooms. I don't know how long it took me to fall asleep, but it felt like a long time. I wondered if Poirot was experiencing a similar mental agitation to mine—not on account of any misplaced spoon, but after the various bewildering utterances and furtive, conspiratorial glances of the previous evening. There was a lot that I wanted to file away for future reference.

Eventually I gave up on sleep. I got up, found my notebook and a pencil and made a list of everything it felt important to remember, planning to draw these things to Poirot's attention at the earliest opportunity.

List for Poirot —January 1st, 1933

1. Matthew Fair described himself as the "intermittently willing victim." What could that mean, apart from that he is occasionally willing to be murdered, or risk being murdered? Why would he be? And why only "intermittently"?

2. Why did Matthew Fair look so very guilty when Poirot admonished all present for keeping quiet about what they knew and failing to clear up the puzzle?

3. Why did Nash Athanasiou, Austin Lanyon, Rhoda Haslop, Olive Haslop, Pearl St. Germain, Thirza Davis and Charles Counsell also look furtive and uncomfortable? Even Belty Ricks, who did not look as if she felt guilty, seemed to radiate a knowing amusement, as if she was harboring a delectable secret. It is also possible that Charles Counsell was not keeping relevant knowledge to himself, since his ordinary expression is already one of unhappiness and mild alarm. (He is perhaps exceedingly shy.) But as for the rest of them: Nash, Austin, Rhoda, Olive, Pearl, Thirza and Matthew himself, I am convinced each of them is in

possession of pertinent information they chose not to disclose.

4. Did the writer of the mysterious twelfth resolution aim to incriminate Pearl St. Germain and Austin Lanyon, by imitating her handwriting and his inclination to write poetry?

5. Has there been a romance between Austin and Pearl, and has it now ended amid much acrimony and recrimination? If not, why do they dislike and gripe at each other?

6. Did "the last and first death of the year" mean "midnight," in the resolution writer's mind? If not, what did it mean?

7. Does anyone plan to harm Matthew? If yes, why advertise the fact and risk interference and the thwarting of your own aim?

8. Why did Nash Athanasiou invite Poirot to Lamperos? And is the answer to this linked to his effort to silence Poirot earlier? (Poirot started to ask a question. He looked at Nash and said: "I wonder, is this perhaps . . . ?", at which point Nash cut him off with a firm "No." His eyes seemed to beg Poirot not to refer publicly to whatever they both had in mind at the time. What is that thing?)

9. Is Thirza Davis in love with Matthew Fair and not her fiancé, Charles? She seemed unabashedly fond of him

The Last Death of the Year

and makes no attempt to hide it. Is this why Charles wears the expression of a condemned man?

10. What precisely is going on between Rhoda Haslop and Matthew Fair? He calls her "Darling" and addresses her in a doting, overly solicitous way. But what does she think about it all—and especially about him having thrown her over for Pearl St. Germain?

11. Does Olive Haslop disapprove of Matthew's manner in relation to her younger sister? When she seemed to move violently in his direction, but said nothing, had she been about to rebuke him for his constant "Darling-ing" of her sister?

12. What are the religious beliefs shared by these "very good friends"?

13. What was Pearl's true reason for leaving the dining terrace and coming to the house? Fetching the bowl cannot have been it, for she knew I had been dispatched to do precisely that.

I put down my pencil and stared at the number 14 on my list. There was something else, was there not? I was sure of it. An important detail—too important to forget . . . and yet I seemed to have done just that.

A noise from outside made me gasp and jump out of my chair at the same time. It was the shrillest scream I had ever heard and it went on and on, losing its shrill, high pitch as it developed and ending up sounding more like the low growl of a dying wild animal.

I had lost all sense of time while writing my list, so I had no notion of what hour it was. Equally, I could not tell you how long I stood open-mouthed, immobile as a block of stone, before throwing open the door of my room and running out into the night.

Poirot was ahead of me, in a navy-and-lilac patterned silk robe and matching slippers. The two of us hurried through Manos's kitchen, in no doubt about which direction the noise was coming from: the dining terrace. *Of course*. It felt inevitable that the next stage of our ordeal (for that was how I thought of it, even before I knew a murder had been committed) would stage itself in the same location as the troubles of the previous evening.

Nash Athanasiou, Austin Lanyon and Rhoda Haslop were already there when we arrived. They were standing in a row beside what looked, in the darkness, like a large heap on the ground, long and shapeless.

On the other side of this thing, whatever it was, Pearl St. Germain was gurgling in distress, bent in half, though the sight of me and Poirot approaching put a stop to the din, finally. "Oh, Edward," she wailed and ran at me with great ferocity, at the exact moment that other people started to appear: Olive Haslop, Thirza Davis, Charles Counsell.

I wanted to follow Poirot to where they all stood, but Pearl was pushing me the opposite way, saying, "No, you mustn't, you mustn't, it's too terrible."

The candles on the dining terrace were burning, I noticed. I was sure they had been extinguished before we all retired for the night. Yes, Olive and Rhoda Haslop had attended to that; I watched them do it. Someone had re-lit them, evidently.

All of the faces of the Very Good Friends were visible in the moonlight; all wore expressions of profound shock. "What on earth has happened?" Thirza demanded. No one else had said a word, at least not since Poirot's and my arrival at the scene.

"God has punished me," said Rhoda shakily. "And there is no avoiding the rest of his punishment, which is what the rest of my life will be. I will be given no more chances at happiness, not now."

"For pity's sake, woman," said Austin, but there was kindness in his voice. "What nonsense."

"The most terrible thing, Edward—that is what has happened," Pearl answered the question as if I, and not Thirza, had asked it. "I cannot bear to look," she sobbed. "There is so much blood—gallons of it. Look, it's all over my feet. Oh, I cannot stand a second more of this horror. How can it be—a murderer, here? Austin was right all along: murder is a terrible thing, always. It cannot be justified, ever. I wish I had spoken up, but I thought everyone would call me silly—"

By now, Poirot was standing right beside the large heap... which, I gathered from Pearl's outpouring, was a dead body.

Belty Ricks. Matthew Fair. They were the only two who were not present and visibly alive. As well as, I supposed, Manos the cook and Rasmus the boatman.

Pearl had glued herself to my side and wrapped her arms around me. I made what I hoped were comforting noises, while trying to peel her off me.

"Poirot?" I enquired.

There was the sound of heavy running footsteps accompanied by panting with a decidedly male sound to it. Then a man appeared at the farthest end of the dining terrace who must have come from the path that curled around the edge of the bay. I recognized our visitor straight away as the owner of the Liakada Bay Hotel, Yannis Grafas, whom I had seen with his wife while Matthew and I were swimming yesterday. He said something urgent-sounding in Greek that had the intonation of a question. I guessed he was asking what the commotion was about; it seemed likely that Pearl's screaming would have been audible even at that distance, in the otherwise quiet night. There was no sound of waves lapping; the sea seemed entirely still for the first time since Poirot and I had arrived at The House of Perpetual Welcome.

The House of Occasional Murder, I said silently to myself, as Belty Ricks emerged from the house blinking repeatedly, shielding her eyes with her hand as if in response to a glaring light, though there was none. "What are you all doing?" she asked. Thirza Davis turned away with a haughty toss of the hair, and it reminded me of something: yes, that's right. She had done the same before our New Year's Eve dinner, when she had arrived on the terrace: made a production of turning away at the sight of Belty.

Yannis Grafas's arrival had put a stop to Pearl's latest outburst, unless it was a coincidence that she ran out of steam at the same time. She said, "Oh." Then in a voice devoid of emotion: "It is Yannis from the hotel" and stepped behind me, as if she expected me not only to protect her from him but also to understand why this should be required.

No one answered Belty's question. Rhoda Haslop was sobbing in her sister's arms.

On Poirot's instructions, Yannis was soon on his way, by bicycle, to fetch the Lamperos police. I shook Pearl off me once more, made my way to Poirot's side and looked down at the sightless, open eyes of the murder victim, trying not to breathe too deeply, for the smell of blood was one I found hard to tolerate and it was not usually quite so overpowering as it was here and now. It made me feel considerably worse to think that perhaps this particular bloodstream had been so full of vim and sheer, unbridled enthusiasm for life that it had possessed, somehow, a stronger aroma.

Any vitality once present was now overwhelming in its absence. The lifeless face and useless body that remained would soon be "cold in the earth," as the poet Emily Brontë would have it, never again to delight in any of the joys the world had to offer. The tragedy of it was too big to grasp. If it had been someone else, a chap who had enjoyed life a little less, maybe . . . Charles Counsell came to mind, and I felt instantly guilty. I did not wish Mr. Counsell any harm, of course.

It was not his life that had been cruelly cut short, however, so I spent next to no time worrying about him. My mind seemed able to produce only three words, which echoed in an endless loop for the next several hours: "You were warned."

Indeed we were; we had been—though in an imprecise manner that had made effective protection unlikely if not impossible. And this horror at my feet was the result: beneath a large thick blanket that had been pulled up to his chin, leaving only his still face visible, the murder victim: Matthew Fair.

CHAPTER 9

An Inspector Suspects

What happened next was rather a blur. Rhoda fainted at least twice and Belty fetched her some water from Manos's kitchen. Everyone said multiple times that it was impossible, could not be true, must not have happened.

But happened it had.

"M. Fair has been stabbed many times. Many wounds," Poirot said to me, stepping closer to the prone body. "No weapon is here that I can see."

"Stay away from him!" Rhoda screamed. "All of you, stay away. Oh, Matthew! My darling Matthew!"

"Mademoiselle Rhoda is right," said Poirot. "None of us must touch him. We must do nothing but wait here patiently for the police to arrive."

My eyes met his and I gave a small nod of understanding: we had here an invaluable opportunity to observe everybody during this crucial period. There are many ways in which a killer might give themselves away while standing around unoccupied.

For instance . . . it was interesting that Olive seemed to have no response of her own, being too busy comforting and restraining her distressed sister. I guessed that Rhoda's misery concerned her more than Matthew's death, though perhaps that was unfair; after all, if one is a caring and helpful sort, one would always do better to attend to the living than the dead.

Austin Lanyon stood a few feet away, his eyes fixed on Matthew's body, one hand across his chest and the other covering his mouth. Nash paced back and forth repeating the same word over and over: "No. No. No." His eyes shone with tears under the light cast by the moon. I looked at Pearl, caught her looking at me, and turned quickly away. She did not seem tearful or even especially shocked anymore. Surely, she could not have recovered so quickly. Yet she seemed composed, more like a detached observer than one who, only minutes earlier, had been screaming the place down.

Charles Counsell and Thirza Davis stood side by side. Tears snaked their way down Thirza's face and her long neck. *A sad swan*, I thought. Her tall, thin frame shook. Charles's features were stretched almost to the point of disfigurement by the atrocity that lay before us. When I looked at him, I thought, *That's more like it*, and my disgust for Pearl's nonchalance increased.

As for Belty Ricks . . . her expression took a while for me to interpret. She appeared regretful more than sad, but also resigned—almost as if she was thinking, "I could have told them this was going to happen."

"Tell me, while we wait for the police to arrive . . ." Poirot looked from one face to another. "Where has everybody been, and doing what, between when we said our goodnights and now?"

"Where do you think we've been?" said Austin. "In bed. Asleep. It's what I tend to do in the middle of the night."

"Forgive the imposition, monsieur." Poirot smiled at him politely. "At least one person was *not* asleep, *évidement*."

"Well, *I* was asleep," said Austin.

"I was too, reckless fool that I am," Nash said. "How could I have been so complacent as to sleep after the threat made to Matthew only hours earlier. I shall ne—" He stopped.

"Were you about to say 'I shall never forgive myself'?" asked Thirza Davis pointedly. "Is that not heresy, according to your rules?"

"*Our* rules," Charles, her fiancé, corrected her. "We all believe equally in our mission here, don't we?"

Thirza said nothing. From the twitch of her mouth, I guessed she might be less fervent a believer than her betrothed.

"I was also asleep, Monsieur Poirot," said Charles.

"Me too," Thirza said.

"And me," said Belty.

"*You* were not asleep, mademoiselle," Poirot said to Pearl.

"No, I was not," she replied. "And neither was Rhoda. Were you, Rhoda? You were at your window, looking out. I saw you as I got closer to the house. You had lit a lamp, I believe, or else I should not have been able to see you."

Rhoda, still weeping, nodded. "I . . . was . . . lying in bed at first, trying to . . . sleep and I think I drifted off for a few minutes, but . . . I think I must have heard something because I jolted awake and . . . that's when I went to the window and looked out. I waited and watched, but I saw and heard nothing . . . not until Pearl came walking along the bay road."

"Where had you been?" Poirot asked Pearl.

"Down on the beach, listening to the waves," she said. "Looking at the sea. It looks so beautiful in the moonlight. I could not sleep. I had the pain of unrequited love in my heart, you see."

"For Monsieur Matthew?" asked Poirot.

"Matthew?" Pearl tittered as if at a joke. "Gracious, no. I stopped loving Matthew ages ago."

Rhoda shuddered at this. Olive looked at Pearl in astonishment, gave a small shake of her head, then wrapped her arms more tightly around her sister.

Pearl St. Germain was loathsome, I decided, and a Very Good Friend to precisely nobody. She had been shocked to see blood and a dead body—that was the only reason she had screamed, because *she*, the only one who mattered, had had an unpleasant experience. She didn't care a damn about poor Matthew.

"So, you were on the bay road walking back from the beach," Poirot asked her.

She nodded. "It is the only way to get back."

"Whatever noise it was that woke Rhoda . . ." Olive Haslop began. "I heard it too. It did not wake me, though. I was already awake, worrying about the nastiness inside someone's head that prompted them to to write that horrible rhyming resolution. As I lay there fretting about it, I heard the faint sound of voices coming from the floor below, where the men sleep. Perhaps it was . . ."

"It might have been Matthew talking to his killer," said Belty.

"That's what I thought," Olive told her. "I heard nothing more after Rhoda woke up and went to open our window. I certainly did not suspect anything like what has happened. I was sure no one was going to hurt Matthew, or else I would have rushed outside as soon as I heard . . ." She stopped and closed her eyes. "The footsteps. Yes, before I heard the sound of voices, I heard footsteps. Two people's footsteps, walking first downstairs and then to the front door."

"Which is your room?" Poirot asked her. "It must be one of these at the front of the house, yes?"

Olive pointed high up and to the right. "The one at the end."

I studied its position and considered it in relation to that of Matthew. It would have been impossible to look out of that window and see his body where it lay.

"Mademoiselle," Poirot said quietly, as he walked slowly toward Rhoda. "Did you, then, witness Mademoiselle Pearl finding the body of Monsieur Fair?"

Rhoda nodded, wiping her eyes. "I saw her seeing him, though he was out of my range of sight. Pearl did not kill him, Monsieur Poirot."

"Of course I did not!" Pearl laughed at the notion. "Heavens above! I am not the sort of girl who trots around murdering people."

"Whoever did it, it was definitely not her," said Rhoda. "I saw her tripping along looking . . . perky, the way she usually does. She was in high spirits I should say. Then she saw . . . she must have seen . . . and her mouth dropped open, and this terrible howl came out. That is how I know it was not her."

"None of us here is the murdering sort." Nash paced restlessly to and fro. "None of us! Please, Dear Lord, let that be the truth. Though we are steeped in murder, and have been ever since—"

"Be quiet, man," Austin snapped at him. "You'll only make everyone feel a damn sight worse."

"I blame myself. I should have—"

"You could not have anticipated this and neither could I," said Austin forcefully. "I didn't kill Matthew. Therefore, I do not blame myself and I never will."

Poirot's eyes widened. At some point soon, he would certainly ask Austin and Nash many questions about what had just passed between them. He must have decided now was not the time.

Not much more of substance was said before the arrival of the police thirty minutes later, though Poirot paid attention to every word and facial expression in the interim and I did too.

I had been expecting several officers of the Lamperos constabulary, but only one arrived: Inspector Konstantinos Kombothekra, a short man of around sixty years of age, wearing a white open-necked shirt with black trousers. "My friend, I am so sorry about the tragedy that has taken place here," he told Poirot, then repeated the same words to Nash Athanasiou and to me.

Yannis Grafas, by the inspector's side, also offered his condolences, as did one of the other new arrivals. The policeman and hotel owner had brought company: Manos the cook and Rasmus the silent boatman, by whose side was either the same diminutive gray horse that had been present at dinner or one that looked identical to it.

"I will cook a meal," said Manos. "It will not take long. One hour is the most it will take."

"No one is hungry, Manos," Nash told him. "It's the middle of the night. Besides there must be heaps of leftovers from—"

"I will not hear of this!" Manos raised both arms in protest. "Death is here at Spiti Athanasiou, yes? Violent death? And where death has visited, must also visit good food. Proper food. The Soutzoukakia, the Stifada. Some Melitzanosalata! Leftovers will not be good enough, not at all." Yannis Grafas nodded his agreement, and Manos disappeared into his kitchen.

Manos might have been brought here for catering purposes, but who, I wondered, had thought to collect Rasmus on the way? And why? Perhaps a boat trip to the mainland was likely to be necessary. Come to think of it, there was unlikely to be any sort of Scotland Yard equivalent on the island of Lamperos itself.

Inspector Kombothekra told me, "God bless Manos. He is one of the best fellows alive. The famous, the incredible, the most esteemed! I am honored to make your acquaintance, Monsieur Poirot." He leaned in so that only Poirot and I would hear him, and said, "We must speak away from the others. I must tell you of my suspicions."

"But... you have not yet looked at Monsieur Fair's body," said Poirot, perplexed. "You have not made the search of the house or interviewed anybody—"

"All of this I will do," said Kombothekra. "First I speak with you alone."

"Very well," said Poirot. "Let us sit over there. And my friend Inspector Catchpool here will accompany us. He works for Scotland Yard."

Once the three of us were seated at a sufficient distance from the others, the Greek inspector said, "All of these friends here at Spiti Athanasiou I know well, Monsieur Poirot. None of them is a killer. They have the too good character. Mister Nash, he tries so hard to do the greatest of work here—yet his father, no, no." Kombothekra's face darkened. "His father is not proud as he should be. He wanted the son to be lawyer or doctor. If Nash were my son, I would be proud."

Poirot and I listened in stupefied silence as he regaled us with stories about all of The Spitty's residents, one after another. Charles and Thirza, the poor things, fled to Lamperos from a very trying and tragic situation in England: both their families turned against them after Charles's father and sister both died within weeks of one another. Evidently Kombothekra thought Poirot and I knew all about this already, so having told us no more than that, he moved on with his narration, first to Belty Ricks—"The lady with the big secret. Nash did the correct and wise thing, I think, in letting her stay."—then to Austin, then Pearl—"The charming and funny American, he makes everybody smile. But then along came Miss Pearl to the house, and there was the big explosion of passions. She is most loving and generous, that young one. But Mr. Matthew was tempted by her, away from Miss Rhoda, who was very sad. Poor Miss Pearl did not mean to hurt anybody of course."

"What about Matthew Fair?" Poirot asked.

"Ah, Matthew." Tears formed in the inspector's eyes. "He was the finest of all living here. The loyal very purest and best character. Of the men," he qualified. "I must tell you, gentlemen, that nobody is finer than Miss Olive Haslop. Her sister Rhoda has a noble soul also, but Miss Olive . . . she is . . . perfect." Kombothekra nodded, happy he had chosen the right word.

"My heart . . ." He placed his hand on his chest. "It is the possession of Miss Olive. I am not married and have not ever been—and only recently did I come to understand why: because my maker knew I had to wait."

"For . . . Olive Haslop?" I guessed aloud.

"Yes. Wait to meet her, yes. But!" He pressed his finger against his lips. "Not to say anything about this to her, please. I tell her myself. Soon. Now, let me examine the body of poor Mr. Matthew. Then, assuming nothing I hear or discover contradicts the whispers of my . . ." he patted his stomach, "I will tell you who I believe committed this crime."

Kombothekra walked briskly over to where Matthew lay. "*Mon dieu*," muttered Poirot. "Does it not make you feel better, Catchpool, to have the wholly impartial perspective, from one so capable of objectivity and with no personal investment whatever?"

I shook my head, temporarily speechless, as we followed the inspector back to the larger group, where he proceeded to ask all the questions I would have asked had I been officially in charge of proceedings. Poirot then contributed some additional ones.

What we learned, assuming the friends were telling the truth (which at least one person was not, obviously) was the following: everyone remembered seeing Matthew on the dining terrace just after we had all agreed to retire for the night, but no one could say that they had seen him go inside or to his room. By the time Inspector Kombothekra went to search The Spitty from top to bottom, demanding that we all remain outside and together while he did so, what seemed to have emerged was that Matthew must have been killed at around two in the morning. Olive Haslop said that she had heard the voices, and the two sets of footsteps a little before two—and no, she hadn't been able to tell if they were both male, both female, or one of each; the stone floor in between was too thick for such precision of identification.

Pearl had found Matthew's body upon her return from the beach, from where she must have set off just after two, since Rhoda first saw her from her window at ten minutes past the hour. Rhoda was certain of this because she had looked at the clock in her room immediately after waking and before opening her bedroom window to look out.

I was in no position to offer an opinion, having been so alarmed by Pearl's screaming that I had neglected to look at my pocket watch.

"I blame myself," Nash kept saying. "I have done everything wrong, made every possible mistake—"

"M. Nash," Poirot interrupted him. "Please accompany me to the terrace outside my room, on the other side of the kitchen. Catchpool and I wish to speak to you alone."

"But Konny said we should all stay here together," Austin protested.

Konny? He was referring to his Inspector Konstantinos Kombothekra, of course.

"Yes, the rest of you stay here together, please," Poirot ordered. "Come, Monsieur Nash. You must tell Catchpool everything you told me when you invited me to come here."

We entered Manos's kitchen, where Nash soon found himself detained by an urgent consultation with the culinary master himself, on the subject of meal timings. As a result, Poirot and I reached our little terrace some minutes ahead of our host's arrival.

"Damnation! I was right in my very first conclusions, Catchpool," he said. "While everyone was busy saying 'The killer might have been imprecise and meant midnight,' I, Hercule Poirot, experienced the great uneasiness inside—and I was wise to do so!"

"You are always wise," I told him.

"How I wish that were true. Like a fool, I did not trust my own instincts. Why not, when they are always the best?" he railed at himself. "The truth is that the killer *does* have a precise mind, and is as aware as are you and I that midnight is one second only, the first second of the new day *only*. Monsieur Fair's murderer hoped to mislead us, *mon ami*. We were meant to assume midnight was when he would strike. He—or she—intended for the scene to play out precisely as it did: all of us guarding the life of Matthew Fair until midnight had safely passed. Then we would all go to bed and only *then*, after he assumed everybody else in the house had fallen asleep, did the killer strike."

"That is what happened," I agreed. "I suppose we oughtn't to be surprised that someone capable of murder is also a liar."

"What lie?" asked Poirot.

I refrained from saying *Isn't it obvious?* "The lie that he would kill Matthew Fair at midnight."

Poirot made a hissing noise. "Still you do not see?"

"See what?"

"The murderer did not lie, Catchpool. He or she tried to be clever."

"How so?"

"If the verse had announced that Monsieur Fair would be killed at midnight then it would have been a lie, for he was not. But 'the last and first death of the year' cannot mean midnight, as I have several times now tried to—"

"Oh, I see," I cut in, sparing him the ordeal of further explanation. "You're saying the murderer meant something else by 'the last and first death of the year,' so there was no lie about midnight involved."

"At last!" My friend threw up his hands in mock gratitude. "Yes, he meant something different—and relied upon us not being clever enough to work out the true meaning. Now Matthew has been killed, and we have more known facts to help us solve this puzzle. How, though, does two o'clock in the morning count as the last death of the year? Does the killer mean he will murder nobody else in 1933, after Monsieur Fair? But then first and last would make more sense, no? This murder would be the first and last death of this year."

"It would," I agreed.

"I cannot shake the conviction that, with this mystery of 'last and first,' the killer has set for us a puzzle to which there is a logical solution, if only we could find it," Poirot said. "Ah, here is Monsieur Nash. I will let him tell you all about why he invited me here. It was to prevent a murder, not to solve one. And the intended victim whose life he feared was in danger . . . it was *not* Matthew Fair but someone else altogether!"

CHAPTER 10

Forgiveness Goes Too Far

"Someone tried to kill Pearl. It was a few weeks ago. That is why I invited Monsieur Poirot to Liakada Bay," said Nash.

"What did you mean before, about this place being steeped in murder?" I asked him.

"Have I not just explained? Someone tried to kill Pearl." My first impression was that he was still lying, or concealing something at least. His answer sounded nervous. Then again, he had seemed permanently anxious since I had first met him.

"How did someone try to kill Pearl?" I asked.

"There's a terrace immediately outside her bedroom," said Nash. "Whoever it was tried to push her off it. No one saw anything. Everyone claimed to have been busy somewhere else at the time. It was impossible to establish who was the guilty party, and the most frustrating thing of all was that Pearl herself strenuously denied it—she claimed a goat, of all things, came out onto her terrace to attack her."

"Ah, yes, she did mention that to me," I said.

"Asked if she had seen the goat, she said no, for she had been facing the other way. She claimed to have heard it galloping away, however." Nash exhaled slowly. "As I told Monsieur Poirot, there are many goats in this area, and not one has ever set foot inside The Spitty—which it would have needed to do, not to mention ascend two flights of stairs. It is nonsense! And Pearl St. Germain . . . well, I'm afraid she is quite the most unrealistic person I have ever known. She enjoys entertaining herself with flights of fancy. Naturally, she was reluctant to face the fact that anyone might wish to hurt her. I invited Monsieur Poirot here so that he could help me to identify the source of the danger, before anything disastrous . . ." Nash broke off with a sigh. "And as we know, it is now too late. Something disastrous has occurred."

"Pearl has not been harmed," I stated the obvious.

"No. Matthew . . ." Nash looked up at me. "I do not feel, presently, that I can go on without him. Nor do I want to."

"I am very sorry that you have lost your dear friend, monsieur," said Poirot.

"I have lost *everything*, Monsieur Poirot. Not only Matthew. Also my beliefs, my way of life. The truth is: if I ever find out who committed this vile crime, I cannot promise that I will not strangle them with my bare hands. What sort of religious leader—what sort of Christian—does that make me? I am supposed to be on a mission to turn the world into a place of mercy and—"

"There is not time now for the soul-searching," Poirot spoke over him, though kindly. "Please describe as succinctly as you can your particular . . . religious philosophy, for the benefit of Catchpool."

Nash did as instructed, and I listened at first out of duty and then, once Nash got going, with increasing interest. Owing to his great distress, his explanation of his religious beliefs and those of the community at The Spitty was somewhat garbled, so I have made my own summary which is easier to digest:

After a conventional Anglican upbringing similar to my own, Nash concluded that traditional Christianity was insufficiently forgiving. It required its adherents first to admit to having sinned, then to stop sinning at the earliest opportunity and do one's best to be good thereafter, in order to earn one's salvation.

According to Nash, forgiveness was not something anyone should ever need to earn. Instead, it must be freely given, always, to everyone—because the moment we allow in its opposite or any manner of harshness (even toward the worst monsters) and justify it on any grounds whatsoever, we are repelling hope and light. This, in Nash's view, will never allow us to create a pure, kind world in which humans evolved to the highest and most enlightened versions of themselves.

Forgiveness had to come first, he believed, and it had to be constant and unconditional. "Forgive the sinners" was a brilliant idea—quite the best part of Christianity, if you were to ask Nash—but it had never been taken far enough. His view was: no matter how badly a person had behaved, the onus was on the rest of us to forgive them *in advance of their contrition* and even if their contrition never materialized. It was our duty to extend our unconditional love and welcome to them.

This, Nash insisted (he was speaking quite passionately by this point) was the only way to inspire the lost and hopeless to save themselves. "Do you understand, Catchpool?" He moved closer to me, as if keen to have my answer as soon as possible. "If I care for you and welcome you in precisely the same way whether you are saintly or the worst sinner, you will notice that your harmful acts yield the same results as would more virtuous behavior. Then and only then will it dawn on you that you in no way *deserve* the riches bestowed upon you, yet—and this is the most vital part—you need not fear they will ever be taken away. You are treated as worthy and loved, no matter what. Given time, you learn that you cannot *undeserve* your way out of love, compassion, mercy. Do you see, Catchpool?"

"Well . . ." I said. "If this is an elaborate joke, you are extremely convincing." Then I worried I had been rude, which was not my intention. It simply seemed incredible to me. A world based around the principles he was suggesting would soon descend into hell on earth.

"No, the only madness is the way we do things presently," said Nash. "My teachings, when put into practice, have a transformative effect upon the spirit. When a person understands that he will never be punished, banished, deprived, no matter what he does . . . why, that is when he strives to deserve the very best. He does not say to himself, as most would guess, 'I might as well be a terrible sinner.' No, he sees that he might as well be *good*. Think about it, man! When you have nothing to lose by trying to become your best possible self, even if you fail over and over again, you run out of all reasons not to try. Why would you *not* be virtuous, if you were received by all as if you already were? Here at The Spitty, we believe the worst sin of all is to be unforgiving."

By this stage, it was abundantly clear that Nash was deadly serious about all of it. Yet had he not said only minutes ago that he would strangle Matthew's killer if he could? As for "Here at The Spitty, we believe . . ." I had felt my lip curl at the pomposity. Was The Spitty on a par with The Vatican? Or was it what I knew it to be: a stone building of dubious design at one end of a pretty bay in Greece, with only nine permanent residents, at least three of whom (Thirza Davis, Austin Lanyon, Pearl St. Germain) I would go to some lengths to avoid taking spiritual instruction from?

"Ask anyone here how our way of seeing the world has freed them," Nash went on. "Matthew broke Rhoda's heart when he chose Pearl, yet she forgave both of them instantly. She might not have been ready to agree to be Matthew's wife, but she soon would have been, with a bit of encouragement

The Last Death of the Year

from me. And look at Belty—she is a good, honorable person now, yet she did something appalling in her past. I do not know what, before you ask—nor do I need or wish to know. We must attend only to who someone is in the present and might become in the future, not who they have been in the past. Look at Charles and Thirza! Did you know they were suspected of two murders? That was in London, before they came here. They were quite innocent, naturally. If they had done it, they would have told me—why should they not, when they know I do not believe in punishment or condemnation?"

This stance of his had worrying implications. I looked at Poirot, but his face was impassive.

"What made it so painful for poor Thirza and Charles is that the ones accusing them were their own relatives," said Nash. "Both families: his and hers. Charles tells me nobody has yet apologized, and I doubt they will, since forgiving oneself is the hardest thing of all. Much easier to pretend one was right all along. Charles and Thirza faced an impossible choice: either forgive what you have previously defined as unforgivable, or allow bitterness to tear your souls to shreds. Happily, they chose to come here and are flourishing as result—which does not, before you raise the objection, mean living up to every ideal all the time." Nash's mouth hardened into a line. "We humans are imperfect creatures. Thirza, for instance, has not yet been able entirely to forgive her and Charles's relations. Apart from Marie Doxford, but . . . That is a quite different case."

His obvious regret at having mentioned the name, followed by the swift and curt attempt to shut off the topic, prompted me to ask who Marie Doxford was and what was different about her.

Instead of answering, Nash replied with a question of his own: "Tell me Monsieur Poirot, Inspector Catchpool . . . Have

97

you ever succeeded in feeling vengeful toward someone who has suffered far worse agonies than the pain they caused you?"

"I have a question too," came a higher-pitched voice from behind me. I turned and saw Pearl St. Germain. She wore a rather desperate expression and was breathing heavily. "May I take Edward away with me. It is something of an emergency."

"Of course," said Nash. "Why? Has something happened, Pearl?"

"Nothing. It's . . . Oh, Edward you must come at once!" she said, then turned and ran off before any of us could say another word.

CHAPTER 11

Another Verse Makes Things Worse

After a few minutes of searching, I found Pearl in The Spitty's dark, wood-paneled dining room, moving back and forth next to the window in an agitated manner. Once she had checked that I had brought no one with me, she reached into her sleeve and pulled out a folded piece of paper. Naturally, I was assailed by unpleasant memories of the New Year's Resolutions game, and of that one resolution in particular.

Pearl held out the paper, her arm quivering, and I took it from her, thinking it must contain something terrible if the look on her face was any sort of clue.

My fingers stumbled over the opening of it, and when I saw four neat lines of verse, I feared the worst: another threat of murder, this time with a different prospective victim. Fortunately, my suspicion proved incorrect. This was an ominous poem, in handwriting that looked identical to that of the murder resolution, but it was not a threat of any sort.

> *There is a monster near us now.*
> *No glimpse of truth will she allow.*
> *Her heart and head are full of lies.*
> *January kills. December dies.*

"Where did you find this?" I asked Pearl.

"I didn't find it," she said. "I wrote it."

"You wrote it?"

She nodded. "You see, I am not the pretty simpleton you imagine me to be, Edward.

"I have never written a poem before in my life—yet look what I was able to do when I set my mind to it. You might say, 'Well, anyone can make the lines the right length and put rhymes at the end of them' but is that true?"

"Miss St. Germain, are you trying to tell me that, contrary to what you said on New Year's Eve, it *was* you who wrote the poem about killing Matthew?"

She recoiled. "Heavens, no! Did you not hear what I said? This is the first poem I have ever written."

"Austin Lanyon might have composed the resolution poem, but did you write it down for him?"

"I did *not*!" It was an anguished wail. "Nor have I any idea who did, or who composed it. I know nothing about any of it."

"But this poem here . . ." I glanced at it again, ". . . was written by the same hand."

"That is not *true,* Edward!"

"All right, all right, calm yourself. I apologize. I did not mean to . . . Perhaps the handwriting is not identical, but it is very similar."

"I told you that! I said, when I saw the resolution about killing Matthew, 'This looks like my handwriting.' Did you not hear me say it?"

"Very well, then: you did not write the threat to murder Matthew," I said. "Tell me about *this* poem. What does it mean? And why did you arrive in such a heated state to show to it me?"

"I wrote it to prove I could," said Pearl with feeling. "Austin's endless boasting exasperates me. And I'm tired of everyone assuming I've nothing but candy floss between my ears. I have never minded until now, but . . . well, your arrival changed that, Edward. I suppose I . . . well, I wanted to prove to you that I am not stupid. And if I looked fearful and had a sense of urgency about me . . ." She tilted her chin upwards in a haughty gesture. "Yes, I daresay I did. It was perceptive of you to notice it, but I am not surprised. You and I have a deeper understanding of one another than is customary after so short an acquaintance—"

"Miss St. Germain—"

"Must I ask you again to call me Pearl?" She smiled. "Can we not at long last dispense with the formalities?"

At long last? I had known her for less than one complete day.

"Who is the 'she' in this verse of yours?" I asked her.

"Oh, I don't know!" she said impatiently, as if it could not have mattered less.

"But . . . about whom were you thinking when you wrote it?"

"*You,* Edward. I think of very little else."

"Me? But I am not a 'she.' This poem seems to be describing a woman."

'Honestly, I despair of you, Edward. The poem is *for* you. It is not *about* you."

"Miss St. Germain, you seem to have written here about a woman who lies. A monster. You must have had someone in mind. If you are aware of someone at The Spitty having lied, you must tell me at once."

Pearl looked angry suddenly. "Maybe I was thinking of all of them," she said. "Most of us have clandestine thoughts that we never admit to, don't we? Though I shall not leave your side without confiding all my secret thoughts to you, Edward—that is a promise."

It landed with the force of a terrifying threat, but I was gallant enough not to say so.

There was a cunning glint in Pearl's eyes as she said, "Rhoda's secret is that she pretends she forgave Matthew instantly when he threw her after I arrived, but I don't believe it for a second. And Olive *must* have a secret—the way she creeps around, watching people closely, as if she is spying on us for the government or something. Maybe she is, now I come to think of it. It's not impossible that the government would send an . . . operative, is it, to keep an eye on an alternative Christian community they're afraid might become too influential?"

I could not help chuckling at this. "You think James Ramsay MacDonald would have made it a priority to keep a close eye on Nash Athanasiou and his eight chums over on the island of Lamperos, do you?"

"There is no need to be unkind to me in a gratuitous fashion, Edward."

I said a quick "sorry," then asked her, "Who else here do you believe is hiding something?"

"Well, we all know Belty Ricks is. She arrived here with a secret and has been allowed to keep it. There was a huge to-do, followed by a vote, and it went her way. Ever since, she has been sitting around with a lazy smile on her face, like the cat who has licked up all the cream!"

"A . . . a vote?" I said.

"Then there is Thirza Davis," Pearl went on. "I don't think Thirza is especially enamored of Charles, her fiancé. It's funny, you know—I did not know it until yesterday, but being madly in love is like having special magical powers. It gives a wonderful . . . *glow* to all the everyday objects around you—with one exception: people who seem somehow to stand against love. They alone do not glow. In fact, they do the opposite—they seem somehow sullied and darker. That is Thirza, without a doubt, Edward. Olive too; she also does not *glow*. Now, Charles, Thirza's fiancé—he is desperately unhappy I think. He knows he lost her love a long time ago, but he has the glow I'm talking about nonetheless, because *he* still loves *her* desperately. Rhoda is the same: heartbroken, but she glows, darkly, because she loved Matthew so passionately, to the bitter end."

Pearl looked impatient as she shook her head. "She really should have said 'yes' to him when he begged her to marry him the second time, once I had tired of him. Oh, Edward, I have been simply beastly to every man I have met on this island until today. Yesterday, I mean. It still feels like the same day as last night, doesn't it?"

"To whom have you been beastly?" I asked her.

"I did not mean to be! But I didn't know, you see. I didn't understand what was wrong with me, not until yesterday, when you arrived and . . . I saw you, and at once life made sense. One look at your face—"

"There are more important matters than my face to consider," I said, trying to steer her in a different direction, fearing I knew what was coming. Sure enough . . .

"I *love* you, Edward. I have fallen more wildly in love than anyone in this world has ever been. Quite giddy with it, I am! The moment I set eyes on you—it really did happen in a fraction of an instant, and do not tell me that it can't happen that way in real life, as it does in the fairy tales, because now I know that's not true. *You*, Edward, are the man I wrote about in my resolution: the man I shall marry before the end of this year—"

"Miss St. Germain, I cannot allow you to—"

"Pearl!" she wailed.

"Very well, if you insist: Pearl," I snapped at her. "I cannot allow you to continue in this vein. I am I afraid I do not—"

"Hush, Edward, please." She ran at me and slapped her little hand over my mouth. "I am not a fool. I know you do not yet feel about me the way I feel about you, but you will. You'll find that in due course a new sentiment will sprout up inside you. The seeds that will soon blossom have been planted already. I see it all, Edward: your discomfort in my presence, your attempts to avoid me. It is overpowering to think of, is it not? So strong that I felt compelled to come and hunt for you in the house last night, when you went to fetch the bowl for the game. You were taking so long in there, and I could not bear for us to be apart any longer."

"Pearl, you are completely wrong about every single—"

"I see it all, Edward. I am not wrong, for it is beyond doubt. I have not been given all these feelings so that I can weep until the end of my days, which is what will happen if you never ask me to be your wife. Suffering myself into an early grave from a broken heart is decidedly *not* my destiny. I refuse to countenance the idea that it might be!" She twisted away from me, making a noise that indicated physical pain. "And I regret most profoundly the anguish I have caused to others. Only now do I see how callously I have treated so many people. I thought I was in love with first Nash, then Matthew, then Austin . . . but I was not. I broke all their hearts—well, in truth I did not break anything of Austin's, but only because he has no heart to break. And Nash had no romantic interest in me, so that was all over very quickly. He is on a higher level, I think—not the level that contains love affairs." Pearl nodded to herself. "I suppose many spiritual leaders must be the same."

I wondered if it this was true of Nash as I recalled how passionately he had spoken of poor, deceased Matthew: *I do not feel, presently, that I can go on without him. Nor do I want to.* Then I thought of Nash's claim that Rhoda Haslop would have agreed to marry Matthew eventually, had he not been killed, and I made a plan to consider all of this properly later.

"I did, however, break poor Matthew's heart," said Pearl gravely. "And Rhoda's too, which she did not deserve. She loved him unwaveringly, and is a thoroughly good person, and I do so admire her for that, though I should not wish to be like her in any other way. She's terribly earnest and dreary, and desperately unattractive." Pearl grimaced. "But she would have loved Matthew forever, whereas I only loved him for six days. Well, five and three-quarters."

"Five and three-quarters," I repeated tonelessly.

"Yes. Oh dear! I must apologize to *everybody*, and also explain that it's not my fault," Pearl said with great resolve. "I have always known, you see, that Fate meant me to play a part in the greatest love story of all time. I have known that was my calling since childhood. Naturally, I looked for the perfect man Destiny must have sent for me to find and . . . well, I suppose I didn't want to admit that I kept failing to find him. No one enjoys feeling like a failure, so I convinced myself time and time again. Poor Mother and Father wasted *so* much money on the two weddings I ran away from at the last minute . . . and then, when I came here, I thought, "Of course, here is where my destiny must be, not in the spoilt, rich circles of my old life, where everyone is vacuous and cares only about money and fame, but *here*, on this beautiful, simple island."

And I was right—because eventually *you* arrived, Edward, my handsome prince. Now I can fulfil my truest destiny. We both can."

"I am not the person you're looking for, Pearl." I tried not to sound too harsh, though I was repulsed by her ramblings. "Be sensible, girl. This is nonsense—a silly fantasy."

A look of such devastation appeared on her face that I decided I had better soften my tone if I wanted to avert a disaster. I gave her what I hoped was an encouraging pat on the arm and said, "I am sure there are many men out there who will fall in love with you on the spot, and whom you will love in return. For my part, I have no desire to marry anybody. Never have and never will. I plan to remain a bachelor. As it happens, I broke this news to my mother at Christmas. She . . . expressed considerable disappointment."

"As would I, if I believed you." Pearl's voice shook. "Fortunately, I do not and I never shall. It would be an annihilation of my whole self to do so, therefore I do not accept it! I *know* we are meant to be married. You will see. You must trust me, and—"

"No, *you* must see," I insisted. "You will only make it worse for yourself in the long run if you entertain false hope."

"Oh, there is nothing false about it." Pearl gave a cunning smile. "You and I are about to enter into a bargain. If you will agree to open your mind to the possibility that you might, one day soon, fall in love with me, then in return I will help you to solve the murder of Matthew." Her smile widened. "There is plenty I could tell you. I'm talking about things you might never get to find out about otherwise."

"Such as?" I said.

"I know what the resolution meant—the 'last and first death of the year' part that even Monsieur Poirot did not understand." Pearl looked pleased with herself. "It means

Matthew must have been killed a little before two in the morning—perhaps only a minute before, but definitely before. But you and Monsieur Poirot will never understand why it means that, unless I explain it to you." She smiled, folded her arms and waited for my response, confident she had me fully under control.

CHAPTER 12

What Pearl Knew

"You will tell Hercule Poirot at once!" my Belgian friend commanded in his most fearsome voice. It was now, in every sense, the first day of January 1933, New Year's Day, and several hours since Pearl had cemented my low opinion of her by threatening me with permanent ignorance if I did not submit to her blackmail. She, Poirot and I had left The Spitty's grounds at eight o'clock and adjourned to the outdoor café that jutted out from the Liakada Bay Hotel's lowest floor. The day looked set to be bright and chilly, and the waves were showing off: every so often dancing up to flick their spray in our faces. Poirot, for this reason, had turned his back on the water, which to my mind was a form of blasphemy.

I had repeated almost nothing of what Pearl had said to me (there was no need, for I trusted her so-called "love" for me would soon blow over; she was as changeable as the Aegean Sea by all accounts). All I had done was show Poirot her poem and tell him she claimed to know what "the last and first death of the year" meant.

"It is unconscionable that you have kept this knowledge to yourself for as long as you have, mademoiselle," he told her.

"I tried to tell Edward last night, as soon as he had read it out," said Pearl. "But someone who thought they were far more important than me raised their voice, as so often happens . . . I don't even remember who it was! All I know is, everyone here believes me incapable of saying anything worth attending to. After a while, one gives up."

Poirot was shaking his head. "This is not acceptable. Do you realize what you have admitted?" He stood up without warning, bounced out of his chair by the indignation swelling inside him. "You *knew* the killer would strike not at midnight but at precisely two o'clock in the morning. This is true, yes? Had you shared this knowledge, Monsieur Fair's death could have been prevented."

"You are being most unfair to me, Monsieur Poirot," Pearl whined. "I believed the resolution in rhyme was no more than an intriguing provocation. If I had known it was in earnest and that someone planned to commit such a horrible, bloody crime . . ." She shuddered.

"The mere intrigue, eh? The riddle?" Poirot sounded a little less angry.

"Yes, and so I didn't want to spoil it for anyone. I knew the others should all have been able to guess too, and I didn't want to spoil their fun in doing so. We were meant to be enjoying ourselves after all. Last New Year's Eve—the one before this one just passed—we had puzzles galore and stayed up till the sun rose." Pearl pursed her mouth. "But I *did* try to say something privately to you, Edward, about 'Matthew Time,' because I knew you couldn't possibly know and wouldn't be able to guess—so nobody can accuse me of trying to keep anything a secret."

"Thirza Davis was by your side when you mentioned it," I said. It was Thirza, indeed, who had started to speak immediately afterward—about how Matthew Fair liked to go to bed early, and had done so the previous New Year's Eve. Matthew had replied that he tired earlier than the rest of them as a result of all his sea swimming.

"Please explain, mademoiselle," said Poirot. "What is 'Matthew Time'?"

"When Nash and Matthew first came here to set things up, Matthew missed home a great deal," said Pearl. "He had lived all his life in England until then and he yearned for it desperately. Nash said he would get over it in time and come to love Lamperos, and he did. And of course he adored Liakada Bay and, like all of us, he believed wholeheartedly in the work Nash is trying to do here . . . but he never quite got over his longing for home. I think that's rather sweet, don't you?" Pearl addressed this question to me. "I was a little envious, having found home stifling since the moment I was born—but then, that was my parents' fault, not England's." A twitch of resentment passed across her face. "Well, they failed to imprison me in their sterile little world. Unlike them, I am a person who cannot wait to have new adventures, explore new, colorful—"

"I wish to hear only about Monsieur Fair and his relationship to the passing of time," Poirot told her.

"Matthew made a point of not acknowledging Greek time," said Pearl. "It was more of a joke than anything else, but there was serious intent behind it. His pocket watch remained set to whatever time it was in England. He wasn't silly about it—he knew when someone said 'Supper is at 7,' they meant Greek 7 o'clock. And he turned up late for everything in any case . . . but he was adamant that his watch would remain set to English time. He once said to me, 'I keep my pocket watch close to my heart, Pearl, so it must always tell my heart's correct time, and that's whatever time it is at home, in Appleby in Westmoreland. That will always be home, no matter where I live.' Oh!"

She wiped away a tear. "I remember, he patted his chest as he said it. Oh, it is too dreadful. Poor Matthew! It is simply impossible that he is no longer here with us, that I shall never again hear his voice. I had quite fallen out of love with him, Edward—you needn't worry about that—but I still cared for him as a friend. It makes me terribly sad to recall how fondly he spoke of his little . . . village or whatever it is. I had never heard of the place and he said it was in the north somewhere, so I cannot imagine it holds much appeal, but he did seem to be very much under its spell."

"So," said Poirot. "We are two hours ahead of England here. This means that it was only ten in the evening according to the time of Monsieur Fair's heart when it was midnight for everybody else at Liakada Bay?"

Pearl nodded. "I'm sure that is what 'last and first death of the year' meant. Matthew's murder, if it happened just before *his* midnight—shortly before our two o'clock, in other words . . . well, then that would have been the last death of *his* 1932, if you see what I mean. While for the rest of us, he died two hours into 1933. That is why I believe he must have been killed a very short while before two o'clock—unless, of course, his killer didn't give a tuppenny damn about accuracy, which I suppose is always possible."

"*Merci*, mademoiselle. You found Monsieur Fair's body on the dining terrace at ten minutes after two, yes? Where had you been immediately before?"

"On the beach," said Pearl. "I've already answered that question."

"So, you came up from there and joined the road that goes from the Liakada Bay Hotel to The Spitty?"

"Yes, and then, as soon as I got to the dining terrace, I . . . I saw him." Pearl wrapped her arms around herself, shivering.

"And began to scream," said Poirot. "*Eh bien*, did you notice Mademoiselle Rhoda at the window of her bedroom?"

"Not at first," said Pearl. "Only when I became aware of something moving. I think I must have heard her window banging against the wall. Then I looked up to see where the sound had come from. I think she was trying to ask me what was wrong, but I couldn't hear her over my own screams which I couldn't seem to stop."

"I see." Poirot inclined his head. "Thank you. That will be all for now, Miss St. Germain."

Pearl looked as if she was considering putting up a fight and refusing to leave.

"Catchpool and I need to speak alone," Poirot told her.

"Tell me, Monsieur Poirot, have I been helpful?" Pearl asked brightly. "Let me tell you: I intend to be even more helpful in the coming days." With that, she hurried away.

"What did she mean by that?" said Poirot. I heard him as if from a distance. I was thinking that Thirza's interjection last night, after Pearl's mention of "Matthew Time," had been quite beside the point. What did Matthew's tendency to retire to bed early have to do with him having left his watch set to English time? Nothing whatever. Yet Thirza had piped up as if the two were connected—as if one had made her think of the other.

"Catchpool. Do not drift away, please," said Poirot. "It could be that Miss St. Germain has more to tell us. You must make the best possible use of your . . . unique position in her affections. Extract anything from her that might prove valuable. Until you have done so . . ."—he eyed me warily—"kindly refrain from telling her that you do not have the same strong feeling for her as she does for you."

"Oh, I've got strong feelings, all right," I said. "None she would wish to hear about, I dare say."

The Last Death of the Year

"I spoke to Mademoiselle Rhoda a short while ago," Poirot told me. "She made a point of seeking me out. She is adamant that she saw Mademoiselle Pearl approach the dining terrace *not* from the bay but as if she had come from the hotel. In the opinion of Mademoiselle Rhoda, it is out of the question that Mademoiselle Pearl had been on the beach immediately before returning to The Spitty and finding the body of Monsieur Fair."

"That's interesting," I said. "One of them is lying."

"*Oui*. We must find out which." Poirot gazed past my shoulder for a few seconds, then said, "Tell me, Catchpool: why would our poetic murderer include such an obvious clue in his threat to kill? Anyone apart from the two of us could have said, 'Ah, I know what this means,' and explained about Matthew Time. Had they done so, Monsieur Fair would have been protected until past 2 o'clock in the morning."

"They perhaps thought 'last and first death of the year' was cryptic enough for no one to guess at its true meaning. But, leaving aside the time, why warn us at all? If the killer meant business, and we now know he did, then why alert us to his intention? I suppose there's a chance our cryptic poet and our killer are two different people."

Poirot gave a small nod. "That is possible. And, if true, raises more questions. Would the murderer have killed Monsieur Fair even without the poem? Perhaps the timing was decided by the 'last and first death of the year' suggestion but it would have happened anyway. Or . . ." He looked at me and waited.

"Did hearing the verse inspire somebody to do what they would not otherwise have done?" I said.

"*Précisément*. Ah!" Poirot stood up and raised his hand. Inspector Kombothekra was standing at the nearest edge of The Spitty's dining terrace, waving his arms. The poor man had been searching the house and its grounds all night, I assumed. Poirot had started to move toward the path that would take us back to the house, but he had taken no more than a few steps when the Greek policeman's gestures made it clear we should stay where we were, and before we knew it he was marching along the path toward us as if he had something important to tell us.

CHAPTER 13

Head in the Sand

Kombothekra lowered himself into the hard, broken-legged, cushionless chair next to mine with an appreciative sigh, as if it were a featherbed. His contentment vanished as soon as he started to speak, however. "The news I have for you is not good," he told Poirot. "I think I know who killed Mr. Fair. It is the person I referred to before, you remember? I would prefer it to be somebody else, somebody still here in the bay, but . . ." He shrugged. "I fear the worst. I and my very good friends have searched the house, and found nothing. Every single bedroom we have explored inch by inch—including yours, and yours, Inspector Catchpool. Also every public room, the terraces, the gardens, the rocks below, at the front. The whole outside. Nothing! No knife that did the stabbing, no evidence of any kind to guide us. This killer, he has shown himself to be the expert in avoiding detection—"

"Your very good friends?" said Poirot. "Who do you mean, Inspector?"

"Mr. Nash, Mr. Austin . . ."

I listened, astonished, as Kombothekra named all nine residents of The Spitty.

"Manos and Rasmus helped with the search also, and so did Yannis Grafas from the hotel," the inspector finished off his list of helpers. "This search, it could not have been more thorough."

Nor more involving of every single one of our murder suspects, I thought drily. Poirot's expression told me he was thinking the same thing.

"Who is this killer you suspect?" Poirot asked Kombothekra. "How do you know he has left Liakada Bay? Could he not be above us somewhere, hidden amid the trees? Is there not dense forest over there?"

"We on Lamperos call him Kefáli Stin Ámmo. This means . . . I do not know how to say in English. It is not his real name. I do not know what that is. I wish I did."

"If you do not know his name . . ." Poirot began rather testily.

"You speak no Greek, I think," Kombothekra asked. "Kefáli Stin Ámmo means the head stuck down in . . . not the sea." He pointed.

"The pebbles?" I guessed.

"No, the other kind of beach."

"The sand?" said Poirot.

"Yes, yes, the sand," said Kombothekra. "We say about this killer, since we cannot find him, that he must have buried his head in the sand. I am pleased now to tell you the story of Kefáli Stin Ámmo?"

Poirot nodded almost imperceptibly.

"He has killed before," the inspector said. "Here, on Lamperos. Not in Liakada—on the other side of the island. A family was murdered four years ago: mother, father, two daughters. Terrible tragedy. No trace or clue was left. And there is *always* left the trace or the clue, always something, as you must know, Mr. Poirot. Nobody who knew this family had any reason to dislike or harm them. We are good, kind people here on Lamperos. Only a depraved stranger with no conscience could have committed this act of barbarism. I worked and worked, searched and searched . . . still, I did not find him. I never found him. That was when I invented for him the name, Kefáli Stin Ámmo. I meant it as a joke: his head must be buried in the sand or else how did I still not know him?" In a half-whisper, Kombothekra added mournfully, "How to find a man whose face you have never seen?"

I cleared my throat. "I would like to check I have got this right, Inspector, if I may: are you saying you were unable to find the murderer of this family and so invented an entirely imaginary character?"

"No, no." He wagged his finger at me.

Thank heavens, I thought to myself.

"He was not the making of my imagination. This family, they were killed. Their deaths were real. The man who cut short their lives, he too is real. Now, I believe, he has struck again."

"But . . . why on earth do you assume it is the same killer?" I said, exasperated.

Inspector Kombothekra gave me a strange look. "Because I find no clue, as I said. No trace."

"Why are you so certain that none of the people living at Spiti Athanasiou could have killed Monsieur Fair?" Poirot asked him.

"Because, Mr. Poirot, never is there a murder without a . . . how do I say it? The compelling force. In the head."

"A motive?" said Poirot.

"Yes, a motive. Exactly. And no one here wants the death of Mr. Matthew. They all tell of their sadness, and I believe them. I know these people, Mr. Poirot. I know them well. Spiti Athanasiou is a house full of love, compassion and forgiveness. All of them, I like, I like very much. Doing the work I do, it is people like those here at Liakada Bay that give me hope." Kombothekra gave an emphatic nod. "Most people are good. This I am pleased to believe. Most people I like, and most people like me."

"I don't doubt it," I muttered, thinking that a murderer pretending to be innocent and motive-less must like him best of all. I stole a glance at Poirot, who looked rather dazed, then turned back to Kombothekra. "Look here, Inspector . . ." Was there any point trying to reason with him? Probably not, but it is hard to relinquish all hope, as many will attest who have encountered tougher conditions than the ones afflicting me at that moment. "You say you believe your Kefáli Stin Ámmo is no longer here at Liakada Bay. In which case, when and how did he leave? Somebody would surely have noticed a bicycle or a boat."

"Nobody saw him," the inspector said fiercely. "Nobody heard him. It is the way of Kefáli Stin Ámmo. How many times must I tell you this?"

"For pity's sake, man, surely you can see—" I began incredulously.

"He cannot, Catchpool," Poirot said quietly. "Inspector, tell us, please, about Manos, the cook at the house. Is he also a friend of yours?"

The question gave rise to much delight. "He is! Manos is the most precious of friends. There is not a kinder heart on Lamperos than the heart of Manos Bourgos. Since we were boys, he is my friend."

When Poirot asked about Rasmus the boatman, Kombothekra's report was equally glowing, and at the mention of Yannis Grafas he almost exploded with joy. "Yannis has the nature of the sun, for which this island is famous," he told us. "My mother attended his birth. He was the most beautiful baby she had ever seen, she told me."

We endured a few minutes more of the same sort of thing before Kombothekra announced that he was needed back at the police station in Lamperos town "to make my report."

As soon as he was far enough away, Poirot said with some force, "If only we had all of that time to waste that we just wasted! Catchpool, find Yannis Grafas inside the hotel. Ask him if he saw or heard anything last night. If Pearl St. Germain is telling the truth about being on the beach before 2 o'clock, he might have seen her. I would like to know if she or Rhoda Haslop is telling the truth about that. He might also have heard voices carried by the wind from The Spitty's dining terrace across to the hotel, as might his wife. Speak to her too. I shall return to the house, where I plan to interview everybody—all of our suspects, for that is what they are. From now on, Catchpool, we are in charge of this investigation. I, Poirot, am in charge," he quickly corrected himself.

I DID AS HE ASKED, and soon found Yannis Grafas in his dark, cramped living room inside the hotel. It was full of too many chairs, each one of which had a multicolored, checked woolen blanket draped over it. Grafas showed no sign at all of possessing "the nature of the sun"; quite the contrary. He had a morose bearing and did not smile once. I know that speaking to a policeman can bring out a person's suspicious streak, but I found it hard to imagine finding this surly chap in buoyant spirits in even the most favorable of circumstances.

"I saw nothing," he said. "I did not hear a thing. I have nothing helpful I can tell you." No doubt unintentionally, Grafas was giving a good impression of a guilty person guarding the truth with great vigilance, determined to let none of it slip out. I asked him if he had seen Pearl St. Germain in the bay at any time last night. At first he said no, then he changed his story when I told him it was possible Matthew Fair had been killed shortly before two o'clock. "Yes, I saw Pearl," he said, abruptly. "On the beach at two o'clock. Before also. She was there from half past one until two o'clock. So she cannot have killed anybody."

Pearl St. Germain would have been regarded by most as a very attractive young woman, and I wondered if this hotelier had a secret yen for her. If so, could I maybe transfer her obsession with me onto him? He was a fine-looking man. He had a wife already, of course, which was an obstacle . . .

At a certain point it became clear that Grafas had used up the total number of words he was willing to allocate to answering my questions, and I made my way back to our side of the bay. As I got closer, I saw that someone had been awaiting my return: Thirza Davis. She was standing on the dining terrace watching me approach, a tight look on her face.

CHAPTER 14

Charles Gets It Off His Chest

While his fiancée lay in wait for me, a tense and haggard Charles Counsell sat opposite Poirot at the small, square table in the music room, between the harp and the piano. Upon hearing that each of The Spitty's residents was to be questioned, Charles had volunteered to have his interview first, and as soon as he and Poirot were alone together, he had got straight down to business: "I should prefer you to hear this from me than from anyone else, Monsieur Poirot. Though it pains me to admit it, the truth must be faced. One can only avoid it for so long."

"I agree, monsieur. What does it pain you to admit?"

"I trust I can rely on your discretion?"

"You may trust that Poirot will take the appropriate action, always."

"Very well," said Counsell. "I . . . I believe Thirza was, and probably still is, in love with Matthew," he said. "Which, I realize, puts me in a hazardous position. A man in my shoes might well decide to remove his love rival from the competition." He sighed. "Not that there was any competition, really. I had—have—already lost Thirza, though she prolongs my agony by refusing to tell me so. Oh, she might still be wearing my ring, but I know that any affection she once had for me died long ago." He raised his eyebrows, as if surprised by a new thought. "She might still be set on marrying me, I suppose. Certainly seems to be—though I cannot think why. I know she does not love me. She thinks I'm no use at all. None of which matters, of course, now that more blood has been shed. I can scarcely believe it."

"*More* blood?" enquired Poirot.

Counsell frowned vaguely, as if the question were a distraction. He said, "Oh, not . . . that is nothing that need concern us. There has been crime and tragedy in my past. That is all I meant."

"Is that so?" Poirot watched him closely.

"Yes, but I would prefer not to rake up all of that now. Look here, I simply felt compelled to make a clean breast of all the relevant facts about . . . well, about Thirza, and Matthew—and I meant to say, also, that he did not one single thing to encourage her. He was an honorable fellow, was Matthew, a thoroughly reliable sort. Last man in the world who would run off with another chap's fiancée. But even if he had set his cap at Thirza, I should not have dreamed of taking a violent revenge. I did no such thing, Monsieur Poirot, no matter how likely a candidate I seem. You have to believe me. I . . . well, there is no need to bring up the gruesome stories of the past, as I say, but . . . if I am overly sensitive, it is because this is not the first time I have been accused of murder. I was as innocent then as I am now."

"I have accused you of nothing," Poirot told him. "I do not believe you killed Monsieur Fair."

"How glad I am to hear it!" Relief spread across Counsell's features.

A small, orangey-brown lizard, about three inches long, darted across the floor. "This is usual, I suppose?" Poirot asked. "The animal life inside the house?"

"Oh, yes, little chaps like him dart about all over the place. I rather like them," Counsell said.

"Do you? I do not," said Poirot. "I found one next to my bed this morning. His head was bright turquoise, and his body was green—a most alarming sight."

"Yes, well, you're on the lowest floor. You'll get more of the wildlife looking in on you than most of us, I expect."

"M. Counsell, you and Mademoiselle Thirza arrived here recently, did you not? Only Mademoiselle Pearl came to live here after you?"

"Yes, Thirza and I joined the community about three months after Belty did," Counsell said. "And then Pearl just two or three weeks later, I think."

"And all was well between you and your fiancée before you came here?"

"What do you mean?"

"The love you claim she no longer feels for you . . . she felt it then, when the two of you first came to Lamperos? Before she met Monsieur Fair?"

"I believed so, yes." Counsell looked doubtful. Then he outright contradicted himself by saying, "No. No, not really. I had started to perceive a difference in her manner toward me even then. We both approached the . . . troubles we suffered in our London life very differently. We are not at all the same sort of person, Thirza and I. As you know, what Nash is doing so brilliantly here . . . well, it's all about forgiveness. That is the virtue that leads the way in all we do. It's why I am here. The moment Thirza told me about this little sanctuary and Nash's mission, I did not hesitate, took no persuading at all. I knew it was the very thing I needed. I hoped, and still hope, it will be my salvation. I was determined to *try*, at least."

"To be happy here?" Poirot asked.

"To forgive those who had wronged us," said Counsell.

"Thirza and me. And . . . I was surprised and disappointed that she did not seem to want to make a similar effort, especially as it was her idea to come here. I wouldn't even have known about The Spitty or Nash Athanasiou if she had not told me. Yet from our first day, she seemed to have set her entire will against it."

"Against . . . cultivating the forgiving spirit?" Poirot was reluctant to break into Counsell's monologue, but wanted to check the two of them were not talking at cross purposes.

"Yes, and forgiving our families," Counsell clarified. "Thirza's and mine. Or 'our enemies' as she still calls them—deliberately, to provoke me. She knew Nash would not permit any such talk here and she makes sure not to use those words in his presence. She has always, scrupulously, pretended to be in complete accordance with the ethos here whenever he or Austin are listening. Or Matthew, or Rhoda. Anyone, really, except me. All the most bleak and distressing things she has to say, she saves for me. And the thing is, I cannot help feeling that her furious tirades against unconditional forgiveness are aimed at *me*—that somehow I am the one she cannot forgive, and . . . well, that she's telling me so in a sort of code. In a way I shall never be able to prove."

"Do you think she would prefer to leave the community at The Spitty?" asked Poirot.

"That's the last thing she'd want," said Counsell. "Unless . . ." He chewed the inside of his lip, thinking. "Now that Matthew is dead and she has no love object here, it is possible . . ." He left the sentence unfinished.

"You said before that she might still marry you—as if you would allow it to happen," said Poirot. "Would you?"

Counsell nodded. "I love Thirza. I would not let her down again. Not that I meant to before, but . . . it was in my family, you see, where the trouble started. And then it contaminated her family too. She did not ask for any of it, so, yes, if she will have me, I will do my best to be a dutiful husband."

"Tell me about this family trouble," said Poirot.

"My father died. And the way my sister Marie reacted to his death was . . ." Counsell stopped, closed his eyes for a second, then opened them again. "Even now, the temptation is to use the word 'unforgivable.' Thanks to Nash, I know we mustn't think of even the worst sins in that way, so I shall say instead that what Marie did was cruel and stupid, though no doubt she could not help herself. Nash teaches that even the worst of us are doing the very best we can in any given moment."

Now was not the time, Poirot decided, to take issue with the more dubious pillars of Nash Athanasiou's philosophy of life, though he did think that the foolish young man might take a different view if he were to meet some of the villains Poirot had encountered over the years, many of whom were not doing anything that could accurately be described as "their very best."

"You say you were accused of murder?" he prompted.

"Yes. More than once, if you can believe it." Counsell's resigned air suggested rotten luck of an ordinary sort and nothing especially remarkable. "After Pa died, my sister Marie told everybody that Thirza and I had murdered him. Scared him to death—that was her precise accusation, for he died from a heart attack, which Marie said we had caused by deliberately frightening him out of his wits. According to her, we were after his fortune, which was sizeable. Marie was itching to get her hands on the money—in fact Thirza contends that she never really suspected us, but wanted the two of us hanged and out of the way so that she could scoop up the whole lot. She had run out of all monies left to her by her husband. Having been widowed young, she already felt Fate had dealt her a cruel hand and the world—and Pa's will, specifically—owed her whatever she wanted in compensation."

"Her husband had died?" said Poirot.

"Yes, in a motorcar accident a mere three weeks after their wedding. Most unfortunate. Thirza's assessment is that on the day Francis Doxford died, half of the good in his wife's heart went with him. Then, when my father died and Marie discovered he had left her nothing, that obliterated all that was left of her goodness, leaving only . . . well, something quite monstrous, I'm afraid. That might sound like an exaggeration—"

"Not to me," Poirot assured him. "I have seen what can happen when the wicked impulse is allowed to dominate. It is a tragedy when this occurs, for the person afflicted and all who know them."

"That's right. A tragedy!" For the first time, Counsell sounded almost cheerful. "Trouble is, when smiles and a gentle voice come from a woman as pretty as my sister was . . . well, naturally everyone assumes she cannot be rotten to the core. Her accusations were so extreme, and of course everyone strenuously denied at first that they believed them, but it was clear that secretly they were thinking, 'Surely sweet little Marie Doxford wouldn't say such a thing unless it were true.' When Thirza told her mother and father about it, and her own siblings, they initially purported to be outraged on her and my behalf . . . at the same time as suspecting in much the same vein: 'Why would Marie Doxford—a respectable widowed lady, after all, who has so far lived a blameless life—make such a claim unless she had proof?'

"The plain fact was, she had none, because she was lying," Counsell said angrily. "And really, when you listened to the detail of what Thirza and I were supposed to have done to scare Pa's heart into stopping, it was a most macabre tale that only a warped imagination could concoct. To this day, Thirza insists Marie must have done those very things herself—that she was the one who scared and tormented Pa until his heart stopped, in the hope of getting her hands on what she imagined would be her share: half of a vast fortune."

"But she did not succeed," said Poirot.

Counsell shook his head. "Not a penny went to Marie, or to me and Thirza. Pa left it all to various charitable foundations. I had known well in advance that this was his intention. I assumed he had told Marie too, but apparently not. When the will was read, she got an enormous shock. And, of course, she was furious with me for having known and not told her. Immediately, she changed the substance of her accusation against us: Thirza and I, she now claimed, had frightened Pa to death for a quite different reason: not to get our hands on his fortune, but as revenge for him having disinherited us. She had already told the whole family, as well as the police, that she had seen and heard us commit this terrible crime—so the onus was on her to come up with a new reason why we might have done so."

"What was the police's response to her accusation?" asked Poirot.

"They saw through the lies, thank the heavens, and judged Thirza and myself to be the more trustworthy parties. Naïvely, we believed our torment was finally at an end." Counsell laughed bitterly. "How wrong we were! Our families started to distance themselves. I would have left them to their own devices and hoped they would come round eventually, but Thirza insisted on having it out with them, and . . . Monsieur Poirot, the things that were said to us! Surely, we could understand their confusion, they simpered, and why would Marie have said it if it were entirely untrue? I ask you, Poirot! Have these fools never heard of a lie?"

"Did these same relatives also distance themselves from your sister?"

"Thirza's lot had no dealings with Marie in the first place, but mine, yes, they avoided all three of us assiduously thereafter. 'Something unsavory going on with that trio,' they must have thought—and, no doubt, that we were all as bad as each other. Make no mistake, Monsieur Poirot: wherever there is someone vile and corrupt and someone blameless, you will find plenty of observers ready to unfurl some species of 'both as bad as each other' nonsense, thinking it makes them sound wise and fair. Then, after Marie was murdered, suddenly the only person who cared about behaving with a minimal amount of fairness or decency was me. None of our relations attended her funeral—I was the only family member present. Thirza tried to talk me out of it—she refused to come with me, naturally—but I was Marie's brother and we had loved each other for most of our lives. I felt it was my duty to see her laid to rest and pay my respects, no matter what she had done to me."

"You mentioned before that you were twice accused of murder," said Poirot. "Were you suspected of killing your sister?"

Counsell's jaw set. "I was, yes."

"By the police?"

"What? No, no. They knew perfectly well I hadn't done it. I was demonstrably somewhere else when Marie was . . . when it happened."

"Then . . . you were accused by your relatives, or Mademoiselle Thirza's?"

"No, not by them either. I have not had any contact with any of them since Marie died."

"I do not understand, monsieur." Poirot eyed him quizzically. "You said that you were accused—"

"Of Marie's murder? Yes, I was. There was someone who did all they could to drag a confession out of me for the murder of my own sister, someone for whom my alibi was, apparently, insufficient proof that I wasn't a savage killer."

Counsell covered his face with his hands as if to shield himself from what he was about to say. "My accuser was my own fiancée. Thirza."

CHAPTER 15

Thirza the Unforgiving

"Of course Charles didn't murder his sister," Thirza snapped, her voice full of scorn. The two of us were sitting side by side on the dining terrace's rough stone wall, which was no less comfortable than any of the available chairs. We faced in opposite directions; me with a view of the sea at its most spectacular—not "wine dark' as Homer described it, but sparkling in the bright sunlight as if its surface were made of tiny diamonds—and Thirza with her back to it.

Her derision, I worked out, must have been aimed at herself, for in the baroque story she had just recounted to me, she was the person who had accused Charles Counsell of murdering his only sibling.

"I think I knew deep down that he couldn't have done it," she said. "Several of his colleagues vouched for his whereabouts at the time. I didn't want to believe them, though. You see, I hoped with all my heart that Charles *had* killed the disgusting Marie. I should have regarded him as quite heroic if he had—that is the truth. If he'd had any sense, he would have allowed me to believe it and admire him for it, but Charles is much too saintly for that. As, I'm sure, are you." She turned to me with a peculiar smile. "Don't bother to deny it. I can see it in your face. You may disapprove of me if you wish, Inspector Catchpool. It will be excellent practice for you."

My face must have asked the obvious question, because she said, "Later on, you will need to do even more disapproving of me, for I am about to tell you all the things I should probably feel guilty about, but do not. So, you might as well make a start now, with that little tidbit. Don't worry, I have no concern whatever for your opinion of me so I shan't be upset. I only want you to know everything so that you can catch Matthew's murderer. And then that person can hang from the neck until dead," Thirza added venomously. "Isn't that what the judges say? Perhaps they do not say it in Greece. Is hanging what they do here? I assume that here, on Lamperos, is where Matthew's killer will be put to death?"

I knew none of the answers to her questions.

"You think I sound revoltingly bitter, don't you?" Thirza said. "Well, I am—and what's more, there's nothing wrong with feeling the way I do. You would too, had you been maligned the way I have. Shall I tell you the truth about how Charles and I treated his father, Inspector Catchpool? We cared for him, entertained him, tended to him for months on end. We did so because we loved him, in spite of his faults, which were *legion*, let me tell you. And we raised not the slightest complaint when he told Charles he would inherit nothing. We had our private thoughts about it, of course, but his testamentary arrangements were his affair. I cannot *bear* those who stick their beaks into other people's private business. We wouldn't have dreamed of causing a fuss, and Charles had a profitable company of his own, one he had grown from nothing, that would have looked after us very nicely for the rest of our lives. We didn't need his father's money. Nor did we want it, if he didn't want us to have it. Though I can't pretend I wasn't angry with him. It was so illogical!"

"How so?" I asked.

"Albert believed it was character-corrupting to leave one's wealth to one's children," Thirza said in a tight voice. "Yet he came by his own wealth in that precise manner, and didn't give it all away in his lifetime . . . so he cannot have worried too much about his own character. By the time he was informed of his illness, Charles was already thirty-five years old and the hardest worker I have ever known. He had already made a far greater contribution to the world, and more money using his own wits, than Albert ever had. Charles is the very last person to be idle or inclined to sponge off anybody. He puts his back into the job at hand, whatever it might be. Always has. Even Marie, in spite of her faults, did everything she could to better her material position after her husband died. Any halfwit could see that *none* of the potential beneficiaries of Albert's will would have been improved or helped by being deprived of the family wealth. My theory is that Albert felt envious and ashamed whenever he compared himself to Charles, who had created all of his own success and prosperity. Charles seemed to find this possibility inordinately upsetting. He could only bear it if *principle* was involved, and not something as base as good old-fashioned jealousy, so I shut up about it eventually."

Thirza gave a derisive snort. "No doubt this is how life will continue once we are married and for the rest of our lives: me buttoning my mouth in order not to shatter his illusions. Charles hates it when I speak my mind—about his father, about this place, Nash . . ." Her laugh was hard-edged. "Sometimes I cannot help it, though. 'Próti Foní'! I ask you, have you ever heard such self-aggrandizing hogwash in your life? I should like to see Nash retain his superior air and forgiving ways if Marie Doxford ever turned her malicious attention to *him*. She can't, of course, because she's dead, thank the Lord."

If she expected me to appear shocked, she was going to be

disappointed. Over the years, I have developed the useful skill of looking as if I'm thinking about nothing at all, and forming no opinions about it either.

"Why did you agree to come here, if you hold Nash's . . . work in such low esteem?" I asked her.

"It was a mistake," she said at once. "I heard about the community from a friend and was foolish enough to mention it to Charles, after which he simply wouldn't shut up about it. And the prospect of putting thousands of miles between me and everyone I loathed in England was tempting. Also, I adore the weather and scenery of Greece, and the people are the loveliest and friendliest I have ever known. Nevertheless," she said quietly, and I heard sorrow in her voice. "A mistake."

"Then why not leave?" I said.

"Charles will not. And I have agreed to marry Charles," said Thirza expressionlessly. "Someone like me needs a husband like him, I dare say."

"What do you mean?"

"It doesn't matter," she said curtly. "I expect I shall rather enjoy my dislike of my married life. Since coming here, my favorite pastime is feeling disgruntled and despising everything. All the claptrap about forgiveness that everyone spouts around here . . . I soon turned my heart into a safely feathered nest to protect my every last grudge. Since arriving at The Spitty, I have been adding new ones at a rate of roughly one a day. The only person I . . ." She broke off. "Never mind."

"The only person you . . . what?" I asked with a breezy casualness, hoping to trick her into thinking it could hardly matter if she told me.

A few seconds passed. Then Thirza said, "Matthew came close to convincing me now and then that . . . well, that perhaps forgiving one's enemies did have certain benefits. He said all the same things Nash and Charles both say all the time, but . . . Do you know, Inspector Catchpool, I have only just realized the difference."

That you were in love with Matthew? I thought but did not say.

"Matthew lived what he preached," said Thirza. "You have heard, I expect, that the people of Lamperos have the sun inside them? Well, Matthew was from Westmoreland in England, but he had the sun inside him all right. More than anyone I have ever known. He shrugged off all unpleasantness as if he simply did not recognize it. It shriveled when confronted with his powerful optimism. Nash and Charles both lumber about as if carrying mountains of gloom on both shoulders."

"Does that mean they are unforgiving?" I asked. "Or necessarily wrong on the topic of forgiveness?"

"The former," said Thirza. "Worried people, miserable people . . . are they not those who cannot forgive life for not giving them the benefits and certainties to which they believed they are entitled? Why not greet each day as if it's your very favorite, as Matthew did, no matter what it contains?" Her brow furrowed and her voice lowered in pitch as she answered her own question: "I'll tell you why not: because we cannot feel differently than the way we do. If anyone could have turned me into an all-forgiving saint, Matthew was that person. Ultimately, even he failed: not to persuade me that there are benefits to ridding oneself of resentment—I knew he was right about that, having forgiven the vile Marie Doxford—but to convince me that I could change my essential nature. I'm like a snake, Inspector Catchpool."

As if to prove her point, she bared her teeth and hissed loudly at me, then laughed. "It is in my nature, I am afraid, to hate forever those who have wronged me. Not to be merciful."

"Yet you say you have forgiven Marie? Whom you are still referring to as 'vile'?" This made no sense to me.

"I like to describe things correctly, and Marie *was* vile," Thirza said. "But yes, I have forgiven her and her only—because she was murdered in the most brutal fashion, and although her murder had nothing to do with her treatment of Charles and me, it truly felt as if the Lord above had allocated to her the worst of comeuppances. I tried not to forgive her—said to myself endlessly, 'Don't be a fool, Thirza. You swore to hate her forever, remember?' But that's quite impossible when someone's suffering vastly outweighs the harm they once inflicted on you. It feels so undeniable that, in a cosmic sense, justice has been done. I explained all this to Matthew and he got terribly excited. He said, 'And how does it feel to be free of that small parcel of hate?'"

Thirza smiled and blinked away tears. "That's what he called it: a 'small parcel of hate.' Bless his heart. I told him it felt wonderful. To contemplate Marie Doxford and feel simply nothing—just an absence of emotion and a feeling of 'Justice was done and the matter is concluded.' Of course it was liberating, but I can hardly arrange the murders of everybody I loathe, can I? And while those who have vilified and betrayed me wander around happily, taking afternoon tea, playing golf, doing whatever they please . . ." Her lip curled. "As I said to Matthew, no one wants to be lugging parcels of hate around, but one simply cannot feel differently from how one feels."

"Hm," I said, for Thirza had given me a lot to think about. And she was not finished yet:

"You might be wondering why I was willing to admit, to Matthew alone, that I, who had taken such pride in hardening my heart, had inadvertently and without my own permission forgiven the very worst of those who had sinned against me."

I waited.

"I was in love with Matthew," Thirza said eventually. "That is why I confided in him and not my own fiancé."

"I see," I replied in a sober fashion.

"I should be grateful if you would not mention any of this to Charles, Inspector Catchpool. It would only distress him. Now, you are going to say that I do not seem as grief-stricken as you would expect, given that the man I adored has just been killed. I strive to appear composed; it is quite deliberate, and of benefit to me—at this painful time, when I feel more shattered than ever before—to be able to watch myself as if from a great height and see that I am getting on with the routines of my life, having conversations in which I remain calm, doing all my usual things. You might not understand."

"I think I do," I told her.

"You must catch whoever did it, Inspector Catchpool."

"I shall do my best."

"Good, because whoever it is, they must hang for it. Monsieur Poirot is a genius, I am told, and I'm sure it is true. But he is French. Everyone at The Spitty is English or American. There will undoubtedly be nuances of language and expression—things he cannot understand."

"He is Belgian," I said.

"Yes, and the language he speaks is *French*," she said impatiently. "I want *you*, Inspector Catchpool, to stop relying so heavily on your friend's abilities and use your own brain to solve this. What would you do if you were here alone and Poirot was at home in . . . Brussels?"

"He doesn't live in Brussels. He lives in London."

Thirza made an impatient noise. "I don't care where he lives! He can live next door to me on the Strand if he wishes—I will happily share with him my view of whatever they are building or knocking down that day. Do not, please, point out that I don't live in London anymore because I live here at present. I am aware of that fact. Now, do you understand what I am asking of you or do you not?"

I told her I did.

"Good." She gave me a rigid, unnatural smile. "Then I am ready to tell you what happened last night. I shall go mad if I do not confess to somebody, and since Matthew is no longer here..."

"Confess?" I said.

"Yes, Inspector Catchpool," said Thirza. "It is my fault that my beloved Matthew was murdered."

CHAPTER 16

The Belty Ricks Vote

In the time it took me to extract from Thirza Davis everything she could usefully tell me, Poirot—as he later boasted—managed to interview not one, not two, not three, but an impressive four people. "Ah, Catchpool," he breathed contentedly. "I took my interrogative aim as rigorously as the scalpel of the finest surgeon."

The first person after Charles Counsell to cross the threshold of the music room (which had effectively become Poirot's headquarters for the purposes of the Matthew Fair murder investigation) was Belty Ricks. She was wearing another exquisite dress today, sea green with gold thread woven through it, and Poirot wondered not for the first time why a woman with such taste and style who was lucky enough to have been christened "Betlinde"—a most elegant name—should choose to go by the undignified "Belty." ("Do I invite those I meet to address me as 'Herky,' Catchpool? Most decidedly I do not!")

He had requested that Belty visit him first and wasted no time in asking her to supply further details in relation to what I had told him about a rather unorthodox sounding vote, of which she had been the subject. He had not been certain she would know what he was talking about (perhaps the vote took place in her absence, he surmised) but her eyes sharpened the moment he referred to it.

"Oh, that," she said. "So, you have heard, then. Tell me, Monsieur Poirot: which way would you have voted?"

He told her he knew none of the particulars: only that there had been a disagreement, resolved in the democratic way.

"Democratic?" She had laughed. "As first invented by the ancient Greeks, you mean, and therefore fitting for the island of Lamperos? Let me tell you, Mr. Poirot, The House of Perpetual Welcome is not a democracy. Nor has it ever pretended to be."

She said this as though it made no difference to her one way or the other, just as she had asked how Poirot would have voted as if she couldn't have cared less. Or rather (Poirot had corrected himself when he'd told me about it later) she had sought his view only so that she could judge him, slot him into the appropriate box in her mental classification system.

"Nash makes all the decisions here," she said. "A spiritual movement needs a clear leader, he believes. I know what you are going to say: why bother with a vote, then? I wasn't there for the meeting—as its main controversial topic, I was deliberately excluded—but I know how this place works. Nash likes to hear things debated in order to know his own mind. He will have allowed a vote in order to test his own response to its result."

"What was the controversy that required a vote?" Poirot asked.

"Oh, you don't know what the big ballyhoo was all about?" Belty looked surprised. "Well, then . . ." She took a deep breath. "One thing and one thing only attracted me to Nash's new spiritual movement: the prospect of unconditional forgiveness. A fresh start, the ability to leave behind not only what I had endured but also the shriveled husk I had become as a result . . . Intolerable unhappiness had been inflicted upon me, Monsieur Poirot, and I had done my fair share of inflicting too." She gave a little laugh. "I wanted the slate wiped clean."

And that is how you appear, mademoiselle, Poirot thought. *Like a slate wiped clean, with no deep reserves of emotion left.*

"Nash has explained so much that I would never have thought of if left to my own devices," said Belty. "Like for instance that forgiveness means far more than most people imagine. We think it only means that we stop being angry with others, but if you forgive everyone from your past to the greatest extent that you can, and if you similarly pardon yourself . . . why, then everything cancels itself out. The past becomes completely unnecessary to remember. It can disappear altogether if we want it to. What a wonderful idea!" Belty chuckled, as if the thing she had praised was nothing more serious than a diverting parlor trick.

"When I first arrived here, I was very frank with my new friends, since I did not wish to present myself dishonestly," she said. "It was important to me to live a good and blameless life from that point forward—which meant no lying, no distorting of the truth. Charles, Thirza and Pearl had not yet joined our little group, but I told Austin, Matthew, Rhoda and Olive what I had told Nash: I had not been a good or moral person before I came to Liakada Bay. Austin seemed delighted." Belty smiled at the memory. "Couldn't wait to tell me all about his own former misdeeds—and boy, does that man know how to turn each little peccadillo into the most charming and hilarious tale!" Belty's smile remained in place, with a slight downward twist, as she said, "He ended up quite beside himself, like a baby whirling around in a tantrum, when I made it clear I was not going to respond in kind and tell him anything about my own past sins. I said to Nash: if the forgiveness here is unconditional, then why must I provide a laundry list of my wrongdoings? What if I don't want to? Would these people not agree to welcome me and be my 'very good friends' if I refused? If so, that was neither welcoming nor forgiving, surely."

Belty leaned forward in her chair. "My past was *gone*, Mr. Poirot. Like it had never existed in the first place. I didn't want Old, Rotten Me following New Me around. And the truth is, no one cared what I'd done before coming here apart from Austin. He was the only one demanding to know . . . until he talked Matthew and Olive round to his point of view, convinced them that my reluctance to share my moral self-flagellation was evidence I didn't trust them, or regarded myself as superior. Silly boy! He'd have said anything to winkle my stories out of me.

"I knew why he kept pushing for lascivious details," Belty said knowingly. "Purely for titillation. Every story he told about his own immorality involved him ending up the arms of the wrong sort of woman." She raised an eyebrow. "He took one look at me, found me attractive no doubt, and decided he needed to hear me expand on all the loose living I must have indulged in before coming to Lamperos. Rhoda took my part, sweet girl that she is, and Nash took *her* side. Hence, I was allowed to stay."

"But Matthew Fair . . . he took the side of Olive Haslop and Austin Lanyon?" asked Poirot.

"Are you asking if I murdered him for doing so?" Belty emitted a lethargic laugh. "I did not. That would have been something of an overreaction, don't you think?"

Poirot said nothing; he felt disinclined to joke about murder.

"I had nothing against the guy, and besides, I had made a promise to myself," said Belty. "If I was allowed to stay at The Spitty, I would not do a single thing wrong ever again. My behavior would be exemplary. And it has been. I have followed Nash's directions to the letter with regard to those who sought to banish me: Austin and Olive. I forgave both of them without the slightest qualm. I could kinda see their point of view, though obviously I disagreed. Olive is a smart lady; she and I have become rather good friends. As for Matthew, I'd have forgiven him too, but he changed his mind the moment he saw that both Rhoda and Nash were in the 'Let Belty stay' gang. Matthew always wanted to make his favorite people happy more than he ever believed in anything."

"Mademoiselle, do you regret the murder of Matthew Fair?" Poirot asked her.

"Why, of course I do," she said easily. "He was the kindest, funniest guy you could hope to meet. But you know what consoles me? Because I do believe in heaven, Mr. Poirot. And I know that's where Matthew is now, and he'll be making the most of it all right. He was better than anyone at grabbing whatever was on offer and just having the best ol' time with it."

Poirot recoiled a little from this description, as if heaven were some sort of fairground Lucky Dip. "Who, in your opinion, killed Monsieur Fair?" he asked Belty.

"Oh, I should say it was probably Austin," she replied smoothly. "You gotta ask yourself, 'Who here is capable of wickedness?' I think Austin is, given the right conditions. Not that I don't like him a lot. I like him just fine. He's so clever and entertaining. He and I are kinda good friends, too, but . . . well, I guess it comes down to a question of capacity."

Belty nodded to herself. "And when it comes to murder, I'd say Austin has capacity aplenty."

FIFTEEN MINUTES LATER, POIROT WAS able to compare and contrast Austin Lanyon's perspective on the famous Belty Ricks Vote.

"Nash doesn't often make a jackass of himself, but gee whiz, did he get that one wrong," Austin said, sitting sideways in the chair Belty had vacated, his legs draped over its wooden arm. His facial expression suggested he was physically comfortable, though in Poirot's estimation this was not possible. "Belty insisting she did not need to tell us a damn thing about who she had been or what she'd done prior to coming here . . . I like the lady well enough, especially to look at, but her determined secrecy planted doubts in me that never went away. And now I'll tell you something that will surprise you, Poirot, and I hope you pay attention—"

"You believe it was Mademoiselle Belty who murdered Matthew Fair," said Poirot.

"Why, you must be every bit as smart as they all say you are!" Austin looked delighted. "Don't get too excited, though. I can't prove it. The way I see it is that clues are nice, but knowledge of character counts for more."

"You are suggesting she has the bad character, Mademoiselle Belty?"

"I am," said Austin. "Nash misunderstood what was at stake when we all took that vote. Forgiveness cannot mean the absence of necessary protections. And we were grievously lax when we failed to protect our community by letting Belty in." Frustration twisted his features. "We could and should have forgiven Belty for all those transgressions she refused to tell us about, and then sent her on her way. Without the ability to recognize danger and corruption, how can our movement thrive, let alone replace all other forms of religion, all over the word? That is Nash's aim, and mine too."

"Ah, just the tiny ambition, *bien sûr*," Poirot commented with a smile.

"Vast, vast ambition," said Austin earnestly, stretching out his arms as wide as they would go. "I won't apologize for it. I wish Nash would be louder and bolder about it, too, but he lacks confidence. Whenever he's not reading us the rules, he seems to be full of doubt and fear. I'll tell you a secret, Monsieur Poirot." Austin lowered his voice. "I ought to be the leader here. I never waver in my belief, and I never forget about joy, either. To listen to Nash or Rhoda or Charles, you could easily imagine forgiveness was a spiritual chore—vital, but difficult. Burdensome, no fun at all. Let me tell you, Poirot: to forgive the most unspeakable acts—why, it is the greatest joy a person can know."

"If you say so," Poirot murmured.

"It's the truth," Austin insisted. "When you finally learn that nothing and no one can stop you experiencing bliss, and that therefore there can be nothing for you to hold against another living soul . . ." He stopped. In a harder voice, he said, "Most people are nowhere near learning that lesson, which is why our work here must not be imperiled. Nash cannot see it, though, and so first Belty was invited to stay and then Pearl." This last name he spat out in disgust. "I'd send them both packing if it were down to me. Thirza too, actually."

"Women, all three," Poirot observed.

Austin laughed. "I like women well enough. Olive and Rhoda are good sorts. And Belty's my Favorite in all kinds of ways, as she well knows." He gave a grunt of satisfaction, in the manner of one who had eaten a large and delicious meal and now could not possibly manage any more. "I would still expel her from The Spitty if I could. She knows that too. And in all honesty, Poirot, and I'm sure you'll agree: liking them is one thing, but I do often wonder if females are able to put aside their own personal, petty preoccupations and focus single-mindedly upon a world-transforming project in the way we men can. I mean, take Rhoda—she used to *live* for this work we are trying to do here. I would even say . . . yes, I am happy to concede that she was the most devout of us all. Still, is, maybe. She forgave Matthew for choosing Pearl and breaking her heart, yet turned down countless marriage proposals from him once he had seen the light—for *his* sake, she said, and I believe she meant it, too. She thought he would soon become unhappy if they married, because he did not love her enough. My point is, Poirot, devout or not, nine-tenths of Rhoda's thoughts were and are Matthew-focused, when this mission of ours requires all of us to be as obsessed with the cause as Rhoda is with her tragic romance. Was," Austin corrected himself.

"Would you exile her too?" Poirot asked.

Austin looked irritated. "Not a chance. Didn't I say? She and her sister Olive are an asset overall. Olive especially." There was admiration in his voice. "If ever there was a lady who thinks like a man . . . Olive is as serious-minded as any fellow I've ever known. Got a way with words too. She ought to try writing poetry, though she's keener on scientific experiments. Still, before we voted on Belty, she summed it up better than I had: she said—I will never forget it—"'Unconditional forgiveness' does not mean that the condition of *knowing what occurred* should not apply.' Damn right! 'Unconditional' means only that we forgive any and every sin, but I mean, we gotta know what it is we're forgiving. Don't you agree, Poirot?"

Receiving no answer, Austin said, "Olive agrees, and that's good enough for me. She and I don't see eye to eye on everything, mind you. That woman takes every chance she can to turn the spiritual advancement of our species into her pet science project."

"How so, monsieur?"

Austin stood up and began to walk around the circumference of the room. "She cannot grasp that *belief* is what is required first, before anything else—faith of the wildest, craziest-feeling kind. She's always seeking ways to test each new stricture and assertion Nash and I come up with, to check there's no possible argument that might undermine it. And when she fails to find one, only *then* does she believe. But it works so much better the other way round. First the crazy, wild faith, then the intense joy, then the unwavering belief—and only if we get that far does the evidence start flooding in. Let the spirit lead!"

Poirot had different thoughts about the relationship between proof and belief, which he kept to himself. "You said 'Nash and I.' Are the principles this community follows not created solely by Monsieur Nash, then?"

"Let us say that I make the occasional *superb* contribution," Austin replied with a grin. "And my delivery is more dazzling than Nash's, which is not hard. I might not be Défteri Foní, but . . ." He stopped. "Well, blow me down! I *might* be the Second Voice, now that Matthew is . . . Not that I am saying . . . Obviously I would far rather Matthew were still with us."

Catching Poirot in the act of watching him carefully, Austin stopped perambulating around the room and said, "You want to, Mr. Poirot. You want to, oh so badly. But the truth is, you don't. Because, like I said, you're *smart*." He tapped the side of his head.

"What, in your opinion, do I want to do?" asked Poirot.

"Why, suspect me of Matthew's murder, of course," Austin said.

CHAPTER 17

What Thirza Knew

"If you know who killed Matthew, you must tell me." I did my best to present this as an unarguable fact, after Thirza Davis had stayed silent for a worryingly long time. I feared she was regretting her bold disclosure.

"It was not I who killed him," she said after a long silence. "I am not about to confess to murder, though I might one day need to. As soon as I find out who killed Matthew, I shall . . . I shall . . ."

"You will do nothing criminal, because you know it would be wrong," I told her.

"'Wrong'?" She sneered. "If I were to get hold of the person in question before the gallows did, would it matter? The end result would be the same. Oh, listen to me. I am pathetic: indulging in fantasies about garroting Matthew's killer because it's easier than facing up to my own guilt. The fact is, I could have saved his life, and I didn't. Worse than that, I *prevented* his life from being saved. I shall never forgive myself. Nor do I wish to be made to feel any less wretched about it." She shot me a warning glance, no doubt suspecting I was just the type to mount an ambush of unsolicited comfort.

"You probably do not remember, Inspector Catchpool, but

on the terrace last night, after you had read out that horrible murder poem, Pearl said something about 'Matthew Time.' And I, God damn me to hell, interrupted immediately afterwards, because I didn't want her to tell you what she had meant by that."

I listened patiently as Thirza regaled me with the very same story I had heard from Pearl, about Matthew having resolved always to keep his watch set to English time.

"As soon as I heard her describe it in that way—'Matthew Time'—I knew what she was about to say, and had what I thought was an inspired idea. Like Pearl, I wondered if the poem's author had maybe meant to suggest, in the most cryptic way, that the killer would strike at *Matthew's* midnight—which would be our 2 o'clock in the morning, and I did not want Pearl to say any more because . . ." Thirza broke off with a strangled noise. "You will think me pitiful when I tell you," she whispered. "I shan't blame you. I could not hate myself more."

"That won't do anybody any good," I told her, and she acknowledged the truth of it with a small nod.

"There was no doubt in my mind that Charles was the writer of the verse," she said. "I didn't think he would hurt Matthew when it came down to it, but I believed he planned to, in a silly, pretend kind of way—that he wanted to see himself as someone who would do whatever it took to remove his love rival from the scene . . . which is quite absurd, for Matthew had no interest in me of that kind. Rhoda was the one he was trying to convince himself he loved, after being told by Nash that swapping her for Pearl had been a terrible mistake. And Pearl was the one he *really* loved, though I am not sure he was aware he still did . . ."

Thirza broke off, looking a little confused, having drifted from her original point.

"Has Charles admitted to you that he wrote the threatening poem?" I asked her.

"Gracious, no. And he never will. He went to great pains to imitate Pearl's handwriting, to no avail. I know it must have been him. No one else had a motive to kill Matthew. Well, except perhaps Rhoda, but she is perfectly pure and good, so that rules her out. Olive, for Rhoda's sake?" Thirza inclined her head. "No. Rhoda will be even more drippy and doomed now that Matthew is dead—forever, probably. Olive is too intelligent to saddle herself with *that*." She started to count off the Very Good Friends on her fingers. "Austin is a scoundrel at heart, but I don't think murder is among the sins he finds tempting. Nash? Out of the question; he *adored* his perfect disciple. Pearl? Hasn't got the brains for a rhyming quatrain, let alone a murder plan."

I thought about the poem Pearl had brought to me and wondered if she had plagiarized it from somewhere. "You have not mentioned Charles," I said. "If he wrote the poem, surely he might have committed the crime."

"He might have, yes, except he did not. That is beyond doubt."

I waited for her to say more.

Thirza said, "I interrupted Pearl, when she spoke of 'Matthew Time,' because I didn't want anyone else to work out that the poem could have meant two in the morning. If they had, and had announced their intention to stay awake until then, Charles would have been far too scared to make his move at that time. I would not have been able to catch him creeping out of his bedroom and remonstrate with him for being so ridiculously melodramatic. Charles is a good man, fundamentally. It would not suit him at all to become a murderer, and I did not believe he would go that far, if it came down to it . . ."

"But you planned to catch him red-handed before he could?"

Thirza nodded. "I was standing at the top of the stairs from half past one. Watching. I could see Charles's bedroom door from where I stood. My plan, if I saw it start to open, was to step back so that Charles couldn't see me, and then follow him downstairs. Then, as he approached Matthew's door—blunt instrument in hand, I imagined—I would leap out and stop him before he did anything too silly. I was going to give him merry hell for his recklessness, naturally."

"And did you see anything, as you watched and waited?" I asked.

"Well, I did not see Charles," said Thirza. "His bedroom door remained closed. But . . . yes, I saw somebody." She turned to face me. "I saw Matthew, two or three minutes after I took up my post. He left his room, went downstairs and to the front door, and from there he went outside. Panic overtook me, suddenly, and I thought, 'What a muttonhead you are, Thirza!' I had assumed Charles was in his bedroom, when for all I knew he had stayed outside when the rest of us came in. Why did that not occur to me? What if he had asked Matthew to meet him somewhere at 2 o'clock—on one of the terraces, or on the beach? I rushed to Charles's room, feeling as if my heart might explode out of my mouth—because if he and Matthew were down at the bay, I feared I would not have time to get to them before something awful happened—but thank goodness, I found Charles tucked up in bed, sound asleep."

"What did you do then?" I asked.

Thirza's face contorted and she said unhappily, "I returned to my room. That turned out to be a poor decision, given what happened to Matthew, but . . . I was no longer worried about him, because I was so sure the threatening verse had come from Charles. It simply did not occur to me that Matthew might be in danger from anyone else."

"Even though the poem talked about the murderer having a female 'helper'?" I said.

"Yes, despite that," Thirza said with a heavy sigh. "I put that down to a desire on Charles's part to create extra subterfuge. And no doubt you will now suspect that Charles did it, and that I was his helper. Of course his fiancée would like to protect him, you will think."

"No, I do not think that," I told her. "Frankly, I don't know what to think or whom to suspect."

"Not Charles," Thirza said firmly. "He is a good, innocent man."

"And . . . not you either?" I asked, to make sure.

She shrugged. "You may suspect me if you wish. I don't care. I've told you I didn't do it, but you don't have to believe me if you don't want to."

CHAPTER 18

Olive's Experiment and Rhoda's Dilemma

Poirot mopped the perspiration from his brow with his monogrammed handkerchief as he followed Olive Haslop through a clearing between two dense clumps of trees. This was the highest altitude he had experienced since arriving on Lamperos, and he had no desire to ascend any further.

"We must be nearly at our destination," he called out.

Olive, marching on ahead, called back, "What's that, Monsieur Poirot? Did you say something about desperation?"

"Not yet, though if we do not arrive soon . . ." he muttered to himself. Olive had insisted on leading him up the little track behind the back of the Liakada Bay Hotel. She had promised that the walk would take "no time at all."

"I cannot risk saying what I need to say anywhere near The Spitty," she had told him, and it had been enough to get Poirot moving. Now, if he looked down through the branches of the olive trees, he could see the many different parts of the roof of The House of Perpetual Welcome and was able to observe once again what a strange shape it was from this elevated perspective as much as any other.

Finally, Olive called out, "Here we are. I told you it would not take long."

Poirot emerged from the trees. He had to admit that what he could see in every direction from this stony plateau was impressive: the most glorious "view from on high"—endless sea to the left and right and, ahead across the Aegean, the shore of what must have been another island: a sandy beach shaped like a long dog's bone, narrow in the middle with wider, curved bits at both ends. Beyond the sand was a green slope, broken up by outcrops of gray rock, perched on which were tiny white dots that must have been houses.

The view immediately before Poirot's eyes was more surprising. There were two red and white striped deckchairs and a little wooden table, squashed into the only flat area on this rocky platform. "I promised you somewhere to sit, and here it is." Olive smiled.

"You carried these up here yourself?" asked Poirot. She had strong, sinewy arms, so it was not impossible. Also, she had scampered up here without once seeming out of breath. Poirot guessed that, if one lived on an island with no proper roads, one might end up rather fitter than if one lived in London with its streets that were all too easy for both legs and wheels to navigate.

"Rhoda helped me furnish the place," said Olive, as if the clearing were a house. "But we did it ages ago, not today. More than a year ago. Just after Charles and Thirza arrived, when The Spitty got noisier and more crowded, and we felt a sudden need for a secret spot of our own, just us two sisters. It can feel rather strange, being part of a little group within a bigger group. Rather like you and Inspector Catchpool must feel!" Olive looked pleased with the comparison. "Rhoda and I are best friends as well as family, and this is where we come to have our private Board of Directors meetings."

"Board of . . . ?" Poirot began.

"It's a little joke between us." Olive smiled. "If either of us needs to make an important decision, here is where we come to chew it over. We both put forward our points of view and examine the issue from every possible angle and then we vote—and we only take action if we are unanimous, since there is no third sister to make a casting vote. If there is disagreement between us, we continue to discuss it until we are of one mind. It's an excellent system, if I say so myself," she concluded.

"Will I be required to vote on something at the end of our conversation today?" asked Poirot with a small smile.

"No." Olive looked sad, and pressed her mouth into a line, perhaps to stop herself from crying. "The knotty problem that has felt like a terrible, inescapable trap for so long had been finally, *tragically*, resolved. No choice is left, now that Matthew has been murdered. If only he had lived—" She broke off. "But, no, that is not why I brought you here. Goodness knows I have spent enough hours of my life discussing Matthew Fair—first as my sister's from-a-distance love object, then as a beloved future brother-in-law, then as a heartbreaker who meant no harm but nevertheless did plenty of it . . ."

Again, Olive stopped herself. "See how naturally it comes to me, to make him the center of my attention? It *must* stop, now he is dead." She sounded anguished. "Though even as I say it, I fear the opposite. I am terribly afraid that Rhoda will *never* now free herself of . . . the hold he had over her. Oh, it wasn't his fault—Matthew was just Matthew, there was no guile to him. He racketed about like a bouncy dog, with never too much going on up here." She tapped the side of her head. "But now he is dead and will no doubt be remembered forever as perfect, as the dead tend to be. I am sure you are familiar with the Thomas Hardy poem: 'Woman much missed, how you call to me, call to me . . .'"

"It is a very touching composition," said Poirot.

"I doubt Mr. Hardy's second wife, now his widow, feels that way about it," Olive said tartly. "But I must not allow myself to be distracted. I did not make you climb up here to debate matters of the heart."

Ah, thought Poirot, *so now she refers to it as the climb and not any more the short walk.*

"I have some information I feel it would be dishonest to withhold," said Olive. "And I know it is impertinent to seek to impose conditions, but I must throw myself upon your mercy and beg you to tell nobody at all. Not even Rhoda." She corrected herself: "*Especially* not Rhoda. She would be horrified. In fact, the love and trust she has for me might not survive such a discovery. And I should certainly be sent away from The Spitty at once—"

"I shall be discreet," Poirot interrupted her catastrophizing. "Though I would ask your permission to discuss it with Inspector Catchpool, if I think it might be important?"

"Important?" Olive looked confused. "Oh . . . No, it has nothing to do with the murder of Matthew. And I'm afraid it will not help you to catch his killer. What I'm about to tell you concerns nothing more than my private beliefs. Nevertheless, when you and Inspector Catchpool are stomping around telling everyone that absolutely nothing must be withheld . . . well, that sort of atmosphere makes any secret one is keeping feel jagged and uncomfortable inside the heart."

"Hercule Poirot does not stomp, mademoiselle."

"Oh, you know what I mean." Olive smiled. "Perhaps it is my secret that is doing the stomping—all over my conscience. I told a lie a long time ago, you see. And then before I knew it, I had a pretense I had to maintain . . . well, forever."

"What secret?"

"I am not convinced by any of Nash's spiritual principles, Monsieur Poirot. I pretend I am, and my performance is flawless, but . . . deep down, I think this new religion that Nash is attempting to create in order to take over the whole world and make it do his bidding is nothing more than bunkum. He has the best of intentions, I have no doubt, but . . . well, it really is foolhardiness of the most astonishing kind. I am *aghast* that so many apparently intelligent people have fallen for it—including my own sister, who, as you know, is the most passionate advocate of *Próti Foní* and his new, improved Christianity. For my part, I have always thought it quite ludicrous. I still firmly believe what I learned in our village church in Salway Ash. That's in Dorset, where Rhoda and I grew up and lived until we moved to Oxford," she explained quickly.

"They have the most magnificent names, your English villages," said Poirot.

"They do," Olive agreed. "How I miss home . . ." She stared out at the sea as if hoping to catch a glimpse of Salway Ash in the distance. "I would return to Dorset or Oxford tomorrow, either one, if only Rhoda would agree. There is little hope of that, I fear, even now Matthew is dead. Rhoda was determined to come here from the moment Nash invited her. I can still picture quite vividly how her face glowed when she told me she was the first one he had invited, after Matthew and Austin. In my eyes, that proved how credulous she was. If someone were to tell me that I was first after two other people, I would point out that the word they were looking for was 'third.'"

Olive stood up and walked to the edge of the precipice. "You will understand, I hope, why I could hardly allow my sister to come to this island without me, with only three deluded young men to make sure no harm came to her. I had nothing else interesting to do and no one making any claims on my time or attention, so I decided that to come here might be an interesting . . . experiment of sorts. I do relish a good old experiment," she said with gusto. "I put it to myself that, though I was not a disciple of Nash Athanasiou, perhaps I might become one over time? I looked forward to seeing his many theories, and my own beliefs, put to the stringent test of practical application. The proper scientific approach involves never, ever assuming one is right purely because one would like to be."

"*D'accord,* mademoiselle." Poirot was beginning to approve of Olive Haslop.

"I was curious to see how things unfolded here, and willing to be open-minded," she went on. "I even hoped that I might end up a little more proficient when it came to loving my enemy, but I'm afraid it took me all of a week to satisfy myself that Nash does not have the solution to all the world's problems, material or spiritual. This community is dangerous. Oh, I know what you're thinking!" She whirled around to face Poirot. "It is easy for me to say that now that Matthew is dead, yes? I promise you, Monsieur Poirot, I felt the danger long before New Year's Eve. I have felt that something was very wrong from as far back as when Belty Ricks first arrived. She has a secret past she refuses to talk about. Tell me, does Betlinde Ricks not sound like a name someone would invent? And then Thirza and Charles came to the house, and then that amoral creature Pearl."

"You disapprove of them all?" Poirot asked.

"Not quite that, no," said Olive. "It is more than that . . . well, with each new arrival, my sense that something extremely hazardous is lurking just out of sight has intensified. As for my original intention in coming here: to protect Rhoda from harm . . ." Olive barked out a laugh. "I failed dismally. Even with me by her side to advise and protect her, she was nearly destroyed." Her voice shook as she went on, "Matthew broke her heart, however unintentionally. He broke *her*, and now his murder has decimated her still further. She will devote the rest of her life to revisiting those brief moments of happiness from her past, when she believed he loved her and always would. If only he had not died, she might have somehow, one day, broken free of his influence. What?" Olive demanded suddenly. "Why are you looking at me like that?"

"It is true, is it not, that you have contempt for Mademoiselle Pearl?"

"Lashings of it, yes," said Olive. "Why do you ask?"

"Please do not take offence when I ask you this: did you, on December 12 last year, try to kill Pearl St. Germain by pushing her off the edge of the terrace outside her bedroom?"

"No, I didn't. I know Nash thinks someone did, someone who was not one of our horned goat friends—speiroeidís. The name comes from the word 'spiral' in Greek." Tears welled up in Olive's eyes, and spilled over. "But Austin is always telling me I must have faith and believe even when there is no grounds for doing so, so I will admit that *every single day* I pray for all I'm worth that it was indeed a goat that tried to push Pearl to her death."

"Why do you . . . ? Ah." Poirot nodded. "I see. You fear that it could have been your sister, Mademoiselle Rhoda."

"I do *not* fear that," Olive said pointedly, wiping her eyes. "My sister is very much opposed to murder and all forms of sin. She has told me so many times, whereas I am afraid I cannot say the same for the goats of Lamperos. They have not been good enough, as yet, to advise me of the moral underpinnings that guide their behavior. I don't know about you, Monsieur Poirot, but I find that to be rather suspicious."

AN HOUR LATER, BACK AT The Spitty, Poirot asked the same question of Rhoda Haslop: was it she who had tried to kill Pearl St. Germain on December 12? She replied with a simple, quiet "No." Unlike her older sister, she did not think to blame Pearl's near-fatal misfortune on a spiral-horned goat—and that, Poirot thought, was because she had no energy or mental space to spare for invention, speculation, theorizing, or indeed for anything apart from the all-encompassing despair that seemed to radiate from her small frame. Only once or twice before had he encountered so palpable a burden of unhappiness. It made it difficult to conduct a conversation in the normal way; the person was both tangibly there and, at the same time, unreachable.

"No," Rhoda repeated with a shiver. "I should be far too afraid to kill anyone even if there were someone I wanted dead, and there is not. Not even Pearl. You might not understand—Olive doesn't—but I loved Matthew, you see. And it was clear to me that he loved Pearl the way I loved him, in that unending way that can never stop no matter what the person does. If I had hurt Pearl, even only by speaking harshly to her, I would have known I was aggressing against the woman beloved by my beloved. I could never have done that."

She shivered again, and Poirot said, "Shall we continue our conversation inside, mademoiselle? You seem to be suffering from the cold."

"It is not cold," she replied at once. "This is where I suffer least, sitting here on this step, with nothing in front of me but a stone wall. I cannot see the sea or any trees, and even the sun's rays do not reach as far down as this—not at any time of the day, winter or summer. That is why you found me here."

The two of them were positioned somewhat awkwardly at the bottom of the small stone staircase that led from the sitting room's terrace down to the tiny, triangular area of dried yellowing grass and pebbles beneath. This little patch could hardly be described as part of The Spitty's grounds; it was a small scrap of nothing between the house's outer wall and the wall separating Nash's family's property from the rest of Liakada Bay.

"You believe, then, that Monsieur Fair's love for Mademoiselle Pearl survived her casting him aside?" Poirot asked her.

"I believe he *wanted* to stop loving her, once he was . . . able to see the truth of everything," said Rhoda. "He also liked to obey Nash, so he did his best to persuade himself it was me he loved after all. Nash told him that Pearl could never make him happy, whereas I could; my love for him would never run out in the way Pearl's had. To Matthew's credit, he really threw himself into the performance of loving me again. He was forever popping up by my side and calling me 'Darling Rhoda,' and he must have proposed marriage at least five hundred times, whereas before, when he and I were truly happy together, he only proposed once and with far less fanfare."

She began to cry. Poirot would have passed her his handkerchief, but she was already clutching two of her own.

"And his pretense was *sincere*—that was why it was such an agony for me," she wept. "Most people know they are lying when they do it, but Matthew believed his own wishful thinking. All he wanted was for me to believe it too—that we could be happy together. And I wanted to believe, truly I did, but . . ."

"You could not?" said Poirot.

Rhoda shook her head. After a few seconds she said, "My sister Olive and I . . . we have a place that we go to when we want to talk and not be overheard. It's up there." She pointed. "Through the trees, past the hotel. There are chairs there, and we sit and look out at the sea. We used to," she amended. "I cannot imagine doing so now. I cannot imagine doing anything ever again. Even taking the breaths necessary to stay alive feels like the most . . . onerous task, in service of a result I am not sure I want. Monsieur Poirot, how does one go on living when all one desires is to stop and cease to exist?"

"One simply goes on," he told her. "One adds it to the list of things one must do, despite not having much of an appetite for it. Then, with luck and the passing of time . . . the appetite returns."

She looked as if she was taking the suggestion seriously enough. "Olive and I used to go off to our secret place any chance we got," she said. "We called them our 'board meetings.' They were *all* about Matthew and what I ought to do—lately, at any rate, since Pearl tossed him away like a broken toy and Nash ordered him to rekindle things with me. I could not say yes to him without consulting Olive. She is so wise, and she and I always agree about everything when I am in my right mind. We both knew Nash was our path to fulfilment and salvation, from the first time we heard of his brilliant, revolutionary ideas."

Poirot did his best to maintain a neutral expression.

"After the Pearl debacle, when Matthew first proposed marriage to me again, I asked Olive what I ought to do," said Rhoda. "I wanted to know if she believed he loved me as he claimed to. Was it possible, after all that had passed between us? Olive said she did not doubt his love for me. 'The trouble is he is *too* loving,' she said. 'And what happens when the next pretty, scheming young girl comes along and flutters her eyelashes at him?' She feared what happened with Pearl might happen again, and so did I. And if Matthew and I were married by then and perhaps had children too. . . ." Rhoda groaned. "My poor children, abandoned by their father!" she said as if these fictional beings existed. "No, I decided, I could not do that to them. Olive advised me to tell Matthew 'No,' once and for all. It would be painful, but then once the pain subsided, I would be free, she said. Quite right, I agreed, and set off to do just that. But when I saw Matthew's face and heard him say again how it was me and me alone that he loved, and what a fool he had been . . . and then when he said later that he would never give up, never marry anyone else . . ."

Poirot heard a ripping noise: fabric tearing. Rhoda had made a hole in one of her handkerchiefs; her unhappy fingers had torn through it.

"After a few weeks, I was forced to admit to Olive that I had failed," she said. "I did not have it in me to turn down the chance to be Mrs. Matthew Fair." A sob burst from her mouth. "Oh, I must not say that name again, the one that can never be mine."

"How did your sister respond to this news?" Poirot asked.

"Brilliantly," answered Rhoda through her tears. "Olive always knows the answer. She took me up to our secret place for an emergency board meeting. She said, 'Now listen here, Rhoda. You know there is nothing I love more than an experiment. The way to look at this is that we have already experimented with deciding to say no to Matthew, and it didn't work. There was a substantial failure, was there not, on the saying no to Matthew front?' Oh, she wasn't trying to make me feel bad, Monsieur Poirot. On the contrary, it was rousing, and it made me laugh. She said, 'What can we learn, then, from this failure? I should say the lesson is that *you do not want to say no*. You want to say yes! In which case, let us try that instead and see if you manage it.'"

"And did this suggestion please you?" asked Poirot.

"No!" Rhoda made a muted wailing sound. "How could I say yes when I believed there was a risk Matthew might fall out of love with me again? I was sure he still hankered after Pearl, no matter what he said . . . I saw the way he looked at her sometimes. He had more desire for her than for me—that much was apparent, and nor do I blame him for it. One cannot help these things, and . . . well, look at me. And look at Pearl."

"You felt unable to accept Monsieur Fair's proposal and equally unable to refuse it," Poirot summarized.

Rhoda nodded. "Olive explained that the experiment she had in mind did not involve me marrying Matthew in the near future. "Say yes to him on one condition,' she advised me. 'That the engagement lasts at least two years. If he loves you, he will agree to those terms without hesitation, and two years is a long enough period of probation, I think.'"

"Did you agree?"

"It didn't matter whether I did or didn't," said Rhoda. "I could not bring myself to do it to Matthew: tie him to me when I *knew* I was not what his heart truly wanted. He would have done his best, you see. He always did, and there was every chance of him succeeding, especially with Nash cheering on his efforts. He would probably have been first a dutiful fiancé, then a dutiful, uxorious husband. Oh, I cannot bear it." Dropping the handkerchiefs on the ground, Rhoda buried her face in her hands. "It can't be true that I will never see him again. I cannot survive it! I no longer care if I am married to him or loved by him or not, as long as I don't have to live without him."

"Mademoiselle, I promise you I will bring Monsieur Fair's killer to justice," said Poirot.

Rhoda looked up at him in horror. "No. Oh, no, you must do no such thing! That would only make things worse. The only true justice is forgiveness, Monsieur Poirot. We must forgive Matthew's murderer. It does not matter who did it. I do not wish to know."

"Mademoiselle, if you will permit me to—"

"*No,* I tell you!" she shrieked. "You must stop immediately, whatever you are doing. Abandon all your plans to catch and punish a killer. How will more killing solve the fact of the first killing? It would be unforgiving, a sin against God, and would only destroy me all the more if it were to be done in Matthew's name. He wouldn't want it either. Please, I beg of you: go back to England and take your Scotland Yard inspector friend with you. You cannot help me. If you care about my survival, please, do as I ask."

CHAPTER 19

A Shocking Confession

I awoke while it was still dark the next day, and decided that, since further sleep was unlikely, I would aim instead to be on the beach in time to watch the sun rise and then to swim while I was down there. Nothing beats eating breakfast with the blood vibrating in the veins, having already had one's cold water dip, and feeling not unlike a Baked Alaska pudding: chilly at one's core, but with a warmer layer on the outside as the skin's surface heats up.

As quickly as I could, I made a bundle out of a towel and some warm clothes to put on afterwards, and headed down to the gently lapping water. I felt a pang of sadness, as I had yesterday, for it was impossible to be here on my way to swim and not recall taking this same route on New Year's Eve, only two days ago, with a happy Matthew Fair by my side.

The sunrise was even more beautiful than yesterday's: a sultry orange that made me think of a very expensive cocktail in one of the world's finest hotels. I might have been an audience of one, but I had sufficient enthusiasm and appreciation for an army of ten. Once the sun was well on its way, I took the plunge. The sea turned out to be colder than I had expected, so I applied myself to some vigorous front crawl and to the puzzle of Matthew Fair's murder. One problem was that Olive Haslop's and Thirza Davis's accounts contradicted one another. Olive was adamant that, while lying awake at close to two o'clock in the morning on New Year's Day, she heard two sets of footsteps and two voices talking. Thirza, meanwhile, said she heard no conversation and only one set of footsteps—Matthew's. According to her, she then saw him leave the house alone as she watched from The Spitty's top floor.

Thinking that maybe the second set of footsteps Olive had heard might have been Thirza's, as she ran to check on Charles in his bedroom after Matthew had gone outside, I put this to Olive at dinner last night. "No," she said. "I definitely heard both the pairs of feet at the same time. I heard two people who were talking and going somewhere *together*."

Was she lying, or was Thirza? Or was it possible, somehow, that both thought they were telling the truth?

The person I suspected most strongly—of dishonesty, of murder, of being by far the worst of the lot in almost every way—was Pearl, yet she had what seemed to be a persuasive alibi in the form of Rhoda having seen her returning, and being shocked to find Matthew's body lying on the terrace. Surely Rhoda would not lie to protect Pearl, the woman on whose account she had been thrown over in love.

One of the biggest unknowns was the whereabouts of the murder weapon, and the clothes worn by the killer when the crime was committed. They would presumably have been covered in blood. Yet they had not been found, and neither had a blood-stained knife, during Inspector Kombothekra's thorough search of The Spitty. He had been helped by the Very Good Friends, he said . . . Had one of them taken the opportunity to throw an incriminating bundle into the sea while his back was turned? Or was it possible that was done in between the killing and Pearl finding Matthew dead and starting to scream? Would there have been sufficient time? And did the murderer then run naked back to his or her room, or were they wearing some other clothes underneath the layer on top, having planned it all out in advance?

Of course, Pearl might be mistaken, or lying, about Matthew having been murdered just before 2 o'clock in the morning. Thirza saw him leave the house two or three minutes after half past one, and he might have been killed almost immediately after that . . . which would have left plenty of time for the murderer to do whatever was necessary before Pearl got back to The Spitty at ten minutes after two.

I became aware that I could no longer feel the tips of my fingers. I needed to get to dry land and warm myself up. I turned, then started as I saw an alarming apparition on the sand ahead—all the more alarming for being real.

It was Pearl. She was holding something aloft: one of the towels I had brought down with me. And—horror of horrors—she was going to drape it around me if I let her. If I did not, I would come across as most ungallant. Better to get it over with, I decided.

"Edward!" she said urgently, entrapping me in the towel. "Have you spoken to Yannis yet? Has he told you yet that he saw me here, by the sea, the night Matthew was killed?"

"He did, yes. Not at first. Initially he said he hadn't seen you at all. I did not find him especially convincing, I have to say."

"Oh, forget about him. Edward . . . oh, dash it all! I promised myself I would be dignified and refrain from asking but I simply must know: do you love me yet?"

"*What?*"

"Do you feel that you would simply *die* if I did not return your love?" she tried again.

"I shall never feel that way," I told her. "I think you're being very silly indeed."

I braced myself for a hysterical response, but she simply nodded. "I had a feeling you would say that. I am being tested. Destiny or Fate or whatever you want to call it . . . It demands that I do better, in order to earn my reward. Very well. There is something I need to tell you, Edward, something I swore I would take to my grave. But . . . if I am not totally honest with you, you will never love me. That is the message that Destiny has delivered to my heart today, and I finally understand it."

"I am not going to fall in love with you—not ever," I told her. "Having said that, I'm grateful to this Destiny chap if he's come all the way to Lamperos, braving the endless boat crossings and inconvenient transport connections, in order to urge you not to obstruct the course of justice for a moment longer than you already have!" What had started out as a joke ended up sounding more like a burst of ill temper. I could not persuade myself to mind all that much; Pearl was an infuriating ninny who clearly had not been given nearly enough dressings down in her life so far.

"I understand why you are angry with me," she said quietly. "I am ready to tell you the full truth."

"Which is?"

"Austin," Pearl said in a hushed voice that I could only just hear over the roar of the waves. "He is the one. I have proof, or rather, I *used* to have proof. Austin made no secret of his desire to see Matthew dead. He . . . he asked me if I would help him to achieve that end."

"I see," I said skeptically, thinking that "used to have

proof" and "have no proof whatsoever" were not so far apart. I was sure she was making it up for attention, but I played along. "To which request you said no, of course."

"I wish I had said no. I wish it with all my heart," Pearl said with a sob. "God help me, I said *yes*."

CHAPTER 20

Poirot Cures His Phobia

"I cannot tell you precisely when all of this happened. I think my . . . pact, shall we call it, with Austin started a few weeks after I first came here and ended a few months after that. But I cannot give you the exact dates of any of it, I'm afraid." Pearl seemed to shrivel under Poirot's stern gaze. Naturally, I had brought her to him straightaway to deliver this vital new piece of information firsthand. The two of us had found him apparently lost in thought on the half-collapsed bench beneath the fat-trunked tree.

"Time works differently at Liakada Bay," she went on. "Almost as if it doesn't exist at all. It scarcely matters on what day or at what hour this or that was said or done."

"You expect me to believe that Monsieur Lanyon, Austin Lanyon, confided in you that he meant to kill Matthew Fair?" Poirot asked her.

"He did more than confide in me," said Pearl. "He said he would need my help, or else he might not get away with it. I said I would—only because I was in love with him at the time."

"You say it as if that is a good enough reason. *Mon Dieu!*"

"Tell Poirot what you told me about the letters," I said. Then, realizing it would sicken me to hear her voice at that particular juncture, I started to do so myself: "She has proof of this conspiracy to murder—or rather, she did until recently—in the form of a written correspondence between her and Austin Lanyon."

"But the letters have been stolen," said Pearl. "I had them safely hidden in my room—and then one day they were gone, just as if they were never there—but they *were* there! Until they . . . weren't." She looked crestfallen. "M. Poirot, you must promise not to think badly of me. I doubt I would have gone through with an actual killing. No, I am sure I would not," she said more decisively, having resolved the matter to her own satisfaction.

"What was the substance of these letters?" Poirot asked her.

She frowned. "Oh, Austin wrote reams and reams, mainly about how we ought to do it. Should we push Matthew into the sea after knocking him out, and hope he drowns, or should we poison him, or should we—"

"*Sacré tonnerre!*"

"Oh, it was awful, Edward," Pearl turned to me. "It was distasteful to have to write about such things, and Austin would go on and on, listing all the possible advantages and disadvantages of each murder method. I kept telling him—writing to him, I mean, for he said we could not risk discussing it in case we were overheard—I told him I could not see why it mattered *how* we did it. If you want someone dead, just do it any which way and get it over with, that was my attitude, but Austin made it perfectly apparent that he did not care what I thought. I've no idea how I could ever have loved someone so . . . pigheaded. Well, I didn't, not really, but I only realized that when I met you, Edward."

I turned away in order to miss whatever nauseating look she was aiming in my direction.

"One day, quite unexpectedly, Austin told me he had changed his mind about killing Matthew," said Pearl. "He did not need my help, he told me—the whole plan was called off. I was so relieved! I see now that I should never have agreed in the first place." Her tone was hopeful, as if she thought she would soon be back in Poirot's and my good graces.

"Did Monsieur Lanyon tell you why he wanted Monsieur Fair dead?" asked Poirot.

"He hardly needed to," said Pearl. "I assumed he wanted the position of *Défteri Foní*—which will now be his, naturally. Austin has always had more power here than Matthew in any case, no matter what titles they had or did not have."

"I see. That will be all thank you, Mademoiselle St. Germain."

"Oh, please call me Pearl."

"I said that will be all. Leave us alone, please."

The moment she had gone, Poirot started to move, and for once I had to hurry to keep up with him. "Let us find the man with whom, according to her, she conspired to commit murder," he said. "We will demand to know if there is any truth in the tale we have just heard. Me, I do not think so. Mademoiselle Pearl is the worst of liars, I fear."

I was not sure if he meant her lies were unconvincing or merely plentiful, but I agreed on both counts. We set off in search of Austin Lanyon, taking, at Poirot's insistence, the long, circuitous and multi-levelled route around the sea-facing side of the house.

Since this involved some clambering—a practice I knew Poirot was not fond of—I could not resist asking him why he was bringing me this way when it would have taken us no more than ten seconds to go the quicker way. *It surely cannot be . . .* I thought.

It was. Poirot confided that he had developed a physical

aversion to Manos's kitchen. "If I have to walk through *ce paysage d'enfer* one more time, I fear I would not afterwards be able to eat another meal cooked by that man, no matter how *delicieux* the taste. *Non, non.* It is better if Poirot avoids that room."

"That is a shame, since you and I are the only two people allowed in it apart from Manos," I teased him. "They do say, don't they, that geniuses tend to be messy?"

"If that is true, then stop listening to them, whoever they are," Poirot instructed me. "Pay attention instead to those who tell stories of tidy, methodical geniuses—like Hercule Poirot! I promise you, only rarely does greatness grow out of the shamble."

Soon—or rather, eventually—Poirot and I reached Austin Lanyon's bedroom door. Poirot knocked loudly, three times.

No answer.

"Where is he, Catchpool? Let us look first in the rooms downstairs."

We did not find him on the lowest floor of the house, so we went back up and knocked on all the other bedroom doors. None of the others seemed to know where he was, though a few of the Very Good Friends had seen him just a minute ago, they told us. "I thought he was with you, Monsieur Poirot," said Thirza Davis. "He was hovering outside the music room about forty minutes ago. He looked rather as if he might have been waiting for you, come to think of it."

If Austin was looking for us, then he might now be waiting outside our rooms, on our terrace, I suggested to Poirot. He nodded. "We will look there. Come. No."

"No?" I said. We were outside The Spitty by now, standing a few yards from the front door.

'Ssshh," Poirot hissed. "Listen. I hear voices. Very faint voices."

The Last Death of the Year

I did too, and there was no doubt about where they were coming from: Manos's kitchen. I glanced down the flight of stone steps to my left and saw that the heavy wooden door was standing ajar; that was the only reason we were able to pick up odd fragments of what sounded like an impassioned conversation. Manos would not be happy. He had impressed it on Poirot and me endlessly that both doors, at both ends, must be kept closed at all times.

It took just a few seconds for me to identify Austin's American accent.

I tiptoed closer, then closer still. Poirot followed. As we neared the open door, the woman's voice, which I now recognized as Pearl's, grew louder. "Get out of here this very instant, Austin, and leave me alone. Leave me alone *forever*, is what I mean. It is not safe for us to speak!"

"Gladly, you silly dope," Austin replied angrily. "I enjoy your company about as much as I used to enjoy the morning trembles, in the days before I quit the liquor."

"I cannot stay here with you—anyone could find us. I must go."

"All I need to know from you is—"

"Let me *go*, Austin! It is not *safe*, I tell you."

"Listen here, you sapheaded imbecile—Don't you dare run away from me, you worthless witch!"

A door slammed. Since the one I could see was still ajar, I worked out that Pearl must have exited the kitchen via its only other door, which meant she would soon have found herself on the small terrace outside Poirot's and my rooms. I had a feeling she was tapping and scraping at my window at that very moment.

"Hideous little jade!" Austin yelled, followed by a string of obscenities.

Poirot stepped in front of me and, before I could ask to

be filled in on our plan of action, he was hurrying toward his least favorite part of The Spitty. "M. Lanyon," he said as he pushed the door open to its fullest extent. "Inspector Catchpool and I have been looking for you."

I could not see Austin's expression, concealed from my view as he was by a teetering tower of cardboard boxes.

"Do I gather that you found your exchange with Mademoiselle Pearl frustrating, monsieur?" Poirot asked him.

"I find every encounter with her frustrating," Austin said. "I wish to God she had never come here." The venom in his voice pushed him to the top of my list of suspects for the attempted murder of Pearl, dislodging the anonymous goat that no one seemed to believe in.

I expected Poirot to ask Austin if he had invited Pearl to help him murder Matthew, then changed his mind. Instead, my friend said, "You are not supposed to be in this room, Monsieur Lanyon. Nor to leave open the door. What would Manos *le chef* say if he knew?"

"He would 'tick me off,' as you English people say, as if I were a schoolboy and he the headmaster."

"I am Belgian, monsieur."

"You're from London, aren't you?"

"*Non.* I live in London, but I am from Belgium."

"I didn't really mean English," Austin said impatiently. "I guess I just meant: not American."

"In any case, you must please now vacate this room," said Poirot with authority. "I need to make use of it myself, and I must be alone. Catchpool wishes me to conquer my fear of it, you see, so that we do not have to walk the longest way around the house to reach the front door or the dining terrace. There is only one way to defeat a phobia of this sort: one has to immerse oneself in the dreaded thing, until the aversion loses its power. Yes, yes, please go outside."

The Last Death of the Year

I watched in astonishment as Poirot made small brushing gestures with his hands, as if trying to sweep Austin out of the open door. "Catchpool has some important questions for you, while I am busy in here."

Did I? Yes, in actual fact, I did. That was lucky.

"Goodbye, Monsieur Lanyon." Poirot gave a small wave. "You and I will speak later."

And with that, he closed the door.

CHAPTER 21

Another Shocking Confession

Austin Lanyon was nothing if not dynamic, as I soon found out. When he wanted something to happen and put his full will into it, it was not long before that thing was underway. His response to my questions was to nod decisively, as if we'd agreed on something, and say, "All right. All right." Then he told me to wait here, and that he would soon be back, before running off. "Don't go anywhere—you or Poirot. You're both going to want to climb on board this ride."

All I could do, I thought, was stand in the spot where he had left me, wonder what the "ride" would turn out to be, and hope that he returned—which was the precise genius of Austin Lanyon, because of course I could have followed him, refusing to let him out of my sight in case his plan was to hurry to the bay and escape Lamperos by means of a hidden boat. Such was his authoritative manner, however—both strict and reassuring at the same time; how could one doubt that a person who declared his intention so clearly and enthusiastically would reappear?—that I did not tumble to perhaps having been duped until I had already stood still for far too long.

Happily, Austin did soon return, and he was not alone. Nash was by his side, and said, "We must go to Lamperos town. Rasmus is getting the boat ready now. There is something you and Poirot need to know. I should have told you much sooner, but . . ."

"The past cannot be undone," Austin said. "But we should not delay."

At that moment Poirot emerged from Manos's kitchen, and soon the four of us were on our way.

We disembarked at the port at Lamperos Town, which was as busy as the day we arrived from England. From there we walked across the beach, then between two dense clusters of trees, and we came out at the end of a narrow, dusty path. This we followed until it became, by degrees, a cobbled street. We walked past little shops interspersed with squat, white houses on both sides until we reached the town square, which I had heard Nash call the *Plateía*. This was also mainly cobbled, and about two acres square. It was also puzzlingly empty, with the feel of a disused parade ground, apart from in one corner where a woman and her three children were serving refreshments to people sitting in solid-looking chairs with embroidered cushions. These customers or guests were mainly very old men playing dominos.

Was it possible . . . ? If there was any chance that I might sit for a few minutes in a comfortable chair, with some padding to separate its bones from mine . . . A quick glance at Poirot suggested that he was hoping the same thing.

The woman in charge of the café was able to accommodate us, and soon we were seated in what felt, by comparison with The Spitty, like lavish comfort, with cups of coffee in front of us.

"What is so important that we must travel this distance to be told about it?" asked Poirot.

Austin said, "I'm happy to tell them if you haven't the stomach for it, Nash." For once, his showman-like tone was absent. Whatever this was, he was disinclined to turn it into a joke.

"No." Nash looked pale and gaunt. Had he eaten a meal since Matthew's death? I could not recall seeing him consume any food over the past two days. "Thank you, but . . . it is my duty, as Próti Foní, to explain the madness and deception that has been tolerated at the house. It is my fault for allowing it to continue. It's my fault Matthew is dead, Poirot."

"No, that is his murderer's fault," Austin corrected him. "We all need to remember that. Though I feel equally responsible for everything that's gone wrong. Like Nash, I am inclined to believe I probably put the idea of killing Matthew into the mind of a killer."

"I should have forbidden the whole scheme as soon as I heard about it, and I did not." Nash put down his coffee cup and clutched at his head with both his hands.

"Please, one of you, explain," said Poirot. "What should you have forbidden, Monsieur Nash?"

The Spitty's First Voice seemed unable to speak.

"I'll tell them." Austin took over. "When we first came to Liakada Bay to start our work here, there were only three of us: me, Nash and Matthew. Olive and Rhoda joined just a few weeks later. For nearly a year, the five of us were the community. No one else—well, apart from Manos, who kept us fed, and Rasmus, and the women who came in to clean, but they weren't part of our mission. Our new hope for the world, our way of living and thinking and believing? That was just the five of us, and we were solid as rock." Austin waved his clenched fist under my nose. "We were unbeatable in those good old days—glowing with purpose, getting ready to bring salvation to suffering people the world over. Nothing could discourage or defeat us. Then Belty arrived. You already know she was determined to keep all the details of her past to herself? All right.

The Last Death of the Year

Then you know I didn't want her here. I thought she was bad news. Nash disagreed and he's the boss—you know all this, we don't need to go over it again. But I thought Nash a fool for letting her stay when we didn't know the first thing about her. I didn't trust her. I know a lot about sin, gentlemen—sin of most every sort." He sounded solemn and boastful at the same time. "I smelled bad character, bad news of the peculiarly feminine variety. Let me tell you, Poirot, that's an aroma I know very well indeed. Nash here, meanwhile, has an unblemished record of charitable works and the sin count of a baby child that goes straight to heaven before it's opened its eyes! Sure, I turned out to be wrong about Belty, I'll admit it. The result of her test was exemplary." He turned to Nash. "Didn't I come to you and say I might have been wrong after all? And she's turned out to be okay. I like her! Boy, have I made that lady feel welcome since she got here! But I was right about Pearl, who failed the test and kept on failing, and I'm now certain she killed Matthew. Nash is too, though he won't admit it. But we need to hand Pearl over to Konny and—"

"Let justice take its course?" said Nash.

Konny, I remembered, was what the Very Good Friends called Inspector Konstantinos Kombothekra.

"Unforgiving justice, which in truth is nothing of the sort?" Nash went on. "An apparatus of justice that murders wrongdoers while calling itself good? Do you truly mean what you are saying, Austin? I cannot believe you are asking me to—"

"You'd better believe I am." Austin banged his fist down on the table. "As the great Robert Frost himself might say: our step has trodden black the leaves of naïve trust and acceptance. We must now pursue the road not yet taken: we stand for and promote forgiveness, yes, but never at the expense of our community's survival. Nash, we have a killer among us, in our house. You and I both know that person is Pearl St. Germain."

"Then who tried to push her off her bedroom's terrace, if she is the killer?" Nash said.

"Nobody," Austin fired back. "That whole damn story's a lie. There was no goat, we know that, it's insane to give that idea any credence . . . so what if there was no anything? What if the whole thing never happened and Pearl just . . . made it all up? Why would she do that? Well, how about if she planned to do away with Matthew and wanted to set it up so that we'd all think there was some other killer at The Spitty who couldn't be her?"

"Ahem." Poirot cleared his throat, to remind Nash and Austin of our presence. "Messieurs, what is this test that Belty Ricks passed but Pearl St. Germain failed?"

"Let me get back to my story," Austin said. "You'll understand everything by the end of it."

"Please." Poirot gestured for him to continue.

"Nash said Belty could stay, and I guess I was a sore loser. Without asking permission, I decided to set a little test for our new arrival. I could see her starting to make eyes at me pretty soon after getting here. So, I did my best to impress her some more. When I was confident I'd reeled her in far enough, I . . . well, I told her I was planning to kill Matthew and . . . I asked her to help me do it."

"*Sacré tonnerre!*" Poirot breathed. I too could hardly believe what I had heard. "Monsieur . . . this too is the test, *n'est-ce pas?* Of the gullibility of Poirot and Catchpool?"

"I'm afraid not." Nash looked deathly pale. "Unconscionable as it is, it is the truth."

Austin proceeded with his story: "I made up a long, cockamamie tale about how Matthew had stolen a large sum of money from me, which indirectly brought about the death of my aunt Dorothy. I don't have an aunt Dorothy and never did, but Belty wasn't to know that. To her credit, she put me in my place good and proper. 'Absolutely not. Murder is a terrible crime,' she told me, as if I might be unaware of the fact. 'You mustn't do it,' she said. 'You must forgive Matthew and then forget get all about it.' Then she called me a silly boy."

Austin smiled at the memory. "She said I had a chance to do only good and no evil now that I was at The Spitty and lucky enough to be under Nash's wing. Her response was exemplary. I duly promised I would mend my errant ways and abandon all thoughts of killing anybody. In turn, Belty promised to forgive me and, more importantly, to trust me. She had one requirement, however: the two of us had to go and make a clean breast of it to Nash."

"Did you agree to her condition?" I asked. Poirot, by my side, was almost frozen solid with disapproval.

"He did," said Nash. "I knew the moment he started to speak that something very peculiar was going on, but Belty was by his side and the message in Austin's eyes was 'I can explain all this, but not in front of her.' So, I waited, and soon afterwards he . . . explained that he had set this . . . test for her. Naturally, I was horrified."

"But I stood my ground," Austin took up the narration again. "I was feeling much happier about the quality of Belty's character, and I'd satisfied myself that she belonged at The Spitty. I told Nash and Matthew I planned to repeat my test, any time a newcomer landed at The Spitty that I didn't like the flavor of, anyone I wasn't sure about."

"I begged him not to," Nash said dully. "Matthew said he didn't mind at all being a theoretical future murder victim if it helped our cause, but I made it clear I thought it a reckless idea."

"To which I replied that he would one day see the wisdom of my little trick and thank me for it." Austin held up his hands. "I was wrong. I'm sorry, Nash. You know I loved Matthew like a brother." To Poirot and me he said, "Matthew's life was the price we paid in order to find out how wrong I was. My little murder challenge worked like a dream with Charles, with Thirza—they arrived together, but I tested them separately. Both acquitted themselves well: refused at once, just like Belty, though neither of them marched me off to Nash to confess to my proposed crime. Charles did spend nearly an hour preaching to me about why killing was always wrong. He was quite right and immensely tedious all at once. And Thirza played a nasty mind trick on me, designed to make me feel like the most venal, nefarious, unscrupulous villain the world has ever known . . ."

Austin chuckled. "I don't mind telling you—Miss Thirza Davis . . . does she ever know how to use words to wound a feller! Subtly, too. It creeps up on you. Yes, sir. In all my days, I don't think I've ever felt ashamed to my core, apart from twice." He prepared to count off the two times on his fingers. "Most recently, when I found out Matthew was dead and realized that if it weren't for me, he'd probably still be alive—because I did my test on Pearl too, which obviously gave her the idea of killing him . . ."

Austin tilted his head as if pondering something important. Then he said more cheerfully, "I am fortunate, though. The Lord blessed me with an outstanding aptitude for self-forgiveness. Nash teaches that we must be ruthless in giving ourselves the benefit of the salvation offered by unconditional forgiveness as well. It's not only for other people, it's for us too."

"What did Thirza Davis say to make you feel ashamed when you did the test on her?" I asked him. "Assuming you can remember that far back."

"Oh, I shall never forget her verbal dissection of me," said Austin. "Even worse was the way she stared at me while saying it, as if she had burrowed into the depths of me and seen nothing but frothing wickedness..." Austin shuddered. "'You are asking me to commit a murder with you, Austin,' she said. 'Even though you could do it quite easily on your own and don't need my help. Yet you seek to make me your accomplice, so that I share your guilt.' She wasn't asking me, to check she'd got it right, Poirot. She was *telling* me in the voice of a furious, offended angel, thoroughly convinced of her purity and my rottenness.

"'Let me be as clear as clear can be,' she said. 'You want this—you want to involve me—even though you and I have only just met. You cannot possibly wish to harm me, yet you seek to involve me in your crime rather than commit it alone, to change my life and character forever by making me part of a conspiracy to kill. And... even if you do now commit this murder on your own, without my help, I will know it was you, which would make me your guilty accomplice—as guilty as you, if I had told nobody and done nothing to prevent it. And... I think you have thought about all of this. Yes, you worked it all out long before you put this proposal to me.'"

Austin recoiled from the memory as he brought it back to life. It was almost enough to make me shudder too. He was an excellent performer, and I could well imagine that he must have wanted to get far away from Thirza after that intense little speech. No doubt he had felt similar to the way I felt after hearing Pearl drone on about her burgeoning love for me. The intense emotion of women is an alarming thing.

Poirot said, "You say you performed this test upon Charles Counsell and Thirza Davis separately—but they are engaged to be married. Did they not discuss between them this unreasonable suggestion made to them by an American they had only just met?"

"Charles did not tell Thirza," said Austin. "I swore him to

secrecy, and convinced him his silence was part of the whole forgiveness package that he wanted to offer me. I had said the same to Belty: no one needed to know. She also agreed. As for Thirza . . . who knows whom she told or did not tell? Maybe she did say something to Charles after tearing me to shreds, but I don't think so. He'd have hunted me down and subjected me to another of his improving speeches if she had."

Poirot made a huffing noise. "Nobody—not one person—has said a single word to us about having been invited in this way to assist with a murder. No wonder you all looked so furtive on the terrace on New Year's Eve, when I asked who had written the threatening resolution. Not everybody had written those words and put them in the bowl, but *nearly all of you knew* that the murder of Monsieur Fair had been . . . put forward as a plan, a possibility. How could you, Monsieur Lanyon . . . ? And, you, Monsieur Nash—you allowed this behavior to continue, this foolhardy test, so obviously the gravest danger?"

"You must think us depraved lunatics," Nash said sorrowfully. "Fanatics and idiots."

I was thinking that the remark about the community at The Spitty being "steeped in murder" now made perfect sense. As did Matthew Fair's throwaway remark about being "intermittently willing to be a murder victim."

"For what it's worth, I think Thirza wrote what you call 'the threatening resolution,'" Austin told Poirot. "She tried to do it in Pearl's handwriting."

"I don't think so," I chipped in. "Thirza agreed with Pearl that it wasn't her writing, and pointed out that the capital letter *F*'s were wrong. Apparently, Pearl's veer off to the left at the bottom, like kite strings in the wind. That rather poetic image stuck in my mind. Why would Thirza attempt Pearl's handwriting and then draw attention to her own forgery?"

Austin frowned for a few seconds, concentrating. "I suppose you have a point there, Catchpool. No, I can't think why she'd do that. I don't pretend to have all the answers. All I know is that after I did the test on Pearl and she failed it by agreeing to help me with my lethal plot . . . well, she pretty thoroughly glued herself to my side thereafter. She also invented the notion that she had fallen in love with me, so of course she was brimming with appetite to pull me aside whenever she could for some secret murder-plotting in a dark corner. There wasn't much I could do to shake her off."

I knew how that felt.

"Thirza noticed all of it," said Austin. "Boy, did she notice! She'd been watching me like a hawk since I tested her, and I just know she thought I had enlisted Pearl as my new accomplice—that I'd lied to her about giving up on the plan to do away with Matthew. When you read out that horrible resolution, Catchpool, my first thought was, 'So Thirza's trying to land Pearl and me in trouble!'"

"Expose you as plotting to kill Matthew, do you mean?" I asked.

"Think about it: a death threat written in verse, and in writing designed to look like Pearl's?" Austin's eyes blazed with fury. "That was Thirza wanting everyone to know Pearl and I were planning to do what the resolution said. No doubt she hoped to make us squirm until we felt we had no choice to confess. I don't know why she didn't go straight to Nash and tell him the whole lot when I did the test on her, but she didn't. Didn't report me to Our Master, but also didn't agree to forgive me when I promised to give up all thoughts of killing Matthew . . ."

Austin shuddered at the memory. "She refused to say anything comforting at all. Just kept staring at me, when all I wanted was to escape her scorching eyes that seemed to be drilling into my sorry excuse for a soul." He smiled weakly. "I vowed to mend my ways and think no more wicked thoughts about poor, dear Matthew. She just stared at me with those... devouring eyes, and I just knew she was going to make life difficult for me. And that poem-resolution... Whatever you say, Catchpool, I'm pretty sure that was the first move in her Make-Life-Difficult-For-Austin campaign—which, as far as she knew, she could have done by informing on me to Nash, but there was no way she was gonna do that. She was too busy reveling in her own power. Over me," Austin clarified his meaning. "Nash doesn't believe it, but I could see it in her eyes: 'I am in charge of you now. I control you.' She wanted to see what she could make me do. That vile resolution was her first attempt."

"But you do not think she killed Monsieur Fair?" asked Poirot.

"Nope. I told you, Pearl did that," said Austin. "Thirza had no reason to—I was the one she despised with an obsessive fervor. Which, to my mind, meant she should have been banished from our midst, but what do I know? I'm not *Próti Foní*, after all." He stole a glance at the man who was. "And now he will defend her, as he always does..." With an elaborate arm gesture, Austin waved toward Nash as if introducing a star guest.

"Thirza had rightly refused to participate in any murder plot," Nash kept his eyes on Poirot as he spoke. "And she had made no direct threat to Austin or to anyone else. She had not *said*, directly and demonstrably, that she refused to forgive him for... what he had suggested to her. It would have been unjustifiable to expel her for the way she looked at him."

"Nor did our leader cast out Pearl, once she had failed the test," Austin told me. "And she had done considerably more than use her eyes as a weapon of harassment: she had signed up most enthusiastically to help me kill a blameless man. And now Matthew is dead." He turned to Nash and said quietly, "It is useless to say it now, but . . . had we removed both Thirza and Pearl from The Spitty in a timely fashion, he would still be alive today. I cannot prove it, but it's what I believe. Thirza's trouble-making resolution put the idea into Pearl's head to commit the crime, even though I'd made it clear to her that I'd changed my mind."

"Ah! You had told her this?" Poirot asked. "You performed *le grand volte-face*?"

"Yes, after nothing else worked to discourage her," Austin said. "I tried other things first. Nash told me to create opportunities for her to realize that what she and I were planning was an abomination. So, I did as instructed: I started writing her letters, all about exactly how we might do it. I described drowning and poisoning and hitting Matthew over the head with a rock from the bay."

"And stabbing him with a knife from the kitchen of Manos?" suggested Poirot.

"You think I'm a scoundrel, don't you?" Austin smiled. "I understand. Maybe I am. But I happen to be a scoundrel who's trying to save the world, just like I tried to save Pearl. When the letters didn't work to repel her, when she wrote back gleefully to each and every one, I called it off, like I told you—made it clear I'd seen the light, preached my ever-loving, all-forgiving heart out to her. 'All right, Austin,' she said, shrugging the whole thing off like it had been nothing at all. 'I don't mind whether we do or don't. It's up to you. It was your idea to begin with.' I think her pretend love affair with me had started to bore her by then."

"Yet you believe that hearing Catchpool read aloud the rhyming threat to kill Matthew Fair on New Year's Eve caused her to do so?" said Poirot. "Why would she behave in this way? Did she have any reason to do so? Any motive of her own for wanting Monsieur Fair dead?"

"Well . . . she's a suggestible idiot," said Austin. "In her mind, she had already made the necessary accommodations once, and declared herself willing to kill Matthew. Don't tell me it couldn't have happened a second time. Maybe she's even vainer and more egotistical than I thought, and didn't like to watch Matthew fawning over Rhoda again. She might have thought he should remain heartbroken and lonely on her account."

Poirot looked as unconvinced by that theory as I felt.

"What about the letters you and Pearl wrote to one another?" I asked Austin. "She says they have gone missing."

"They might have," said Austin. "Or she might be lying. One really never knows with Pearl. If they were stolen from her room, as she claims, then Thirza was the thief. She perhaps has a spot of blackmail in mind."

Poirot said, "M. Lanyon, when Catchpool and I found you in the kitchen of Manos earlier, attempting to compel Mademoiselle Pearl to speak to you, were you hoping to persuade her to admit that she had killed Monsieur Fair?"

"And to find out why, yes," said Austin. "Maybe she did it for your sake, Catchpool."

"What on earth do you mean?" I asked, taken aback.

"You're a fancy murder detective from London, aren't you?" His voice, all of a sudden, was laced with hostility. "Pearl knew it, we all knew it, even before you arrived. We knew Hercule Poirot was bringing his friend Inspector Edward Catchpool from Scotland Yard."

"I still do not understand—" I started to say.

"Pearl's telling anyone who'll listen: she fell head over heels in love the moment she clapped eyes on you. She'd do anything for you, according to her, idiot that she is." Austin leaned in closer. "What if she decided a murder detective would relish having a murder to solve, even while on holiday? What if she saw the chance to help you solve it, or pretend to? She mighta thought that would provide the perfect opportunity to bring the two of you closer together."

I said coldly, "What I hear when you say that, Mr. Lanyon, is that you can think of no reason that is not utterly ridiculous for why Pearl should have wished to kill Matthew."

"Oh, it's an absurd motive for murder, all right," Austin agreed. "Laughable! But then, that's Pearly: the most unserious person I have ever known, and the least deserving of anyone's respect. Disbelieve if you want to—"

"I do and I shall," I said.

"—but there's nothing more plausible, to my mind, than a person acting entirely in character," Austin concluded.

CHAPTER 22

Kitchen Trickery and Burning Questions

The beach at Lamperos Town was very different from the one at Liakada Bay. It was both shorter in length and wider, with sand instead of pebbles—and a generous portion of that sand was visible and usable now, at high tide. There were many more people here too: hairy-faced men in black hats and white-haired women in shawls and heavy coats, come from the white houses dotted all around this most inhabited part of the island, no doubt, and walking back and forth as if this were merely an extension of the Plateía, kindly provided by Mother Nature.

Nobody was swimming. Unhappily, that "nobody" included me. Poirot was doing his valiant best to talk me out of attempting any such thing. "Look at the Lamperos natives, *mon ami*. Are they throwing off their attire in an undignified fashion and propelling themselves into the water like the fish suffering from a fever? No, they have not forgotten that it is January and the waters are cold enough to turn the veins to ice. Besides, you have neither a towel nor your bathing suit."

"Tell me something," I said. Nash had asked for a moment with Austin in private, so Poirot and I could speak freely. "You mentioned the killer 'taking a knife from Manos's kitchen.' Is

that what you think happened? Because it occurs to me . . ."
As always before I gave voice to an idea, I imagined it being mocked and derided; this had been my habit since childhood, and it was only Poirot's gratitude for my occasional useful contributions that spurred me on.

"Go on, Catchpool," he urged me now.

"Well . . . I was thinking that if the knife came from there, it might have been hidden there afterwards. If I wanted to hide something at The Spitty, my first thought would be of that room—so messy that it's almost impossible to see even what *hasn't* been hidden but is right under one's nose, because there are ten thousand things under that nose. Sorry, I'm not explaining myself very well."

"Yet you are correct," said Poirot with a proud smile. "Now, on that subject . . . You have not asked how I fared in Manos's kitchen earlier."

"Oh—yes, indeed. Did your phobia cure work? Will you be sauntering through that room from now on without a care in the world?"

"Oh, Catchpool." My friend looked disappointed: my least favorite of his expressions. "I had hoped you of all people would not be deceived by my little trick. Of course that was not why I went into the kitchen. And I shall continue to walk around the house to avoid it. It grieves the soul to observe such disorder unless it is strictly necessary. Today, it was necessary. I knew, you see, that I would find there the murder weapon, and suspected I would find, also, the clothes the killer wore. In regard to both, I was proved right."

Noticing my wordless admiration, he said with uncharacteristic modesty. "To think of a kitchen in such circumstances is not a brilliant deduction. It is obvious: one would expect to find quantities of water there, stored in containers ready to use for cooking. One would expect to find bowls too—very handy for the washing away of blood. Then one simply opens the window and pours the bloodstained water into the earth outside—and who is ever to know? Furthermore, is not this room described by everybody at The Spitty as *Manos's* kitchen? We have seen for ourselves how *le chef* drives away anyone who goes near. You and I have the special dispensation, but no one else has permission to enter, *n'est-ce pas*? Now, think back to New Year's Day, and to what precisely was said by Inspector Kombothekra. It made an impression on me because it sounded as if he had been pleasingly thorough. He told us that he had searched thoroughly: all the bedrooms and all the public areas too, inside and outside. Yet would he have searched Manos's kitchen? It is not a bedroom, but . . . would he have considered it a public area? Would he have thought of it as a room that might ever have been used or visited by anyone who might be a murderer?"

"No. No, he wouldn't," I said. "Kombothekra and Manos are good friends, and we know Kombothekra refuses to entertain the possibility that anyone he knows and likes is a murderer. Goodness me, Poirot!" I puffed some air out of my lungs, feeling as if we might be on the verge of a breakthrough. "And of course Manos would have hated the idea of even his friend Konny rummaging around in his kitchen . . . and so the two men would have agreed that there was absolutely no need."

"*Précisement*. 'Only Poirot and Catchpool have been in here," they must have said to one another, 'and they obviously did not kill anyone.'"

"Tell me at once, Poirot: what did you find in there?"

"Two things of interest," he said. "Number one: fragments in the grate of the stove. Clothing was certainly burned there. Only the tiniest scraps were left, so it was impossible to know if the garments had belonged to a man or a woman. Number two: all but one of the knives in the room were either in drawers or scattered about. Only one—the largest and sharpest—was inside a container with a lid on. This container was at the bottom of a tall pile of many such. I opened them one by one, a long and tedious process. But I was rewarded for my effort in the end."

"Oh, well done, old boy."

"I believe the killer cleaned this knife thoroughly, then hid it in a place where only the most determined person would find it—so that no Greek police inspector could stumble upon it, in the event of him searching the room, and decide to check its blade size against Matthew Fair's wounds."

"Poirot, I've been thinking . . ." I said.

"This is excellent news, *mon ami*."

"Pearl encouraged us to believe that Matthew was killed only a few minutes before two o'clock in the morning on New Year's Day. But . . . there is no evidence of that being true. He might have been stabbed at, let us say, twenty-three minutes before two. Given that Pearl found the body and began to scream only at ten *past* two . . . Why, that would give the murderer plenty of time to do everything he or she needed to do in Manos's kitchen: burn the bloody clothes, wash and hide the knife, return to their room and put on new clothes . . . and then come rushing out to the terrace in their nightclothes as if they had been in the house asleep all that time."

"Yes, indeed," said Poirot. "Yet according to the two people we know for certain were awake . . ." He made a noise of dissatisfaction. "Olive Haslop says she heard no further footsteps after the two sets she heard at first. And Thirza Davis also did not hear any movement after Matthew Fair went outside shortly after thirty minutes past one."

"Well, that's easy to explain," I said. "The first feet that were heard were either just Matthew's, or Matthew's and his killer's. That person presumably did not wish Matthew to know they were about to stab him to death, so they would not have risked arousing his suspicion by tiptoeing silently."

Poirot nodded. "You could be right, Catchpool. Whereas after the crime was done . . . yes, then the murderer would make a great effort to proceed silently through the house." He made a noise of dissatisfaction. "If only we could be certain . . ."

He stopped walking and rounded on me. "But we can, Catchpool. We can! Not about everything, but about some things. When one seeks the certain answer, it is of no benefit to dwell too long in the unknown, so, please, repeat to me one more time: everything you have heard and been told, and I will do the same. These things, we can be sure of—that they have been said to us, and by whom. If they are lies, *cela n'a aucune importance*, for it is a fact that they have been told."

Having worked closely with Poirot for several years, I was used to this sort of memory test being sprung on me, and I had a far more capacious memory these days. I provided an account of everything that had been said to me, and then Poirot did the same. After nearly five minutes of silence, weaving up and down the beach amid overheard snatches of conversation in Greek from those around us, Poirot stopped, "Catchpool. You said, if I am not mistaken, that Yannis Grafas told you Pearl St. Germain was on the beach between half past one and two o'clock the night Monsieur Fair was killed?"

"That is right."

"This accords with what Mademoiselle Pearl told me when I interviewed her," said Poirot. "Meanwhile, Thirza Davis saw Matthew alive and going outside at half past one, which is also when, according to Olive Haslop, she heard *two* sets of footsteps . . ."

"It seems almost certain Matthew was killed between half past one and two," I chimed in.

"When Mademoiselle Pearl was on the beach, yes?" said Poirot. "Tell me, Catchpool—if that is so, then how is it possible she saw and heard nothing, as she claims? Furthermore, how is it possible she was not seen by the killer? You have stood on the dining terrace of The Spitty, I have stood there . . . The whole beach is visible from that vantage point, exactly as it is from Yannis Grafas's hotel. Would you consider stabbing a person to death while there was somebody down in the bay?"

"No," I said emphatically. "No, I would not! I suppose if Pearl had been facing in the other direction, and if the wind and the waves were making a racket, then she might not have heard anything, but . . ."

"But the killer would have seen her, and been deterred from taking action. He would have known Mademoiselle Pearl might turn round and see him, or return to the dining terrace at any moment. Unless . . ." Poirot left it to me to finish.

"Unless Pearl was not on the beach between half past one and two, but was on the terrace instead," I said. "Unless Yannis Grafas lied to protect her, and Austin is right, and Pearl St. Germain is the killer."

CHAPTER 23

Pearl Strikes a Deal

The repellent creature herself sprang out at me from behind a tree within twenty five minutes of my arriving back at The Spitty, and I had no doubt it would have happened even sooner had I not hidden in the Aegean Sea for the majority of that time. "Oh, Edward!" she breathed "You are home! What a relief! Austin tells me he spoke to you and explained everything?"

"Not quite everything," I said.

She looked distinctly afraid.

"Never mind, you can fill in the gaps for me," I said. "Tell me: if you and Austin had already abandoned the project of killing Matthew, then why did I overhear you in a frightful panic in Manos's kitchen earlier today, saying it wasn't safe for the two of you to speak?"

All the fear left Pearl's face as suddenly as it had appeared; indeed, I believe I witnessed the moment of her deciding my question could be answered easily. "Ever since Matthew died, Austin has been trying to trap me all over the house and force me to have secret conferences against my will," she said. "If anyone had overheard us, they would have thought we had something to hide, which I do not. Naturally, I did not want anyone to leap to that conclusion, especially knowing our letters might surface one day, so I tried to persuade Austin to leave me alone—but he would not listen. I'm *so* glad he has finally told you the whole story! It is so much better to be honest."

"Then why have you been the opposite?"

"Oh, Edward, do not sound so heartless! I know you have a heart in there somewhere. You cannot hide it." She blinked her wet eyelashes at me. "There is much I need to say to you. I have decided that, though my love for you remains as strong as ever, I shall refrain from mentioning it again."

"How marvelous," I said, and I meant it.

Pearl titled her chin upward and said, "I ask only one thing of you in return: that you listen to what I'm about to say, without interruption, until I'm finished."

"All right, but . . . can your uninterrupted saying last no longer than . . . shall we say ten minutes? I was hoping to have a hot bath and a rest before dinner."

"I did not kill Matthew," she said. "Do you believe me?"

"Unfortunately, I do, yes."

She still looked unhappy. "When you left for Lamperos Town earlier, I felt more desolate than I ever have in my life. You had said you don't love me, and everything felt so bleak . . . and then shame and misery gripped me like a vice, and when I finally broke free of them, I was not the same, Edward. Not the same at all. I understood things that previously I had not. I realized that . . . well, that I cannot force you to love me. You either will or you won't."

"Won't," I said.

"Maybe so," Pearl conceded. "I cannot make you. I can, however, change my own behavior. The truth is that until now, I have not deserved your love. You could never love an habitual liar, and that is what I have been all my life so far. For as long as I can remember, I have been cunning and devious and downright dishonest if it served my purpose. And then before, when I was seized by an impulse to tell you the truth about Austin's plan and the letters we wrote to each other . . . that felt so wonderful, Edward! Oh, it truly did. It felt like salvation. I thought to myself, 'What if, from now on, I resolved to be completely and utterly honest with Edward, and tell him everything I know, everything I *did*?' I knew in my bones that, however much I would rather not, that is what I must do. So, here I am, ready to tell you the full truth about . . . what I did the night Matthew died. If I hope that one day you might love me—and I still do, Edward, I can't help it—then I must first become someone who deserves your love. I must rise to your level."

Pearl sighed. "I am not stupid, contrary to what you believe. I know fine well that I have never been a person of excellent character. That is what I must do, and I will. I shall tell you everything, and in return you must promise to trust me from now on—fully and unquestioningly, in the way that you trust Poirot."

It was all I could do to stop myself from laughing. Not having any particular skill when it came to acting, I must have looked like a clown as I worked my way through a series of facial contortions. Finally, I managed to say, "I'll trust you when you start telling the truth. Do go ahead, please."

"I lied a beach . . . I mean, I lied about being on the beach," Pearl said, her words tripping over her nerves. "When all the others went to bed, I went to the hotel. To Yannis."

"Why? Oh." The answer was apparent from her face.

"What did you expect me to do, Edward? *You* had retired to your room, oblivious to the whirlwind that had overpowered me the moment I saw you. You left me to deal with a tornado of emotion, all on my own. I do not like to be alone, and in the past when such moods have come upon me, I have always . . . well, the thing is, Yannis is simply marvelous at making a girl feel appreciated. I often say to him, 'If there were an Olympic Gold medal given for the ability to console . . . ' And the thing is, Yannis's wife, Irida . . . Have you met Irida?"

"I have seen her," I said.

"She is the tiniest thing, but she sleeps so heavily and snores like a horse, Yannis says. Nothing wakes her. Anyway, now you know: that is where I was," said Pearl. "I left the hotel a few minutes before two o'clock and hurried back to The Spitty."

That, I thought, explains why she didn't see or hear Matthew's killer and why they did not see or hear her on the beach.

"You do believe me, don't you?" said Pearl.

"I've never found it easier to believe anything in my life," I told her.

"Good. If you at least trust me then that will do for now," she said. "It doesn't matter if you are cruel about the person I used to be. I am no longer that liar. You will hear no more untruths from me. Only complete honesty from now on! I have become the woman who deserves your love, Edward."

Even if you have, you're not going to get it, I thought but did not say. Nor did I point out that believing someone about one very particular matter was quite different from trusting them. I could think of no one on earth I trusted less than Pearl St. Germain.

"But she didn't kill Matthew," I muttered to myself as I strode away from her as fast as I could.

CHAPTER 24

Miscellaneous Motives

I looked for Poirot, since I now had something new to tell him, but failed to find him. Both Belty Ricks and Charles Counsell, whom I encountered during my search, told me Poirot must be somewhere nearby, for they had only just seen him. Apparently, he had asked each of them the same rather strange question: had they placed anything on his bed while he was away in Lamperos Town? Both had answered in the negative, and neither could tell me what sort of item he had been thinking of.

Since I could not find him, the next thing on my list was the Liakada Bay Hotel and Yannis Grafas. When I got there, his wife, Irida Grafas, was awake and in charge—not that there were any guests to be in charge of, as far as I could make out. "Yannis rest," said Mrs. Grafas. "He resting more. You not wake him."

My attempts to imbue her with my own sense of urgency failed dismally, and I ended up sitting uncomfortably on a broken chair for forty minutes before Yannis finally appeared: barefooted, with wet hair and wearing a long, buttoned dressing gown—at which point his wife flung a "Now I go rest!" at him, then swept out of the room. It seemed that running a business with no customers was exceedingly tiring for both of them.

I wasted no time—or rather, no more time—in confronting Yannis with the suggestion that he might have given me a wholly false account last time I spoke to him. He demonstrated not one shred of remorse, and only shrugged with his face as well as his shoulders, as if to say, "Yes, this might well be the case."

"How about giving me the truth this time?" I said in what I hoped was a jaunty tone. *You never know, it might be fun!* was the mood I hoped to convey.

"You know already," Yannis said. "Or you would not be here."

I repeated the story I had heard from Pearl and he gave me a lazy smile. "She told you this, yes?"

I nodded.

"First she tells you other story, now she tells you this one?"

"Yes."

"She changes her mind without warning, always. Often." A throaty laugh emerged. "Every day a new decision, a new story. She is exciting."

"If you like that sort of thing," I said. "Mr. Grafas, what is the *truth*? Was Pearl here, with you, between half past one and two o'clock on New Year's Eve? New Year's Day, I mean, or the middle of the night—whatever you want to call it."

"She was, yes. Normally she does not stay so long. I like her to leave soon, not to wake my wife. There is no need to upset my Irida," Yannis added sternly, as if I were the one in danger of doing so. "But that night Miss Pearl talk, talk, talk! She stay long to talk about *you*. She say—"

"I don't wish to know what she said about me," I said. "Tell me instead what she was wearing?"

The hotelier frowned, trying to remember. "A dress, then nothing, then a dress," he said eventually. "The same dress."

"Was it light purple, with a frill here in the shape of a V, sloping down on both sides, like the roof of a house?"

"Yes," said Yannis decisively. "That was the dress—I see it now."

When I had found Pearl on the terrace at ten minutes past two, she had been wearing that very same lilac-colored dress. There was no blood on it.

I tried to disbelieve that she and Yannis Grafas had been together when they both said they were, and failed, despite them both being untrustworthy and of dubious character. There was also Rhoda Haslop, I reminded myself, who had seen Pearl return to The Spitty's grounds and find Matthew's body.

I left the hotel and made my way back to The Spitty, though I no longer felt in the mood to rest, so I walked on, past the house, in the only other direction it was possible to take. If I had remembered correctly from our arrival by boat on New Year's Eve, there was a small, pebbled beach, about half the length of the one at Liakada Bay, over to the east and not too far away. I decided I would walk there and back to use up the nervous energy that was accumulating inside me. For no reason at all that I could think of, I had been experiencing a growing sense of trepidation ever since I awoke that morning.

I passed two goats and no people as I walked, worrying that we might never know who had killed Matthew at twenty or perhaps fifteen minutes before two and then taken themselves off to Manos's kitchen to clean up and hide the evidence. As far as I was concerned, everyone but Pearl was now under suspicion. Apart from her—and Rhoda and Olive, who shared a room—everyone else claimed to have been alone and observed by no one at the time the killing must have occurred. And frankly, if Olive or Rhoda had done it, would not the other have covered for her sister by pretending they were together in their bedroom when it happened? A sibling vouching for a sibling was hardly reliable. And the Haslop sisters had a motive: revenge for the heartbreak Rhoda had suffered on Matthew's account.

Austin Lanyon had a motive too: I sensed that he might have wanted very much to be "Second Voice," if not in the top spot. As ludicrous as it was that anyone should covet such a made-up role as *Défteri Foní* at The Spitty, Austin struck me as a man who craved power, as much as he could get his hands on. If he was the guilty party, then Nash's life might well be in danger too. For how long would Austin agree to play second fiddle? (I wondered what the Greek word, or words, was for "Second fiddle.")

Nash himself struck me as an unlikely killer. He seemed to have worshipped Matthew, and one would need to be stupid beyond belief to invite Hercule Poirot to join one's little island commune if one hoped to commit murder and get away with it.

Belty Ricks, as far as I was aware, had harbored no grudge against Matthew. Also, she moved in a slow and languid way, and seemed by far the least physically energetic of the house's residents. If Belty were to commit murder, I felt sure she would do it in a way that did not require quite so much dashing about, up and down flights of stone steps in the middle of the night.

My thoughts turned to Charles Counsell and Thirza Davis. I couldn't rustle up any motive at all for Thirza, who professed to be in love with Matthew, and her story was that she had found Charles sound asleep when she had checked on him. I doubt she would have given him an alibi if he had done away with her beloved.

That seemed to rule out both of them, then—Thirza and Charles. The trouble was, there was nobody left to suspect. If

I had been compelled to guess at that moment, I should have plumped for Rhoda Haslop (who could have hurried back up to her bedroom after killing Matthew in time to be seen at the window by the returning Pearl), but I couldn't have told you why, apart from that she seemed too virtuous, in some ways, for it not to be a sham.

As yet another unattended goat passed by on the rocky track, glancing up at me, I thought to myself: *And what about the goat incident?*

Who might have wanted Pearl dead?

I had no time to ponder this before I heard someone calling my name. It was a woman's voice. I looked around and soon spotted a figure, on the beach and a few yards behind me. Yes, here was my intended destination; I had arrived. I had been so preoccupied, I had almost missed it.

The figure turned out to be Olive Haslop. She was waving at me, rather vigorously. What on earth was she doing here?

I felt a terrible sense of foreboding, as if there could be only one explanation for her presence: something terrible had happened at The Spitty, and Poirot had sent her to fetch me back.

CHAPTER 25

A Bundle of Letters

I did not know it when I set off on my walk to the beach called Agios Dionysios (this, I discovered later, was its name), but Poirot had taken himself up to the same secret spot that Olive and Rhoda Haslop used for their "board meetings'; that was why I had been unable to find him. After being told by all The Spitty's residents that they had left nothing on his bed, he had removed himself to a more private location in order to read what he had found there: a bundle of letters.

There was no disputing that someone had left them for him, and that the leaver must have entered his bedroom while he and I were in Lamperos Town with Nash and Austin. This unexpected gift appeared to be the entire correspondence between Austin and Pearl, in which they discussed their plot to murder Matthew Fair.

Imagine Poirot's alarm when, high above the trees and halfway through the sixth letter in the sequence, he heard the sound of a woman giving a polite little cough behind him. He turned. It was Pearl.

"What are you . . ." She started to move toward him. Seeing what was in his hand, she took an abrupt step back. "Oh. Those."

"Yes, these. Letter after letter in which you write about ending a man's life as if it were no more momentous a thing than polishing the silver."

"I would never have done it," said Pearl. "Not really."

"You should be ashamed. Yet you do not appear to be."

"That is only because I am now a new and improved character." Her tone suggested she was happy to have all the unpleasantness out of the way and forgotten. "Ask Edward. He trusts me now—would trust me with his life, I believe. Just now, we—" She stopped in response to an eruption of laughter that Poirot could not repress.

"Catchpool would not trust you with a postage stamp, mademoiselle, and certainly not with his life," he said. "If he said that and you believed him, then he is a far more talented liar even than you."

"How dare you speak to me as if I am . . ." Pearl gathered herself. "No, I must not allow myself to be provoked. I see how you've arrived at your . . . misunderstanding. I did used to lie a lot, you are right."

"What about the goat you claimed tried to push you to your death?" Poirot asked her. "What story will you tell now about what happened that day?"

"There was no goat," she said quietly. "Someone pushed me. It must have been someone from The Spitty, though I do not know who. By the time I had righted myself, recovered my balance, they had gone."

"And why did you not say so at the time?" asked Poirot.

"I was scared." Pearl's voice sounded hollow. It might have been genuine fear, or a deliberate act, Poirot thought.

"I wanted whoever had attacked me to know I had protected them so that they wouldn't try again to kill me." She leaned to one side and looked past Poirot. "What is that blue thing over there?"

"The Aegean Sea," Poirot told her.

"No, I mean down there. On the ground." She pointed.

"There is nothing there. Wait . . . now I see it." Poirot crouched down and looked more closely. "It is a lady's ribbon is it not, for the hair? Your and Monsieur Lanyon's letters were bound by it when I found them in my bedroom. It must have fallen to the ground when I removed it. Is it yours?"

Pearl looked caught out.

"You cannot think quickly enough, *n'est-ce pas*? There is the strong urge to deny . . . but remember, I have read the words you wrote to Austin Lanyon. *That* is what incriminates you, not the hair ornament you used to tie the letters together."

"Yes, it is mine," said Pearl. "And so are these." She lunged and grabbed the letters. Poirot tried to stop her but she was too far away to catch. As she hopped down the path away from him, she called out over her shoulder, "You had no right to them, Monsieur Poirot. They were stolen from me, and now I've stolen them back—which isn't even stealing, if they were mine in the first place."

CHAPTER 26

Olive's Opinions

"You have found my favorite beach," said Olive, smiling.

"Is everything all right?" I asked her. "Did Poirot . . . send you to find me?"

"No." She looked surprised. "This is my favorite island walk—up here, then back to Liakada. I do it at least three times a week. The Spitty can become a little . . . overpowering. Walking on a beach, watching the waves lapping . . . It's such a pleasure."

"The very best," I said.

"And the trouble with our beach next to the house is that one feels under surveillance all the time—Irida, Yannis's wife, is often watching from her bedroom window at the hotel, or there's someone on our dining terrace staring down at you. One feels rather assailed by curiosity from both sides."

"I know what you mean," I told her.

"Shall we walk together?" she suggested. "I like to go right up to the top over there, before turning back. It's high tide now, so we won't be able to walk quite as far as the big rock, but let's get as close as we can."

"All right, then," I said.

"Are you sure?" Olive asked. "Do please tell me if you would rather be alone. I don't wish to intrude upon your solitary time."

"That is considerate of you. I should be glad of your company."

She smiled. There was something motherly about her, and I couldn't help thinking that if she, and not Cynthia Catchpool, had been my mother, I would almost certainly have had a happy childhood. Though Rhoda was anything but happy, so perhaps I was wrong.

"Tell me, Inspector Catchpool," said Olive. "What is your opinion of Nash's teachings? Do you agree with our community's ethos: an unconditional welcome for all, even the worst and least repentant miscreants? Unconditional forgiveness, always?"

"Oh, well . . ." Quickly, I debated how forthright I wished to be. It did not feel dangerous to tell Olive the truth, so I said, "No, I am afraid I do not. I try to be a good Christian, and I believe in forgiveness, of course, but not without conditions. Though I am no theologian," I added hastily. "I would not be at all surprised to discover that Nash knows more than I do about these things."

"The trouble with Nash's theory lies in its practical application, and the consequences," said Olive. "I expect Poirot has told you that I am only here because I couldn't think of letting Rhoda come to Greece unsupervised? I will admit, I was also deeply intrigued by Nash's forgiveness experiment, which was how I put it to myself. I like to think I gave it—and, in fact, am still bending over backward to give it—a fair chance. However . . ."

A note of sternness entered her voice. "We have now had a murder, and Nash believes someone tried to kill Pearl a few weeks ago too. So perhaps forgiving everybody willy-nilly and inviting possibly violent individuals into one's community and home is, on reflection, not the best approach."

"I agree with every word of that," I told her.

"And yet . . . and yet . . ." Olive sighed. "Nash is certainly onto something. When one can manage it, forgiving an enemy feels most invigorating. The trouble with his theory, however—an insurmountable obstacle—is that it's based on the incorrect assumption that everyone has a reserve of goodness inside them that can be brought out in the right conditions. If that were true, his prescription might work—and what a cheering world that would be for all of us."

"But . . ." I began. We had reached the beach's farthest point and could go no further, so we turned and started to walk back.

"*But*," Olive said. "Evil people exist. And some of the good ones are just as bad. Good people, I'm afraid to say, do at least half of the harm, which complicates matters considerably."

"Who do you think killed Matthew?" I asked her.

"Belty or Pearl," she said without hesitation. "And I am not only saying that because of the conversation I overheard before leaving the house just now. I swear I am not. Long before today, I have had concerns about Belty and Pearl. I don't think either of them possesses what my mother would have called 'strong moral fiber.' And that rather makes them stand out in a place such as The Spitty, where strong moral fiber is meant to be *de rigeur*."

"Might I ask . . . Do you believe that everyone else has it, all apart from Pearl and Belty?"

"Well, they are none of them perfect," Olive said thoughtfully. "I mean, Austin can be what he would call 'a prize jackass.' Nash is terribly pompous sometimes, and also secretive. And Thirza tends toward being rather judgmental and ill-tempered. Killing is not her thing, though. I know that for a fact."

"What do you mean?" I asked.

"I imagine you have heard by now about Charles's sister? The one who was murdered? A very unpleasant story."

"Horrible, yes," I agreed.

"When Thirza first told me the killer was never caught, she said, 'I wish I had killed Marie myself, but I am not the sort who ever could.' Now, I know what you are thinking: that a murderer would say exactly that. But I believed her."

"Why?"

"Because she elaborated in a way that convinced me. She said, 'The truth is, Olive, the worst harm I could ever imagine doing to anyone I hated—the harm I would enjoy inflicting upon an enemy—would *have* to involve words. The thought of killing someone is tedious. Physical violence bores me. There is no art to it. Besides, I should want anyone I despised to live forever, remembering how I eviscerated them verbally and how painful it was.' Golly, listen to me!"

Olive laughed and looked a little sheepish. "Anyone would think I was on stage at the Dorrills' theatre on George Street."

"May I ask you another question?" I said.

"Please do."

"Do you think Thirza is in love with Matthew? Was, I should say. Because her fiancé Charles is convinced of it. Goodness me!" I exclaimed. "I ought not to have told you that."

"Don't worry, I shan't breathe a word," said Olive. "Thirza, in love with Matthew? No, I wouldn't have thought so. Not at all. She liked him well enough, but . . . actually, I did notice, on New Year's Eve, that she was paying an awful lot of attention to Matthew."

"I did too. So did Charles."

"Oh, I don't know," said Olive. "I'm the last one you

should ask. Not being a romance person myself, I perhaps would not notice romantic yearnings in others. Mercifully, I am quite cured of them myself, too and have been for many long years—which is just as well, since I am not the sort of woman to inspire amorous longing in anybody." She chuckled at the absurdity of the idea.

I should not have said what I said next. It was reprehensibly mischievous of me. "Inspector Kombothekra disagrees," I told her. "He is rather taken with you. He told me so himself."

"Konny? Oh, how harebrained of him." Olive shook her head disapprovingly. "I am not cut out for anything like that." Surprisingly, she then shook her left hand in front of my face and said, "Look at these hands. Sturdy and dependable, ideal for scrubbing pock-marked stone steps at The Spitty, but absolutely nobody's idea of beautiful."

"I can only tell you that, in my opinion, Inspector Kombothekra would be unlikely to see it that way," I said.

"Well, I don't know what he was hoping to achieve with his little joke," Olive said briskly. "I can assure you, Edward—and I do not say this in a self-pitying way, since I am relieved to be undisturbed by the emotional maelstrom that afflicts so many . . . No chap has ever fallen in love with me. I am simply not the sort who gets fallen in love with. Funnily enough, that is what I heard Pearl and Belty discussing on the stairs, immediately before I left for my walk. As self-absorbed as they both are, they gave no thought at all to the way any tiny sound echoes throughout the whole building when one stands in that precise spot. Oh, I couldn't see them but I knew exactly where they were. There is only one place it could have been, close to the top of the first landing."

"I hope they were not making disparaging remarks about you?" I said.

"It started as a conversation about Pearl's dress," said

Olive. "Belty observed that it would not have suited most people but Pearl had such a nice, curvaceous figure and how lucky she was—and then I was mentioned as an example of bad luck on the figure front, having no curves at all, but not being slender either. Pearl described me as a 'shapeless lump' and Belty agreed."

"Inexcusable," I said.

"I was offended mainly by the inaccuracy of it." Olive smiled. "I might be a lump but I do have a shape. Lumps have shapes. They are lump-shaped, are they not? Oh—" Olive broke off with a laugh, then covered her mouth with her hand. "I am so sorry, Edward. I see that I have upset you on my behalf. Please do not fret. I am very happy to be a lump with a brilliant brain—for that is what I am, if I say so myself. The professor always used to say so, and it was the best compliment he could have given me. My contribution to his experiments was invaluable, he said, and it was true—and, what is more, he made sure to give me credit whenever he could. Do you know, Inspector Catchpool . . ."

"What?"

"In my fantasies and dreams, I do not meet handsome princes," said Olive. "Instead,—and you must promise not to tell Monsieur Poirot this. Instead, I help you and him to solve the puzzle of who killed Matthew. And . . . in the very best of those fantasies, I work it out before Monsieur Poirot and he is consumed by envy. Funnily enough, you never mind. You are always full of admiration and congratulations for my achievement."

"In your dreams?" I sought to clarify.

"Yes." She gave a little laugh.

"Well, that is exactly how I would feel," I told her. "I will happily congratulate you all day long if you can tell me who at The Spitty is a murderer." The house was by now visible in the distance.

"I can't, I'm afraid," said Olive. "Not yet, anyway. Though I can tell you . . ." She stopped and stared down at her moving feet as we picked up our pace. "Never mind," she said. "A Scotland Yard murder detective who is also Hercule Poirot's right-hand man doesn't need advice from me, I'm sure."

"I have always needed, and also wanted, advice from as many people as possible," I told her. "Please do go ahead."

"Well . . ." Olive began tentatively. "Thanks to my work with the professor, I have always been a great believer in experimentation. It is the only way, truly, to arrive at reliable truths that do not crumble at the first sign of a challenge. The whole of science is based on this principle."

"I don't quite see how this relates to—"

"I will explain." There was an increased air of authority in her voice now, as she warmed to the topic. "It seems to me that both you and Monsieur Poirot are seeking to *know* things. You both believe that you require more knowing of things, and then eventually there will be enough for you to be certain of who killed Matthew. If you don't mind my saying so, this is quite the wrong approach. It is impossible to know for sure until you *try*, until you experiment—which you will not do if you are sitting around waiting for knowledge to come to you."

"Well now . . ." I chuckled. "You are being a little unfair. We are not merely 'sitting around,' Poirot and I. Apart from anything else, there is nowhere comfortable to sit at The Spitty. You have surely noticed that we have conducted many interviews with—"

"Asking questions is not the same as conducting an experiment of the sort I would recommend." She spoke over me with such gusto, I could hardly mind. "You need to proceed *as if you know*. That is the experiment. Do it and you will soon find out if you are right."

"Are you recommending I send some pour soul off to be hanged for murder when—"

"No, no. Not at all," said Olive. "But in your thoughts, in your heart, in the story you tell yourself. Try it on me, I don't mind. Experiment with believing I killed Matthew. Imagine: you are in a new world, a new reality. You are in Olive-killed-Matthew world. What is the first thing you think?"

"It's impossible," I said. "This world cannot exist."

"Why not?"

"You seem too . . . civilized to commit murder."

"No one is civilized, not deep down," she said. "Can you come up with a better reason for declaring this world to be impossible?"

"Well, I . . . yes, I can. Rhoda adored Matthew and is now terribly unhappy. You would not cause her such pain."

"What if I believed she would get over it in the fullness of time and then find a man who loved her properly, instead of wasting her life on one who had already proved he did not?"

"No," I said decisively. "You would not bet on her being able to get over it. She seems . . . I hope you will not mind my saying so, but your sister seems extremely sensitive. You would have known that to kill Matthew, even assuming you wanted to, would risk destroying Rhoda—which you would never do. I therefore declare this invented world impossible."

"Very good," said Olive. "You see? Now you know in your guts and your bones that I didn't do it. You have attempted to inhabit the *reality* of my being guilty and found it to be impossible—the opposite of a reality. Before, when all you had done was entertain the possibility and ask me questions, you did not know it."

"Clearly, I must now repeat the same experiment in relation to everyone else at The Spitty," I said.

"I should advise that, yes."

"Have you done it?" I asked her.

"Not yet. I have been too busy looking after my sister and besides . . ." She seemed to be weighing her words. Finally, she said, "I am still very much occupied with my forgiveness experiment here, which seems to sprout new branches and require more of me all the time. Seeing Rhoda so utterly demolished by this tragedy . . . I'm afraid it has put a certain amount of rage in my heart. Nash, Austin . . . How can they not see the danger they're stoking? Throwing together all these strangers who were so miserable and desperate that they had to flee their own lives, telling them they are the special chosen ones who will save the whole world, and, at the same time, that they may commit any sin of their choosing and get away with it, without consequences . . . It is madness!"

"Quite," I said.

"And yet . . ." Olive muttered. "When it feels as if I am starting to suffocate in my own anger and disgust, then I remember all the eloquent, persuasive speeches Nash has given over the years, about how forgiveness is freedom and the ultimate gift we can give ourselves . . . and that is when I realize that I cannot, quite yet, declare my experiment with forgiveness to be at an end. I recall, for example, Nash's teaching that sometimes, often, we first need to reach an intolerable extreme of hatred or fury or sadness before we can make the switch to the bliss of unconditional forgiveness for all. And I feel myself nearing that extreme, and . . . well, what if admission to that state of endless bliss is just around the corner for me? It might be; I cannot know the future. The scientific method requires that I continue, therefore, with this exhausting Is-Nash-right-or-wrong? experiment that I have been conducting ever since arriving on Lamperos."

Seeing my concerned expression, Olive smiled and said, "Oh, don't worry about me. I'm fine. My mind needs something to keep it occupied while I try to stop Rhoda from dying of anguish."

As we came closer to The Spitty, I saw that the dining terrace was looking rather crowded. Why were so many people standing outside?

"Oh!" Olive had no doubt noticed the same thing.

"Is there supposed to be some sort of meeting?" I asked.

"Not as far as I . . . oh, dear."

"What?" I asked her.

"I do slightly wish you had not told me . . . Look, there he is."

She was referring to Inspector Kombothekra. What was he doing here?

"Perhaps he has news about Matthew," said Olive.

"If so, it must be bad news," I said, close enough now to be able to see Poirot's face, which left me in no doubt: something was very wrong.

"What is it?" I asked him breathlessly as soon as I was by his side.

"You did not see? On the rocks, as you and Mademoiselle Olive passed by?" He pointed. "I think, *peut-être*, that your *tête-à-tête* was too fascinating and you did not look very far."

"I saw nothing," I told him. "What about the rocks? Has something happened?"

"There has been a further tragedy, I am afraid." Kombothekra's voice came from behind me. The Very Good Friends were standing in a huddle a short distance away, close to the house's front door. They all looked shocked and unsure of what to do.

Except . . . not everyone was present who ought to have

been. Yannis and Irida Grafas were both there and so was Manos, who looked as if he had been propping Rhoda up in Olive's absence... but someone was absent, someone from The Spitty who should have been there with the rest of them...

I realized who was missing at the exact moment that Poirot, said "I'm afraid, *mon ami*, that something terrible has happened here at The House of Perpetual Welcome. Or, as we must now call it, The House of a Second Murder."

CHAPTER 27

Murder Strikes Two

"It is Mademoiselle Pearl. She is, I am afraid, dead. Catchpool? Please, sit for a moment. I see that you are shocked."

"No, no. I am quite all right." Pearl? It seemed impossible. *She is too infuriating and obnoxious to be dead*, I thought, irrational though that was. "And . . . she was murdered?"

"I strongly suspect so, yes," said Poirot. "I think it happened exactly as before, when the first attempt was made. She was pushed from the terrace outside her bedroom and fell down to the rocks beneath."

"She might have fallen, mightn't she?" asked Nash, who had walked over to join us. "I mean . . . I agree, it is unlikely, but we cannot rule it out."

Poirot looked impatient. "Monsieur, you were the one who summoned me to Lamperos because you believed—"

"Yes, I know. I know." Nash held up his hands in a self-protective gesture, as if Poirot were firing jagged stones at him, not words.

"Inspector Catchpool, I must say to you . . ." Kombothekra took my arm and pulled me further away from the others and toward a tree, in front of which a large box had been placed. I hadn't seen it before and wondered what it was doing there, but now didn't seem the best time to ask. "I must tell you what I have just told Mr. Poirot," said the Greek inspector. "I made a mistake. Kefáli Stin Ámmo cannot be the killer—not of Mr. Matthew, nor of Miss Pearl. Though it kills me to say it, somebody here at The Spitty must be guilty of these terrible crimes."

"I see. I see. How alarming," I said, as if Poirot and I had not known it all along.

"What I have found inside the house during my most recent search has changed my mind," the inspector started to explain, then stopped when he heard Poirot make a general announcement:

"Ladies and gentlemen." He clapped his hands together. "Allow me to inform you all of what, at present, is known only to Hercule Poirot and Inspector Kombothekra. All of you are, of course, aware that Mademoiselle Pearl fell to her death a short while ago."

Shocked noises were made by most of the group.

"I believe she was pushed—and luckily, we know the precise moment at which this happened—"

"We do?" I exclaimed. "Sorry. I interrupted. Carry on."

"*Oui, mon ami.* How do we know the time at which this crime was committed? Because, by fortunate coincidence, Madame Grafas here was down by the water, in the bay. She heard a loud exclamation of horrified shock—from Mademoiselle Pearl, I imagine, as she was shoved—and then saw the falling of her body, down to the rocks beneath."

"Oh, Irida, you poor thing," said Rhoda. "It must have been quite dreadful. How horrid for you. I should never be able to get something like that out of my mind, not ever."

"Yes, very bad," agreed Irida in a matter-of-fact tone. "Though I be all right, also." She directed a sideways glance at her husband.

"If you could all please, one by one, tell me what you have done today, and at what times?" said Poirot. "Madame Grafas was down in the bay, and her husband was at the hotel. It is he who was in the room that also contained a clock. He tells us that it was fifteen minutes before three that he saw the change in his wife's demeanor as he watched her from the window. He looked at the clock when she started to run as if her life depended on it, back to the hotel. *Fifteen minutes before three.*" Poirot looked from face to face.

"I will go first," I said. I knew I was not a suspect. Still, it would not hurt to show willing and lead by example. "I think I had set off on my walk by then. I think I left at half past two or thereabouts."

"Earlier," said Olive. "Because I set off on that same walk at *exactly* half past two, and you were ahead of me."

"Where were you when it happened, Poirot?" I asked him.

"Asleep," he said. "I was woken by Monsieur Grafas, when he and his wife came here to inform us all of the tragedy."

"I have been in my room all day, Monsieur Poirot," offered Charles Counsell. "I left it only at around midday, to have a small meal. I missed breakfast this morning. I'm reading a most compelling book, and I did not want to put it down."

"I was in my kitchen," said Manos.

"He was," Austin confirmed. "Nash and I could hear him clattering about and singing. We were sitting on the bench, round the corner." He pointed to the farthest part of the terrace, from which the bay was not visible. "We went there in order not to be seen or overheard while we discussed what ought to happen now—now that Matthew can no longer fill the role of *Défteri Foní*, I mean."

"We were still there, arguing about it, when Rhoda came to tell us what had happened," said Nash.

"And where were you at fifteen minutes to three, mademoiselle?" Poirot asked Rhoda.

"I . . ." She looked at her older sister. "I'm sorry, Olive, but I must tell them. I cannot lie. Olive and I have a secret meeting place that we go to sometimes, to talk. It's up there." She nodded in the direction of the hotel and the hill beyond it. "I went there at about eleven this morning and stayed there for hours."

"Doing what?" Poirot asked.

"Thinking. Yes, just thinking, for hours and hours. And, what is more, I have many more hours of thinking left to do," she added with a touch of defiance. "I did not even begin to get to the bottom of any of the things I need to work out. I only came down from my hiding place when I heard a commotion coming from below. It wasn't close enough for me to understand what was going on, but I heard voices and they sounded upset and frightened. I hurried down and saw Irida and Yannis running along the bay road toward The Spitty. I knew then that something was terribly wrong."

"She come from behind us, yes," Yannis Grafas confirmed. "It could not have been her who did this killing."

"Thirza and I were in the sitting room," Belty told Poirot with a smile. "Playing gin rummy. We started at two, after lunch, I think."

"A little before," said Thirza. "Perhaps ten minutes before two. Neither of us left the room until we heard Irida and Yannis in the hall, saying, 'She's dead, she's dead.'"

"Is this true, Miss Ricks?" I asked Belty. "You did not leave The Spitty's sitting room between ten minutes to two and . . . whenever Mr. and Mrs. Grafas arrived here? What, three o'clock, it must have been, or five minutes to three?"

Yannis nodded.

The Last Death of the Year

"That's right," said Belty. "I didn't leave the room and neither did Thirza. The cards we used are still spread out on the table in there. Go and look if you don't believe me."

I wondered if Olive was thinking what I was thinking. When I looked at her, I found her waiting to catch my eye. She gave me a small nod as if to say, *Yes, you are quite right. Well remembered.*

"Immediately before I left for my walk"—that's what Olive had told me, which meant a little before half past two. And the plain fact was: if she had overheard Pearl and Belty on the stairs just before half past two, criticizing her lumpy shape or shapeless lumpiness or whatever nonsense, then Belty and Thirza had both just lied to Poirot.

I was wondering how I might get him on his own in order to tell him this when Olive saved me the trouble by making a public announcement: "I think you must be misremembering, Belty. You and Pearl were on the stairs when I went out. You were discussing Pearl's pretty dress: how well it suited her figure."

"No, I don't think so." Belty produced a charming smile. "That might have been a different day."

"No, it was today." Charles Counsell made no attempt to conceal his distaste. "You and Pearl conducted that particular exchange outside my bedroom door. I heard every word of it."

There was a short silence. Then, as relaxed as ever, Belty said, "Oh, yes, that is right. I did leave the room once, it's true. I met Pearl on the stairs. She was on her way up to her room."

"Then it's likely you were the last person to see her alive," said Olive.

"Oh, yes, I remember it now," said Thirza. "Belty was gone for no more than five minutes, I should say."

Poirot attended carefully to all of this back and forth, but said nothing.

My mind whirred with furious activity. Apparently, both of these women, Thirza and Belty, were willing to lie at the drop of a hat. But why? Had Thirza pushed Pearl to her death, and had Belty agreed to provide her with an alibi? Or was it the other way round, with Belty as the killer and Thirza in the role of supporting liar?

My main problem with both theories was that the two of them struck me as the most unlikely conspirators. I had not seen them exchange so much as two words since Poirot and I arrived here. Twice, on New Year's Eve, I had seen Thirza walk past Belty as if she were a piece of furniture that required no attention or consideration.

Olive had said that Thirza would never commit murder, that she found violent acts tedious, or words to that effect. Nevertheless, if Thirza had been in love with Matthew Fair . . .

I wondered if she had perhaps been rather violently in love with him: enough to want to kill both him *and* Pearl: him for the sin of not loving her, and Pearl for being the one who inspired him to fall head over heels in a way that Thirza knew she herself never could or would.

"I shall now make the way for Inspector Kombothekra to speak," said Poirot. "He and I have searched the house thoroughly. Many interesting things, we have found, have we not, Inspector?"

Kombothekra nodded, then bent down to open the large box in front of the tree that I had speculated about earlier. "First, we found a yellow knitted scarf that we have been told belonged to Miss Pearl," he said. "At least, it was yellow once. Now, it is mainly red. Red from blood."

Most of us recoiled a little from the sight—though not, I noticed, Belty or Thirza. Their faces did not move in response to this new stimulus. Nor did Austin look distressed by it; his expression was one of avid curiosity. Charles was tight-lipped and disapproving, Olive looked anxious and both Nash and Rhoda gave every appearance of being completely devastated by what was unfolding in front of them. I should not have been surprised if one of them had fainted to the floor.

"Where did you find the scarf?" I asked Poirot. "Is it definitely Pearl's?"

There was a general murmur of assent.

"I found it in bedroom of Matthew," said Kombothekra. "Also, I found there one other possession of Miss Pearl, also covered in blood: a pearl earring."

"This has also been identified as belonging to Mademoiselle Pearl," Poirot told me. "Inspector Kombothekra has assured me that these items were *not there*, in Monsieur Fair's room, when he searched the house the first time, after the first murder."

"All right, so this is starting to make sense," said Austin. "Pearl killed Matthew, got his blood on her scarf and earring while doing so, then hid both somewhere in the house or in the grounds. Someone else found them, realized Pearl was the killer, and pushed her off her bedroom terrace as comeuppance—then left these two clues in Matthew's room for us to find, so that we'd know Pearl was the guilty party. How am I doing, Poirot?"

"Badly, monsieur."

"I think you're jealous," said Austin. "I like my theory. Do you have a better one?"

"Mine is infinitely superior, yes," Poirot said quietly. "I arrived at it after reading many letters that somebody left for me on my bed."

From the box, Inspector Kombothekra pulled out a thick wad of paper. "Letters, yes!" he said. "These are all to and from, from and to, Miss Pearl and you, Mr. Austin."

"I was wondering when they would turn up." Austin sounded entirely unbothered. "My little creative writing project. I hope you admired my prose style, Konny."

"I did not admire the sentiments expressed within," the inspector said. "And I will say, also, this—that if there is a murderer among us now, and I have formed the conclusion that there must be . . . I believe . . . I am afraid that my opinion is . . ."

"Spit it out, Konny." Austin smiled at him, at Poirot, at me. "You think I did it. Probably you all do. That's okay by me. It feels even better than I thought it would."

"To be accused of two murders?" I asked him.

"No, my friend. To be suspected, condemned even, and wholly innocent. Like our Lord Jesus Christ, who got almost everything nearly exactly right. You'll never understand, Catchpool, but when you have known, grown up with, been entangled in soul-corroding sin as I have, and then you've been lucky enough to escape it . . . why, there is only one thing you fear after that. Can you guess what it is?"

I had no interest in participating in another one of his games, so I kept quiet.

"You fear that the guilt and shame and sin, your natural elements, will come for you—pursue you, make you their plaything once again. Compared to that terrifying fate . . ." Austin grinned ". . . being innocent and accused? That's my happy soul's idea of a walk in the park."

CHAPTER 28

Yellow Scarf Complications

"Here's what I don't understand," I told Poirot as soon as I could get him on his own. The two of us were in his room, sitting on two hard-backed wooden chairs by the window, looking out at our terrace and the slope of forest in the distance beyond it. "*Why* would Pearl kill Matthew Fair?" I said. "She had no motive."

"That we know of." My wise friend's words flowed seamlessly from my assertion, as if their rightful place was at the end of my sentence.

He was correct, however. Pearl might well have had a motive we knew nothing about. But she was also with Yannis Grafas at the hotel when Matthew was killed. Even if she hadn't been, the matter of her bloodstained yellow scarf was yet another facet of this puzzle that I could not lever into place in any way that seemed logical; if she had worn the scarf to stab Matthew, why not then burn it in Manos's kitchen stove along with the rest of her bloodied clothing? It would be madness to keep it and hide it somewhere it might be found.

If anyone would have been inclined to keep an item of great sentimental value, Pearl seemed a likely candidate, but the scarf was hers, not Matthew's—a perfectly ordinary item of her own clothing. Would it not have made more sense to keep a possession belonging to him, the man she had once loved?

I was about to say all of this to Poirot when there was a knock at the door, and I rose to open it.

Charles Counsell was standing outside on the terrace, breathing very deliberately, as if he believed himself to be in danger of forgetting to do so if he didn't make a conscious effort. "Is it true about the scarf?" he said, before I had had a chance to invite him to come in. "That a yellow scarf belonging to Pearl was found, covered with blood?"

Had the man lost his memory, I wondered.

"You saw it yourself," said Poirot. "Inspector Kombothekra showed it to all of us."

"I made a point of looking away. I barely heard a word he said," Charles muttered. "This whole awful nightmare feels unreal. Tell me: was the scarf a knitted sort of thing? Holes in it? Thick around the neck, with two sort of . . . leaf-shaped protuberances sticking out at either end, like two leaves of a four-leaf clover?"

"A most accurate description," Poirot told him. "You know this scarf, then?"

Counsell nodded. "I saw Pearl wear it many a time. Yellow was her favorite color, she once told me. She said you only had to look at it and you felt happy and I replied that bright colors tend to give me a headache. It is one of the things I find difficult about living here."

I could well imagine that Pearl might have needed to increase her yellow intake substantially after conversing with this gloom merchant.

"How much blood was on the scarf when it was found?" Counsell asked. "What I mean to say is, if one were looking from a distance, could one easily miss the redness of it, or—"

"No," I said. "It was soaked in blood and more red than yellow. At any distance, that would have been impossible to miss."

"I see. In that case . . ." Counsell looked relieved, and I expected him next to say that there was nothing to discuss. Instead, he took us all in the opposite direction, and I soon worked out that he was relieved to discover that he was not, after all, making a fuss about nothing. "M. Poirot, I saw Pearl wearing that scarf this morning," he said. "There was no blood on it then. It was entirely yellow. Therefore, since there was none of Matthew's blood still on the premises this morning, how did the scarf turn from yellow to red? In what blood was it immersed?"

"It is indeed the conundrum," said Poirot.

"I wish I could tell you that I am certain Thirza did not . . . contrive something," Counsell said quietly.

"What do you mean, monsieur?"

"Is it not apparent? What if somebody dipped that scarf in blood from somewhere else? The kitchen seems the likely place. I have walked past once or twice and seen Manos carving up large animals . . ."

"Are you suggesting that, if this happened, your fiancée was responsible?"

"Not necessarily." Counsell sounded unconvinced. "Though I cannot help but fear—"

"That it was she who killed Monsieur Fair," Poirot finished his sentence for him. No correction followed.

"She loved him," said Counsell. "I know that for sure. From the moment we got here, she was . . . different. Changed. It was unmistakable, the sudden new energy inside her. She was full of passion and . . . well, I knew I wasn't the one who had inspired it. But she could not have Matthew because at first he was going to marry Rhoda, and then he fell for Pearl.

Then when Pearl tired of him, he turned his attention back to Rhoda again. Thirza said several times, 'Of course Rhoda will agree to marry him. She claims she will stand firm, but it's impossible. He is her entire world; I have never seen such an all-consuming obsession. Mark my words, Manos will be planning their wedding feast before too long.'"

"I see," said Poirot. "You think she found the prospect of Monsieur Fair and Mademoiselle Rhoda marrying too much to bear, and killed him to prevent it?"

"I don't know." Counsell looked haunted. "I do not wish to have any of these suspicions in my head, but the thing is, I overheard a conversation between Thirza and Olive Haslop some while ago, and of course I might have misunderstood it, but . . . I'm afraid a small part of me has always wondered whether Thirza . . ."

He seemed to make up his mind to say it. "Whether she might have killed my sister. Marie."

"Tell me about this overheard conversation," Poirot said briskly. "When did it take place? What did you hear your fiancée and Olive Haslop say to each other?"

"It was . . . perhaps three weeks ago?" said Counsell. "I am afraid I cannot recall. Olive was accusing Thirza of having done something unforgivable, but it did not sound as if she meant it or was angry. It sounded rather jovial. Olive said—or at least I thought I heard her say—'That cannot be true, and really, you must stop pretending it is, Thirza. It would be quite evil to mislead people about something . . . well, so life-endangering for all concerned. And, since I do not believe you are evil . . .' Then Thirza interrupted and said, 'I am not lying. I swear to you, Olive, on my honor. It is quite true.

"'You had better not be lying about something as heinous as murder,' Olive replied, sounding a little more serious. I was not meant to have overheard, and my initial plan was to proceed as if I hadn't, but my curiosity got the better of me, I'm afraid. And since I had not eavesdropped deliberately—"

"You asked Mademoiselle Thirza to explain?" said Poirot.

"I did, yes," Counsell said. "Some days later—and she pretended to have no memory of any such conversation. I assumed I must have got the wrong end of the stick somehow and forgot all about it. Naturally, the dreadful events of the last few days have raked it up again in my memory, so I decided to ask Olive about it, which I have just now done."

"And?" I said.

"She too denied any such conversation had ever taken place."

"Which makes you even more suspicious," said Poirot.

"Yes, yes. I see."

"The strangest thing of all, and I remember thinking it at the time, was that Olive was not suggesting that murder was the primary danger. It was the danger of *believing* that she was warning against. The way she said it . . ." Charles looked bewildered. "I had the distinct impression that she thought someone believing something was the life-endangering threat."

CHAPTER 29

Olive Opines Again

Olive Haslop, summoned by Poirot to the music room, arrived carrying a plate with something long and rectangular on it, as well as a small fork. "You have not yet sampled Manos's wonderful Galaktoboureko, Monsieur Poirot. It is high time you did. Please do not tell me you have an aversion to custard in puddings."

"Thank you—but I must solve two murders before I think about entertaining my stomach." Reluctantly, Poirot smiled. "You have ensured, at least, that I will never forget you, mademoiselle. The name of Olive Haslop will lodge forever in the mind of Hercule Poirot. No one has ever brought for me a delicious pastry to an interrogation until now."

"Interrogation?" The elder Miss Haslop looked concerned. "Goodness me, that sounds uninviting."

"Deliberately so." Poirot had reverted to his original sternness. "Catchpool and I have just spoken to Thirza Davis, about a conversation she either did or did not have with you that was either overheard, or not, by her fiancé Charles Counsell."

"That sounds complicated, if not impossible," Olive replied.

"According to Mademoiselle Thirza, this exchange between the two of you never occurred."

She was not the only one suffering from memory problems, I thought drily; I must have been too, for I had no memory of this alleged interview Poirot and I had conducted with Thirza Davis. It was pure invention on his part. Upon Charles Counsell's departure, Poirot had immediately sent me off in search of Olive, whom I had found easily and within minutes. Neither of us had spoken to Thirza in between.

It is a habit of mine to try to learn from Poirot whenever I can, so naturally I was curious about this tactic he had chosen to employ. To my mind, it would have made more sense to say something like, "Thirza Davis has already told us everything," but of course I trusted my brilliant Belgian friend's judgment more than my own.

"I used the word 'interrogation' to remind you, mademoiselle, of the gravity of our situation. Two murders remain unsolved. It is imperative that I am told only the truth. *Eh bien*, you have observed that Hercule Poirot, he enjoys *les délicieuses gourmandises*, and you bring them to sweeten things in your favor—*n'est-ce pas*? You think you can tell me lies and I will not notice, if my tastebuds are dancing in delight?"

"I will tell the truth," Olive said simply. "I find that it's the truth that generally needs sweetening, don't you? Lies are the sugar we pour on top of reality to improve it." After a short pause, she went on, "I think I know which conversation you mean—Thirza told me Charles had asked her about it."

"It happened, then?" said Poirot.

"Yes, but before Matthew was killed," Olive said. "Weeks before. Our discussion was not about that."

"Then what, mademoiselle?"

"Thirza was talking about the unsolved murder of her sister-in-law, Marie Doxford. For some reason—I don't quite know why—each of Charles and Thirza suspected the other of killing Marie, for a time at least. He suspected her after she told him about our community here at Liakada. Suddenly, immediately after Marie's death, she was enthusing about a place where all sins and sinners are instantly forgiven and made welcome. And she suspected him because in her eyes he was so obviously the main victim of Marie's lies and betrayals."

Olive nodded. "What Charles heard was Thirza describing her suspicions to me. Luckily, he didn't hear his name mentioned or seem to realize it was about him. And I told her: 'Charles is a good and decent man, the very last person who would kill in cold blood.' What I meant, when I made the remark Charles overheard about beliefs being life-endangering, was that Thirza needed to be more careful. There she was, sprinkling hints around all over the place that she suspected Charles of murder—an *unsolved* murder, for which, in theory, he might still hang . . . Well, I told her it was irresponsible. Someone might have believed her, after all."

"But Scotland Yard had satisfied themselves that Monsieur Counsell could not have committed the crime," said Poirot.

Olive shot him a regretful look. "You evidently trust the justice system to get it right. Occasionally, mistakes are made and blameless men hanged. What if the police changed their minds after learning that Charles was suspected by his own fiancée?"

Poirot nodded. "Thank you for your cooperation, mademoiselle. And your honesty."

"You will not blame Thirza, I hope, for pretending our conversation never happened?" Olive's brow furrowed. "She might have been acting on my advice. You know: not wanting to

The Last Death of the Year

express her suspicion of Charles to you or Inspector Catchpool in case that led to the very disaster I had warned her about."

"I see," Poirot murmured. "Thank you. That is all, for now."

"I *do* feel you have now done enough interrogating to have earned your dessert, Monsieur Poirot," said Olive. "I shall leave you in peace. Oh, there is one more thing I wanted to say . . ." She looked at me. "You asked me if Thirza was in love with Matthew. It made me think about the flirtatious way she behaved toward him on New Year's Eve. It was odd—almost as if she were . . . well, trying to imitate Pearl. I know it sounds strange, and I cannot think why she would, but I had never seen her treat Matthew in that way before, purring and simpering over him like that. Those were Pearl behaviors, not Thirza behaviors. Thirza is an intelligent, serious person. She would behave with more dignity, more subtlety, even if madly in love."

"What if she was madly in hate?" I asked, not knowing quite what I meant. It was something related to the possibility that Thirza-in-hate might, for a strategic reason, mimic Pearl-in-love. The thought was too vague and woolly, so I abandoned it.

"What if you never find your answers?" Olive asked this as if she felt sorry for Poirot and me. "It is a worry I have had from the start."

"Poirot always gets to the correct solution," I told her.

"I'm sure that's true in normal circumstances," she said. "The Spitty is abnormal, however. Most of our group—even Rhoda, perhaps her most of all—will be determined to stop you from getting to the truth, good disciples that we all are. Nash teaches that any system that punishes and kills is the opposite of justice. Do you not see?"

"You mean that, at The House of Perpetual Welcome, everyone has been brainwashed to believe that *protecting* a murderer might be a more virtuous course of action than helping us to catch him?" I said.

"Precisely that," Olive said in a tone of weary resignation.

CHAPTER 30

The Capital F Puzzle

Once Olive had left us alone and Poirot had ceased rhapsodizing about the divine pastry concoction she had brought him, I suggested he and I might leave the grounds of The Spitty and go somewhere far away for an hour or two—or at least, as far as this little island would allow.

"Could we persuade Rasmus to take us to the *Plateía* in Lamperos Town?" I said, feeling the need to be in a busier place full of people whose minds were occupied by things like fish and washing and the weather and their families' ailments and who were not trying to invent a new religion with a view to imposing it on the whole of humanity. "Or maybe we could go and take a look at poor old James Gresham-Graham's grave. It would be a shame not to see it while we are here."

"I am pleased to escort you to the town by boat," said a deep voice. Poirot and I turned and found Inspector Kombothekra smiling at us through the room's open window. "I have made a discovery that I must tell you about at once," he said. "May I enter, gentlemen?"

"We will meet you outside," I said.

"Yes, let us go to the town," said Poirot. "I believe there might be a telegram awaiting me there, sent from the mainland.

"This telegram, Catchpool..." Poirot said as we went out onto the terrace. "It will provide the useful confirmation of some of what I already know, which is everything. All the answers. You too must be close to working it out, eh?"

"As close as Liakada Bay is to... my home in London," I told him.

"Ah, London," he said, sounding sharp and portentous all of a sudden. "A most important city. *The most* important, of all the world's cities."

"I wouldn't expect you to say that. What about Brussels?"

"*Non, non, non,*" he said.

"I see." This was a turnup for the books indeed; I had heard him say many times before that Brussels was more advanced and impressive in many ways. Still, he did not seem to want to elaborate, so I said, "What I meant to say is that I haven't the slightest idea who killed either Matthew Fair or Pearl St. Germain."

"Ah," he said noncommittally. "And what I meant was: you do not think enough about the city of London. Think of it a little more, and you might soon find yourself on the way to untangling what looks like a complicated mess but is in fact very simple."

"No, I won't," I was happy to admit. "We both know by now, Poirot: my lot in life is to remain in the dark until you choose to enlighten me."

My friend chortled into his famous moustaches, as Inspector Kombothekra marched toward us, arms open. "We go now," he said. "Rasmus will make the boat ready. When we get to town, I show you this. Not until then." He was holding a piece of paper, which I recognized at once.

"That's one of the letters, isn't it?" I said. "From the Pearl and Austin correspondence, planning the murder of Matthew. I recognize her handwriting."

"Ah," said Poirot. "Very distinctive handwriting it is too. Indeed." What the devil was he hinting at?

"Not here." Kombothekra frowned as he moved the paper out of Poirot's reach. "It would not be safe."

A few minutes later we were clambering onto Rasmus's little boat, and the inspector struck up a one-sided conversation with the silent oarsman on the subject of weather conditions.

Poirot turned to me and said quietly, "Tell me something, Catchpool—when did you first see the handwriting of Mademoiselle Pearl?"

"You're talking about the New Year's resolution murder poem, aren't you?" I said. "Do you think Pearl wrote it?"

"Here is a puzzle for you: on New Year's Eve, after you read out the threatening poem, Mademoiselle Thirza said something about Mademoiselle Pearl's handwriting, did she not?"

"Yes. She said that the bottoms of Pearl's capital letter *F*'s were like a kite strings blown sideways by the wind or some such. Wait, I see what you're driving at!" Excitement coursed through me. "There were no sideways-leaning capital *F*'s in the letters Pearl wrote to Austin."

"Correct," said Poirot. "The downward lines of her *F*'s are all perfectly straight. Why, do you think, would Thirza Davis lie about the handwriting of Pearl St. Germain?"

He watched me expectantly for a few seconds. When I said nothing, he sighed. "You do not yet understand. Never mind. *Poirot, il comprend tout!* Well, perhaps not quite all," he quickly amended. "I do not, for instance, know why Inspector

Kombothekra has picked out one letter from the collection as being more significant than all the rest. Do you have any theories about why it might be, Catchpool?"

"Not a one," I said. "But we are nearly at Lamperos Town, so with any luck we will soon find out."

CHAPTER 31

A Trilogy of Murders

Inspector Kombothekra proved to be as good as his word, and Poirot and I did indeed find out, without undue delay, why he believed this one letter to be so important. We had been incorrect in one of our assumptions, however. The writing was Pearl's, but the addressee was not Austin Lanyon. The first three words of the letter were "Dearest beloved Edward . . ."

Which is to say: Pearl had written the wretched thing to me, and the date and time in the page's top right-hand corner made clear that she had done so between twenty minutes and an hour before she fell to her death, immediately after she spoke to Poirot and was told by him that I did not and never would trust her.

After writing it . . . well, in the letter, Pearl explained why she did not push it under my bedroom door but instead deliberately mixed it up with her and Austin's correspondence in the hope that I would not find it any time soon. Her explanation enraged me—as did the fact that she had written it at all; it was quite the most infuriating communication I had ever received, and, though the time is soon coming when I shall have to tell you all about it, believe me when I say that I would far rather pretend it had never existed in the first place—which was exactly what I did for the next three days. That was how much time elapsed before anything else happened at The Spitty apart from the ordinary daily routine, or at least as ordinary as it could be given that two murders had occurred.

Twice during that seventy-two-hour period, Poirot left Liakada Bay by boat and was absent for most of the day. He refused to let me go with him. Then, finally, toward the end of the third day, he asked me to round up all of The Spitty's residents and persuade them to assemble on the dining terrace.

Soon everyone was outside, seated around the long, outdoor table. The fires had been lit in the stone basins to keep the chill in the air at bay, and Manos had brought out the same pile of colorful blankets that I recognized from New Year's Eve for us to wrap around ourselves. "M. Poirot forbids me to cook the proper feast tonight," he told me sorrowfully as he placed a large plate of pastries down on the table. "This small snack is all he will allow. He says the seriousness of what he has to say will take away the appetite from everybody, but Manos thinks not true! You will eat my *Spanakopita* and *Kotopita*, Mr. Catchpool, yes? Even if nobody else does?"

I assured him I would, but he still looked dejected. I felt suddenly ravenous, but did not feel I could reach for a pastry concoction if no one else did, and the others all seemed to be focused entirely on Poirot as he stalked up and down at a steady pace, preparing to speak.

Charles and Thirza sat at opposite ends of the table from one another. Austin and Nash sat side by side opposite Thirza, both looking like condemned men awaiting further sorry tidings. For once, Austin seemed to have no interest in asserting his authority or putting on any kind of show. On his left sat Belty Ricks, who kept looking at him out of the corner of her eye. He appeared not to notice.

Olive and Rhoda were opposite Charles Counsell, their

arms linked. Rhoda looked pale, her face lined with worry. Every few seconds, Olive whispered something in her ear and patted her hand, as if to calm her, though Rhoda looked, if anything, too calm—almost as if she had given up on life altogether. Charles kept shaking his head as if trying and failing to work something out.

Also with us were Inspector Kombothekra, who looked excited—like a man who had just arrived at the theatre in anticipation of an unforgettable show, and Yannis and Irida Grafas, who looked wary and a little bored respectively.

"Thank you all for responding to my invitation," said Poirot, "and for coming here to listen to what I have to tell you."

"I thought it was an order, not an invitation," Thirza said.

"It will be over soon enough, mademoiselle. For your sake, I shall proceed with efficiency. Let me start by saying that we have here the most unusual situation. Two murders at The Spitty and not one killer, not even two killers. Messieurs et mesdames, there are three murderers sitting here now, on this terrace."

"Three?" Nash repeated, and he forgot to close his mouth afterwards.

"Is that all? A mere three," Belty drawled. She looked around to see if anyone was going to laugh at her joke. No one did.

"Do you mean that . . . one of the murders was committed by two people?" said Olive.

"*Non*," said Poirot. "Matthew Fair and Pearl St. Germain were killed by two different people. And the third murderer here today is the one who killed Marie Doxford, the sister of Charles Counsell."

"What? How can that . . . ?" Austin broke off. He looked at Thirza in disgust. "That must be you! Charles is too soft for violence, but you—"

"You know nothing about me," Thirza told him. "Or about Charles."

"I am not soft," Charles almost growled at Austin, as if trying to prove it. "M. Poirot, please explain at once. You claim to know who killed my sister, and you . . . you say that person is one of *us*? That cannot be. It was not me or Thirza, and nobody else here knew Marie."

"All of that is true, yes," Poirot said. "Your sister's killer decided to murder her before the two of them had met. Their first meeting was the occasion on which the crime was committed."

"You are speaking in riddles, man!" Charles covered his face with his hand.

"It must appear so, yes," Poirot agreed. "On the face of the matter, there seems to be much complexity. At first, I could not see a way to unravel the many tangled threads—not until I decided to concentrate on the large number of contradictions involved. *Eh bien,* I compiled for myself the list and set myself the task of working out what each one meant.

"The first contradiction was this: murderers do not like to get caught. No, they do not like it at all! This I know. Why, then, would the killer of Matthew Fair announce in advance the crime he or she planned to commit? These two details seem to contradict each other, do they not?" Poirot looked from face to face as he spoke. "Our killer wished to kill, and, we must assume, to get away with it . . . yet also issued this clear warning.

"Contradiction number two . . ." he went on. "Mademoiselle Thirza described in a particular way the capital letter *F* of Mademoiselle Pearl's handwriting: like the kite with the string going to the left. Yet this is not true. There was nothing remarkable about the upper case *F*'s of Mademoiselle Pearl. And contradiction number three, also relating to Mademoiselle Thirza..."

"I do so love to be the center of attention," Thirza said coldly.

Poirot came to a stop in front of her. He said, "Your fiancé, Mr. Counsell, told me you fell in love with Matthew Fair as soon as you met him. Olive Haslop, however, says this was not so and that you were not enamored of him at all."

"I am not responsible for what people say about me," said Thirza. "Of course I wasn't sweet on Matthew. You must have me confused with Rhoda. Or Nash," she muttered under her breath; but I'm sure I was not the only person who heard it.

"Contradiction number four," Poirot proceeded through his list. "The disagreement about how many sets of footsteps were heard at around half past one, the night Matthew Fair was murdered. Did he leave The Spitty alone, as claimed by Thirza Davis, or is Olive Haslop right that he had someone with him?"

"You really have taken against me, haven't you, Monsieur Poirot?" said Thirza. "Your biased way of presenting things is quite something. I merely make *claims*, whereas Olive is *right*—no, you did not say that, and yes, I am twisting your words—but you are clever enough to anticipate the effect created by positioning this particular word close to that particular name."

"How well you choose *your* words," Poirot told her.

"What is that supposed to mean?" she said impatiently.

"Only that you have just demonstrated the ability to communicate clearly and directly. Yet when Austin asked you to help him commit a particular crime soon after you arrived here... when he asked you to help him kill Matthew Fair..."

"What?" Rhoda gasped. "Oh, no. Please, that cannot be true, Monsieur Poirot. Austin, it's not true, is it? It *can't* be!"

"Austin?" Olive looked as shocked as her sister. "You and Matthew were so fond of each other. At least, I thought—"

"Yes, we were, and that's the truth—the only truth that matters." Austin was staring at Poirot in a way that suggested he might have been contemplating knocking him to the ground. I watched as those angry American fists clenched and unclenched, feeling my muscles tense; was I going to have to rescue my Belgian friend from a physical assault? I sincerely hoped not.

"I had no intention of killing Matthew, Rhoda, I swear it," said Austin. "Poirot is referring to a silly game."

"The test, yes," said Poirot. "And when you subjected Mademoiselle Thirza to this test, her response was unclear, was it not? She did not say, for instance, 'No, I will not help you to murder anybody. I find the idea abhorrent, and I shall do whatever it takes to stop you.' Did she say any of those things?"

"I've told you already," said Austin. "She dealt with me more skillfully and subtly, inviting me to consider that I was seeking to make her my accomplice and . . . compel her to share my guilt. She said that she couldn't believe I wished to harm her, yet clearly I meant to involve her in a bond between guilty conspirators."

"*Oui, oui*," said Poirot. "You also described her as addressing you in the voice of 'a furious, offended angel' as she spoke, *n'est-ce pas*? No, wait, I remember now: you said 'Her scorching eyes were drilling into my sorry excuse for a soul.'"

"That's right," said Austin. "How is this relevant to anything?"

"You believed Mademoiselle Thirza was trying to make you feel ashamed?" Poirot asked him. "That when she stared at you in her piercing way thereafter, she meant you to feel threatened?"

"She certainly did," said Austin.

"Non, monsieur. In fact, she did not. But I shall return

to this subject later. First, I must return to my list of contradictions, which is not yet complete. Here is yet another one. Again, it involves you, Mademoiselle Thirza." Poirot glared at her. "And Mademoiselle Belty too—how could she have been in the sitting room playing gin rummy with you on the day Pearl was killed, and not once leaving the room, at the same time as talking on the staircase with Pearl St. Germain?"

"That's been explained already," said Belty. "Thirza and I made a mistake. We both forgot that I left the room. Then, when it was pointed out, we remembered."

Poirot gave a small shake of his head and said to her, "How fascinating that on the day of Mademoiselle Pearl's murder, you and Mademoiselle Thirza decide to spend hours playing a game of cards together, when I had not seen the two of you exchange so much as a word before then. I had even seen Mademoiselle Thirza avoid you once or twice, in a way that seemed undeniably *un*friendly."

I nodded, for I had too.

"Yet all of a sudden, you spend hours playing a card game together?" said Poirot. "This sudden change in the relationship between the two of you felt like an . . . implausible contradiction. So, which was it, I asked myself: were you studiously pretending *not* to be friends before, or pretending to *be* friends once Pearl was dead and you both needed an alibi? It could not be both. Interestingly, both of those possibilities are consistent with one of you giving the alibi to the other."

"Okay, I'll admit it," said Belty. "The gin rummy story was made up. Thirza and I aren't friends but we're friendly enough. And neither of us killed Pearl, and we didn't want to get blamed for it, so . . . we teamed up."

"You silly fool, Belty," Thirza snapped. "He will now use this against us, you watch."

"No, he won't," said Belty calmly. "He understands, don't

you, Monsieur Poirot? We were both on our own when Pearl was killed, with no one to vouch for our innocence. So, we decided to help each other out. Think of it as the innocent coming to the rescue of the innocent."

"Friendly enough," said Poirot. "That is how you describe your relationship, yes? Friendly enough for two people who met here at Liakada Bay for the first time, you mean? No other connection between you, before then?"

"That's right," said Belty.

"No, it is a lie," Poirot said simply. "There *was* a connection prior to you both coming here—yet at first I could not put my finger on what it was, or why I was so sure . . . until I remembered London!"

Naturally, my ears pricked up. This—whatever Poirot was about to tell us—was the reason he had encouraged me to think of my home city. Still, I could not anticipate what was coming.

"Since I arrived here on Lamperos, I have heard many of you talk about where you are from in England, or America," he said. "Places I have not heard of before—Appleby in Westmoreland—that is where Monsieur Fair came from, is it not? And Oxford and Dorset—these were both home to Olive and Rhoda Haslop. You, Mademoiselle Belty, have the American accent, like Austin Lanyon. It is therefore all too easy to think of you as coming from America, as you must have at one time . . . but your home in England, before you came here, was London. At dinner on New Year's Eve, both you and Monsieur Charles Counsell mentioned famous London landmarks. You said you regularly went to the Savoy Hotel, and Monsieur Counsell indicated that his home was close to the now demolished Hotel Cecil."

Poirot approached Belty with an accusatory look in his eyes. "Is it not the case that the Hotels Savoy and Cecil were extremely close neighbors, side by side, until the Cecil was pulled down? And if Charles Counsell and Belty Ricks both lived near these establishments, was it possible, I asked myself, that they knew one another in London, before coming here? And that perhaps Belty Ricks was known also to Thirza Davis?"

I was staring at Poirot with my mouth open at this stage in the proceedings. *Marie Doxford*, I thought. Could Belty have known Charles's sister as well as Charles?

"Once I asked the right questions, with the help of my connections in London, it all started to fit together," said Poirot. "I discovered, when I went to the mainland yesterday and telephoned to Scotland Yard, that Thirza Davis's alibi for the murder of Marie Doxford was provided by several people—among them was a Miss Betlinde Ricks."

Charles Counsell pushed his chair back from the table and stood up. He stared coldly at his fiancée. "You killed Marie, and you had the nerve to pretend you thought I had done it?"

"No, monsieur. Sit down," said Poirot. "Mademoiselle Thirza did not kill your sister. Marie Doxford was murdered by Betlinde Ricks."

"B-Belty?" Charles stammered.

"*Oui*. In giving Mademoiselle Thirza the alibi, she gave herself one too. You all know, I am sure, that when Mademoiselle Belty arrived here, she admitted she had done something terrible—something she was unwilling to tell to anybody. She it was who recommended The Spitty to Thirza, once the two of them became friends. Tell me, ladies, when was that? How did the two of you meet, and realize you had in common the loathing of Marie Doxford?"

Neither woman spoke.

"*Why* did Belty kill Charles's sister?" Olive asked. I wanted to know this too.

"Ricks is her maiden name," Poirot said. "Now, once more, it is the name by which she is known, but there was a different name in between, was there not, mademoiselle?" Poirot was staring at Belty. "You were married as a young woman, to a man who left you for Marie Doxford, after being persuaded by her that he would be happier with her than with you. I am told by my friends in London that he ended up considerably more *un*happy and regretted his decision."

"He sure did," Belty said quietly. "That woman was poison."

"And also pois*oned*," Poirot emphasized the last syllable. "By you, using strychnine. Then, while dying an agonizing death, chopped into pieces with an axe. Also by you."

"Heavens above." Olive winced.

"Will you admit it, or will you lie and hinder us in our attempts to unearth the truth?" Poirot challenged Belty.

Slowly, she started to nod. "Yes, I killed Marie. I was quite wild with rage, and evil had got into me, under my skin—a yearning for retribution. I know what I did was an offence against both God and mankind, and I am willing to face whatever justice has in store for me. I have been forgiven unconditionally by these Very Good Friends I have had the pleasure of knowing since I came to Lamperos. Their welcome was my salvation. My soul is loved and free, no matter what the law does with me."

"You *fool*, Belty!" Thirza said in a shaky voice. "Without your confession, he would have had no proof at all. Monsieur Poirot, if ever a creature deserved to be poisoned—"

"I shall also answer your question about how Thirza and I first became acquainted," Belty told Poirot. "I was following Marie one day—I was in the habit of following her, waiting and hoping for her to trip and break her neck, or be crushed to death by an enormous coal lorry. Then one day I was about fifty yards behind her and a very angry woman marched up to her and gave her the most vituperative scolding I had ever heard in my life."

"Thirza," I said.

"Thirza," confirmed Belty. "Well, I just had to stop following Marie and run after this impressive lady who had said everything I'd been thinking for so long about Marie—that she was a monster and a liar and deserved nothing but strife forever after what she'd done. When I found out what she'd done to Thirza and Charles . . . well!" Belty aimed a knowing look at Poirot.

"You decided she did not deserve to live too much longer," he said quietly.

"I acted entirely alone," Belty answered the very question that was in my mind. "I only told Thirza once the deed was done."

"And you . . . you said nothing to the police?" Charles rounded on his fiancée. "You furnished this . . . this *creature* with an alibi?"

"It is my fault that these terrible things are happening," murmured Nash. "Everything is my fault. There are . . . Charles, there are terrible people here."

"Don't say I didn't warn you, buddy," Austin muttered.

"No one should listen to me about anything ever again," Nash announced. "I have been the most reprehensible idiot."

"I could not have put it better myself," said Thirza.

"You are a wise man, Nash," said Belty. "You must not lose faith. Do not forget the Trilogy of Forgivings."

"What's that?" I asked.

"It is one of the greatest gifts and lessons," said Rhoda fervently. "It's the epitome of the all-forgiving ideal. First you forgive the other person, then you forgive yourself . . . and what you always find is that once you have completed those two stages successfully, then everyone forgives you. It's how it always works, once the spirit is properly attuned."

"I don't know if I would ever have succeeded in forgiving poor, dead Marie if I had not killed her," Belty leaned over and said to me in a confiding tone. "It sounds dreadfully callous, I know, but what I did to her . . . well, it kinda set me free. Put a stop to the anger and the hate then and there."

"Ah yes!" Poirot sounded excited. His eyes shone a vivid, bright green. "Yes, this is the theory, is it not? Your theory, which is also espoused and promoted by Thirza Davis: that killing your enemy, or learning of his gruesome demise, helps you to forgive—because how can one refuse mercy when one's enemy has suffered worse agonies than those they inflicted? The idea that the person has got away with it is completely removed. Only pity can remain; you hate them no longer. Remember, Catchpool: were we not told that Mademoiselle Thirza, while unable to forgive her and Charles Counsell's other relatives, was easily able to forgive Marie Doxford? And why was that so? Because Marie Doxford had died a horrible, painful, terrifying death. Her own suffering was, in the final calculation, greater than the pain she had caused to Thirza Davis."

"Exactly that," said Belty.

"This theory is a dangerous one indeed," Poirot said quietly. "Indeed, if it had never been theorized into existence or put into words, Pearl St. Germain would still be alive."

CHAPTER 32

The Third Murderer

"It was only by accident that you and Mademoiselle Thirza discovered this theory was true," Poirot told Belty. "Only once you had . . . violently removed from both your lives this enemy that the two of you shared. Then you found out about the community Nash had set up here on Lamperos, and you told Thirza Davis about it. She, in turn, persuaded Monsieur Counsell to come here with you . . ."

"It seemed like a sensible place to go," said Thirza. "When one has recently helped to cover up a murder, one tends to feel that normal life cannot and should not simply continue as if nothing has happened."

"Naturally, the two of you took the precaution of pretending not to know each other once you were both here," Poirot said.

Belty nodded.

"I suppose we could have come clean," Thirza said as if it had only just occurred to her. "This place would have held neither our subterfuge nor our criminal activity against us. Not that we planned to tell anyone the details of our . . . various misdeeds," she added. "But we could have, and we'd have been welcomed every bit as heartily, or so the propaganda goes. That's the whole point of The Spitty, isn't it, Nash?"

"I am coming round to the opinion that there is no point at all, to anything," he said in a low voice.

"I wouldn't go that far," advised Thirza. "There is some merit to your teachings—though I cannot utter the word without grimacing, I'm afraid. 'Teachings'—it sounds so dreadfully pompous. I will concede, though, that I was surprised by how wholesome and liberating it felt to find myself able to forgive and pity Marie after hating her and wishing her dead for so long. That is why I decided to come here and give Nash's monomaniacal enterprise a chance."

"That is a most unfair description," Charles admonished her. "Nash, you must not give up on what you have built here. I will help you. It will be all right in the end. We can still make this work."

"Charles is right," said Rhoda, nodding as if she did not know how to stop.

"Hold on just one minute there, folks," said Austin. "We haven't yet been told who the other two murderers are. Has everyone forgotten about that?"

"I have not," said Poirot.

Thirza said to Charles, "Austin has a point. Might it not be an idea to find out who else is going to end up with a noose around his or her neck, before we make any exciting new plans to save The House of Vainglorious Delusion? Or whatever it will be called in its next incarnation."

Poirot bowed admiringly in her direction. "Once again, mademoiselle, you demonstrate the facility with language, the precision of expression. Yet you did not use this after Austin Lanyon subjected you to his test and asked to help him commit a murder. Instead, you communicated with your eyes, predominantly—the looks full of meaning, glances laden with suggestions and implications. We shall soon discover why."

"M. Poirot, I am quite sure no one is interested in my precise methods of communication on various different occasions," said Thirza. "It hardly matters."

"On the contrary, it matters most profoundly," Poirot insisted. "What is said, what is meant, what is overheard... yes, it all matters a great deal. Your fiancé, Monsieur Counsell... he overheard a conversation between you and Mademoiselle Olive. You had said something to her, I think, to which she replied that it could not be true—that it would be evil to mislead people about something so life-endangering."

Poirot turned to face Olive. "When I asked you to explain the meaning of all this, mademoiselle, you told me a lie. You said that you and Thirza Davis had been discussing the murder of Marie Doxford. You were trying to persuade her that she ought not to suspect Charles, or to discuss her suspicion of him so openly. Of course, we now know these suspicions of hers were a sham, for she knew Belty Ricks had killed Madame Doxford. Leaving that aside, however... your explanation of this overheard fragment of conversation was not at all plausible. Where, *précisément*, did this danger to life reside? Marie Doxford was already dead, and when I telephoned to Scotland Yard yesterday from the mainland, I was assured that Charles Counsell had been most thoroughly investigated as a suspect in the case of his sister's murder. His alibi was provided by four of his colleagues, all trustworthy men of good standing—and in any case, ladies and gentlemen, I simply did not believe that a woman of Mademoiselle Olive's intellectual capacity would fear that Thirza Davis voicing her suspicions with regard to her husband, on the small island of Lamperos, miles and miles from London..."

Poirot shook his head. "No, I could not credit that Olive Haslop truly saw this as a danger to the life of Monsieur Counsell. Where, then, was this danger to life? And if Olive Haslop had lied to me, did that mean she was the killer?"

Olive had paled considerably, I noticed. She kept eyeing Rhoda anxiously.

"I knew she would kill forty innocent people before she would ever dream of killing Matthew Fair, with whom her sister Rhoda was deeply in love," Poirot went on. "But what if she might try to kill . . . somebody else? That is what I began to wonder . . ."

"Pearl," I said before I could stop myself, sensing we might be about to solve the third murder before we got to the second one—assuming we were treating Marie Doxford as the first, that is.

"Yes, indeed." Poirot clapped his hands together twice. "Mademoiselle Pearl. *Mes amis* . . ." He took a deep breath. "The conversation Charles Counsell overheard between his fiancée and Olive Haslop concerned the philosophical conundrum—or perhaps I should say spiritual more than philosophical—of whether or not killing someone, or knowing they have suffered and died, as in the case of Marie Doxford, helps you to forgive that person. Monsieur Counsell overheard Olive Haslop tell Thirza Davis that it would be profoundly irresponsible of her to pretend this is true if it is not. Because it might tempt a person to commit murder in order to test this theory, *n'est-ce pas*?

"Think about it, ladies and gentlemen: might it not persuade Mademoiselle Olive to try a new experiment? We know how fond she is of the scientific experimentation; it excites her greatly. Now, I expect she had already forgiven Matthew Fair for having broken her little sister's heart, or was well along the way to doing so. She saw how, daily, he strove to repair the damage he had wrought. Pearl St. Germain was a quite different matter, however. Mademoiselle Olive told me herself: she does not believe in Monsieur Nash's principle of unconditional forgiveness. What, then, would be her incentive to forgive the amoral and irresponsible woman who had destroyed her beloved sister's happiness by stealing away the heart of the man Rhoda Haslop loved?"

Poirot shook his head vigorously. "There was no such incentive. Forgiving would have felt impossible—and then we must consider that there was a very good reason to want Pearl St. Germain out of the way. If she were no longer around, the chances of Mademoiselle Rhoda making at last the happy marriage with Matthew Fair were much better, if he were not distracted by the presence of the woman he had once loved more."

"Are you saying that Olive killed Pearl partly to clear the field for Rhoda and Matthew, and partly to test whether what Thirza had told her was true about forgiveness being easy once your target has suffered enough?" I asked.

"No. No, no, no," Rhoda whimpered.

"Olive, my friend, please say this is not true." There were tears in Konstantinos Kombothekra's eyes.

Olive said nothing for a long time. When she spoke, her voice was calm. "It had nothing to do with clearing the field," she said. "Matthew was finished with Pearl. It was all over. No, it was the experiment that got me fired up, the unpredictability of it. I truly had no way of guessing what the result might be. Also, Monsieur Poirot, you will disapprove, I know . . . but there was a great deal of *altruism* involved. I knew the world would be a better place without Pearl in it, you see. Isn't that what we are supposed to be doing here—making the world a better place? When I thought of the suffering so many would be spared if she were to be . . . removed from the equation. And what Thirza insisted upon seemed too good to be true. She was convinced I would forgive Pearl instantly if only she were to die some manner of gruesome death. 'What if she is right?' I thought to myself. And then, 'What if I were to enjoy forgiving Pearl, and forgiving myself for murder, and what if I were to become, after all of it, a heaps better person?' I thought it wildly unlikely . . . yet Thirza seemed pleased as Punch to have forgiven Marie. Called it her 'greatest accomplishment.' Maybe I too could have a new greatest accomplishment! As I speculated about it, I felt as if I might actually be one step closer to salvation. I became curious about what salvation might feel like and wondered if it would be a feeling deep in my soul, or more of an attitude of mind . . . and suddenly, I felt like a young woman again, the way I felt when Professor Yaxley and I conducted our scientific experiments together. The good old days!"

"Olive, please, tell me you didn't do it," Rhoda wept.

"I'm afraid I did, dearest Rhoda." Olive reached over to squeeze her sister's arm.

Inspector Kombothekra groaned as if in physical pain.

"I see." Charles Counsell nodded. "Yes, I see. Goodness me . . ." He looked livelier and more optimistic than I had ever seen him. People really did respond to things in the oddest of ways, I thought. To Poirot, Charles said, "So what I heard Olive tell Thirza, in effect, was: 'Do not pretend this will definitely work unless you are certain. That would be evil, for it would endanger Pearl's life and also mine, if I were to be caught.'"

"*Éxactement*," said Poirot.

"Was it also you the first time someone tried to kill Pearl?" I asked Olive. "When she blamed it on a goat?'

"Yes," said Olive. "I was the goat."

"No!" Rhoda wailed. "You are pretending. I will not believe it." Though she was seated, her body seemed to sway and buckle. Charles Counsell walked over to sit by her side. He took both of her hands in his and said, "Be strong, Rhoda. You are the strongest of all of us. You simply need to recognize that quality in yourself."

"Tell us what happened the day Pearl St. Germain died, mademoiselle," said Poirot to Olive.

She appeared happy to oblige. "I overheard the conversation on the stairs between Belty and Pearl, the one in which they disparaged my physical appearance. That was at twenty minutes before three, and it was really only the briefest of exchanges. Once Belty had gone, I followed Pearl to her room and . . . well, I'm sure I don't need to spell it out." She lowered her eyes. "That was at fifteen minutes to three, exactly as you said, Irida. Very well observed. Oh, and I lied to you, Edward." She looked apologetic as she said, "You didn't know the exact time you had left here to walk to Agios Dionysios beach, so I told you when it was and you accepted it as the truth. In fact, you left quite a bit later than I told you, and just as I was positioning myself to give Pearl a good shove. Which I then did, and I must tell you all, friends, that I was pleased. I *did* feel free—liberated, as Thirza had promised. You were wrong about the forgiveness part, though, Thirza. My hatred for that despicable woman did not shift one inch, and I have not forgiven her, not even a little bit. Still, I don't regret trying, even though it will cost me my life. I am proud to have given this most daring experiment a chance. I just know the professor would be proud of me too."

"Dear God in heaven," Nash murmured.

"Well, quite," Olive said with enthusiasm. "You should be proud of me too, Nash—for trying, even if I failed. If forgiveness is the highest good, as you are always saying, then I must deserve some credit for being willing to try the only thing that might have made a difference when it came to my forgiving Pearl."

"What about Matthew?" Nash's voice was barely a whisper. "Who killed our dear Matthew?"

"Ah, yes, indeed. The final murderer," said Poirot. "Regrettably, I fear that our third killer will not be nearly as cooperative as our first and second have been. Never mind: that careless person imagined they had thought of everything, but they in fact left two of their bloody fingerprints on a piece of their clothing that they subsequently attempted to burn in the stove in Manos's kitchen. How lucky it was that this small piece of cloth escaped the flames."

"Tell us who killed Matthew," Rhoda demanded, in a stronger voice than I had ever heard her use before. "Tell us at once."

"I am afraid to say that Matthew Fair was murdered by Miss Thirza Davis," Poirot said.

CHAPTER 33

A Letter from Pearl

"That does not sound right at all." Charles Counsell frowned. "Why would Thirza kill Matthew? She was in love with him."

"Ha!" was his fiancée's response to that. Ex-fiancée by now, surely.

"It is quite correct," Poirot assured him. "I shall now read aloud, if you will permit, a letter from Pearl that she wrote just before she was killed. She wrote it to Catchpool, but she hid it somewhere where he would not, at first, find it. Here is what she wrote:

Dearest Beloved Edward,

I am sure you know by now that your ever so clever but not very nice French friend, Mr. Poirot, found the entire correspondence between Austin and me, all about Austin's silly plan to kill Matthew—which I am sure he was never entirely serious about, by the way.

That is not the point of this letter, however. I am writing to inform you that, as soon as I learned that the letters Austin and I wrote to each other had turned up (they were left on Mr. Poirot's bed by the thief who stole them from me) I quickly worked out exactly why Matthew was killed and by whom. Plainly, his murderer wished to implicate me and Austin. That is why she wrote that silly verse resolution in poetic form, and in handwriting deliberately distorted to look like mine. She knew when she did that that she would very soon afterwards kill Matthew and then, a short time later, leave Austin's and my letters for Mr. Poirot to find. Of course, this would lead to Austin and me being blamed for Matthew's murder—or so she thought.

I did not kill Matthew, Edward. Neither, incidentally, did Austin. The person who stole the letters killed poor Matthew, and I know exactly why she did it. (Here is a clue as to her identity: tell Mr. Poirot not to forget the blue hair ribbon in which the letters were contained when he found them. I told him it was mine, but that was a lie. I would have told him the truth, except I fancied keeping what I knew to myself for the time being.)

Edward, if you had only trusted me, I would have rushed to tell you everything, as soon as I had worked it out: the whole truth, every single bit of it. But Mr. Poirot said that you do not trust me at all, even though you sort of promised to.

Well, I wanted to know if you did or didn't before I told you anything more, so I laid a little trap for you: I found rather a lot of blood in Manos's kitchen, left over from a quite revolting looking piece of meat that he had carved up while preparing a dinner. I dipped two of my personal possessions in that blood, though it sickened me to do it—a pearl earring and my lovely yellow scarf. Then I hid both somewhere I knew they would soon be found. And now I cannot wait to find out if you will bombard me with accusations all over again once they are discovered, and call me a cold-hearted killer, or whether you will come to me and say, "Darling Pearl, I know you are no murderer. I trust you, as I vowed I would. Now, who can it be that is trying to implicate you in this dreadful crime?"

Edward, if you can only pass this test, I have so much that I am desperate to tell you and discuss with you. Poor Matthew's death and what led to it is a fascinating story, really—one that is about love from start to finish, which makes it by far my favorite kind of story. But there is also some detective work required, and some unexpected turns in it, too. I could not at first work out why someone determined to see me blamed and hanged for murder should attempt to speak up on my behalf and protect me from blame when they do not care for me at all. Now, though, it makes perfect sense—and I worked it out all on my own. I hope you will be proud of me, and maybe consider that you have underestimated how sharp a mind I possess.

When I have finished writing this, I shall bury it deep inside Mr. Poirot's stash of letters between me and Austin. I assume those are in his room and won't be too hard to find. It's lucky none of the doors at The Spitty are lockable.

I hope this particular letter will not be found or read by you for at least a few days after my scarf and earring turn up. That should provide me with ample opportunity to see how you respond to the discovery of some bloody items that seem to incriminate me.

Please do not let me down, Edward. I am a better person thanks to you, but it is all wasted if you do not recognize my worth.

Yours in love forever,

Pearl

Poirot took a small bow, then returned to his chair.

"How does that letter prove Thirza killed Matthew?" asked Austin.

"She has a blue hair ribbon," said Charles quietly. "Had, I should say. I have not seen her wear it for some time. Now I know why."

"I ought to have known Thirza Davis was the killer of Matthew Fair much sooner than I did," Poirot said. "There was, as I have said, the contradiction between what Olive Haslop said she heard that night—the footsteps of two people—and the alternative account given by Mademoiselle Thirza. Olive Haslop would not have lied to protect the person who killed her sister's beloved, therefore: Thirza Davis must have been the liar. Then, also, there were the two inexplicable behaviors of Miss Davis during the game of the resolutions: one, she prevented Pearl St. Germain from explaining what was the meaning of 'Matthew Time,' in case that might lead to Matthew Fair being protected *after* midnight. Two, she lied about Mademoiselle Pearl's handwriting, saying that it had the capital letter *F* that looked like the kite tail blown by the wind. If Thirza Davis did not murder Matthew Fair, then what explains these strange behaviors?"

"That doesn't make sense." I frowned. "If Thirza killed Matthew, surely she would want to implicate Pearl. Why would she try to make us believe Pearl didn't write the rhyming death threat?"

"An excellent question," said Poirot approvingly. "The answer is, of course, that she knew her handwriting could never be an exact match for Pearl St. Germain's. And if we were to conclude it was a forgery, who would we be least likely to suspect of having done it? Why, naturally, it would be the person who spoke up and said, 'This is not Pearl's writing.'"

"Yes, I see," said Charles Counsell.

"You won't get an apology out of me," Thirza announced, setting off a chorus of shocked exclamations around the table. "I have not one single regret."

"Not even falling for the oldest killer-catching trick there is?" Poirot asked her. "The bloody fingerprints I referred to earlier? I invented them. Thank you, all the same, for your confession."

Thirza gave a haughty shrug. "You still don't know why I killed Matthew, do you? And you never will. I shall never tell anyone my reason."

"Allow me to explain it on your behalf," said Poirot. "You may correct me if I make an error. It was love that made you do it, was it not? Fierce, passionate love that soon turned to burning hatred when it went unrequited. Not love for Matthew Fair, however. No, not him. Neither your love nor your hate was for him."

Thirza's mouth had dropped open. It was sometimes very satisfying, as it was now, to observe the reactions of those who realized, suddenly, that they had underestimated Hercule Poirot.

"You loved somebody else," he told Thirza. "You only aimed your flattery and attention at Monsieur Matthew on New Year's Eve, in order not to come under suspicion of stabbing him to death. This was one of the contradictions on my list: Charles Counsell told me that you had been most clearly in love with Matthew Fair for some time. Yet according to Olive Haslop, you had shown no particular interest in Monsieur Fair. This caused me to wonder . . . what if they both were correct? What if you had indeed been in love for some time, but with a different person at The Spitty? Austin Lanyon, for instance."

Austin snapped to attention, as if someone had jerked his head on a rope.

"When I tested this theory, I immediately deduced what Monsieur Lanyon still does not understand," said Poirot. "The puzzling words you addressed to him after he asked you, as part of his bizarre character test, to help him kill Monsieur Fair . . . that was the coquette-ish *indirect* communication of one who loved him, *n'est-ce pas*, mademoiselle?"

"Damn you to hell, Poirot," Thirza snapped. "I hope you die!"

"You loved me?" Austin asked her. "*You?*"

"She did," Poirot confirmed. "Very much. You did not expect her to, since she came to Lamperos with a fiancé in tow. For many, that would have been a barrier. That is why you believed she was trying to make you feel guilty, when in fact she was sending you a quite different message: she was suggesting to you that, since you could easily have murdered Matthew Fair without her help, you were obviously requesting her assistance in order to 'bond the two of you together in secrecy forever' or whatever it was that she told you. You believed she was horrified that you would try to endanger her soul and moral fiber in this fashion, *mais non*. She was flattered! Overjoyed, even, to be specially selected for this important task, this unique honor. Her manner toward you became suddenly intense, did it not?"

"Yes." Austin frowned. "It did. I thought—"

"You described how she stared at you with such intensity, while sounding like the 'furious angel.' How you misinterpreted this gaze of hers! Her eyes that would not stop following you around the place . . . just as the eyes of Pearl St. Germain followed Catchpool! That is when it became obvious to me: your description of Mademoiselle Thirza's behavior matched *exactly* the comportment of Mademoiselle Pearl in the company of Catchpool here, which I had witnessed with my own eyes. So, how did Thirza Davis feel when she saw Austin Lanyon huddled together and whispering with his new accomplice, Pearl St. Germain—her replacement, as she must have seen it? That was when Mademoiselle Thirza's envy and hatred of you commenced, Monsieur Lanyon."

Poirot looked around at the assembled faces. "Remember, ladies and gentlemen, Thirza Davis did not know that Austin Lanyon's plan to kill Matthew Fair was a fabrication, a pretense. She believed he was serious. He then told her he had changed his mind . . . so imagine her shock when first she sees him having furtive conversations with Mademoiselle Pearl and then, soon afterwards, she finds a bundle of letters the two have written to each other.

"What do these tell her? That Monsieur Lanyon has *replaced* her with Miss St. Germain! She does not know he is now testing the newest arrival at The Spitty. Naturally, she concludes what anyone would: that she was deceived, and the plan to kill Monsieur Fair is still very much alive; it was simply that Monsieur Austin wished to substitute Mademoiselle Pearl for her. There she was, willing to risk everything for him by committing murder, and he had the audacity to choose a different accomplice, one who was younger and perhaps prettier, but a far less substantial person."

Poirot addressed Thirza: "I do not know when your love for Monsieur Lanyon turned to a desire to see him hanged, but it was before this last New Year's Eve, when you wrote the rhyming resolution, hoping it would be mistaken for the creation of Austin and Pearl. That was quite a puzzle at first, until I realized: there had to be a warning of the murder, and one that implicated your two targets. You had to make sure that both Pearl's handwriting and Austin's habit of writing verse were associated in everyone's minds with the threat to Matthew Fair's life, so that when he died, they would be blamed."

"You'd have let them hang me, Thirza?" Austin said. "I don't believe you'd have been able to resist saving me at the last minute."

"Oh, believe it, sweetheart," she said. "Hating you is so much more enjoyable than loving you ever was."

"Why did you lie about seeing Matthew go outside alone, and checking on Charles?" I asked her. "Why not pretend you had been asleep at the relevant time, or corroborate Olive's account? Or, come to think of it, say you had seen Austin and Pearl accompany Matthew outside?"

"That would have been too much," she said. "I did not want to overplay my hand—and frankly, I was certain I had done enough. I was in no doubt Austin and Pearl would hang for it, once I made sure those letters got found. And . . . I wanted to tell as much of the truth as I could, I suppose. The truth was: I wasn't asleep. I had asked Matthew to meet me on the dining terrace at half past one, told him I had something important I needed to discuss with him. He agreed, of course, and promised to mention it to nobody. Matthew loved nothing more than to be obedient, to almost anyone.

"He was, for once, prompt, and appeared at the correct time. The two people's footsteps Oliver heard leaving the house were his and mine."

"Very well," said Poirot. "I believe all is now clear, at last."

"I do greatly regret that Matthew had to die." Thirza, looked around the table. "But you will never persuade me to blame myself for what became of him. I blame you, Austin, and you, Nash, and that little bitch Pearl, who I'm heartily glad is dead!"

"I am not," I said, surprising myself. I had, I realized, forgiven Pearl for all her silly behavior. It seemed so tragic that her life was over at such a young age, and after her having used it so unwisely. A double tragedy.

Goodness me, was it possible Nash was right? I mused, as I felt the distinct easing of an internal burden of resentment. My dislike of Pearl had metamorphosed almost entirely into compassion. I had none at all—not a shred of pity—for Belty Ricks, Olive Haslop or Thirza Davis. It remained to be seen whether that would change once the Greek authorities had done with those three wicked women what would it would, in due course, do.

Epilogue

Was that the end of the story? Not for everybody, thankfully. I am happy (yes, genuinely, however strange their beliefs might be) to be able to report that Charles Counsell married Rhoda Haslop and the two of them now run The House of Perpetual Welcome at Liakada Bay, which has several new recruits, including the former police inspector Konstantinos Kombothekra, now retired from police work.

The Spitty has new, comfortable, modern furniture, I am told, and although, tragically, Matthew Fair's murder was not the last death of the year at The House of Perpetual Welcome—Pearl St. Germain's was—peace and enlightenment have prevailed there ever since.

Apart from Charles and Rhoda Counsell, none of the Very Good Friends are still there at the house. Austin Lanyon returned to America soon after the two murders, and Nash Athanasiou went with him. The two of them have for the past six months been working on a farm owned by Austin's uncle in Moniteau County, Missouri.

I expect that some of you with keen memories are waiting

to hear how, in my opinion, the list of New Year's resolutions that I shared with you at the start of this account could have solved our two Liakada Bay murders, if I had only thought to make a serious study of them. It is very simple: everybody apart from Thirza Davis and Olive Haslop had a resolution to do something concrete and tangible: change a habit, perform a task, eradicate an unhelpful character trait. Both Olive and Thirza, by contrast, wrote down very vague resolutions: "to be open to learning new things and never be closed minded" (that was Olive, thinking about her experiment of killing Pearl in order to see whether doing so inspired forgiveness); "to promote a just and fair world" (that was Thirza, referring to her attempt to get Austin and Pearl hanged for a murder they did not commit. This, in her eyes, was justice, since both of them had offended her and that was all that counted in her moral reckoning.).

I feel duty-bound to tell you that, to this day, Poirot pooh-poohs my claim that the murders were solvable from the list of New Year's resolutions alone. "What about Mademoiselle Belty Ricks?" he caviled. "She had the specific behavior change in her resolution—the getting up early—and she too committed murder."

"Ah, yes," I told him. "But her murder was in the past, already done. She had no need to talk in riddle-like abstract terms about what she *planned* to do—unlike the two killers who had yet to commit their crimes."

"What about your resolution, Catchpool? To live by the sea. Will you do it?"

"Would you still invite me to solve puzzling cases with you if I did?" I asked him.

"*Bien sûr, mon ami.*"

"Well, then. Good." This gave me no excuse not to do it,

which, in turn, filled me with fear. "We shall see what transpires," I said.

"I believe there is now a vacancy for the position of police inspector on one of the small Greek islands," said Poirot, trying to hide his smile. "Now, what is it called? Ah yes, Lamperos! Home of the impossible to catch master criminal, Kefáli Stin Ámmo . . ."

Acknowledgments

I am hugely grateful, as always, to James and Mathew Prichard and the Christie family, all at Agatha Christie Ltd, David Brawn, Millie Kiel and the team at Harper Collins UK, everyone at HarperCollins US, the many international publishers of my Poirot novels, my agent Peter Straus and all at Rogers Coleridge and White.

Thank you to Emily Winslow and Kate Jones for their editorial interventions as always, and to Alex Crompton for his help with the chapter-by-chapter plan. Special thanks to Dan Jones for his help with Greek island landscaping and the invention of fictional Greek Myths!

Thank you to the Skyros Holidays company, whose beautiful house at Atsitsa Bay (equally welcoming but much less murderous) inspired The Spitty. I am also very grateful for the encouragement of friends, family and my lovely Dream Authors!

DON'T MISS THE NATIONAL BESTSELLER

MARPLE: TWELVE NEW MYSTERIES

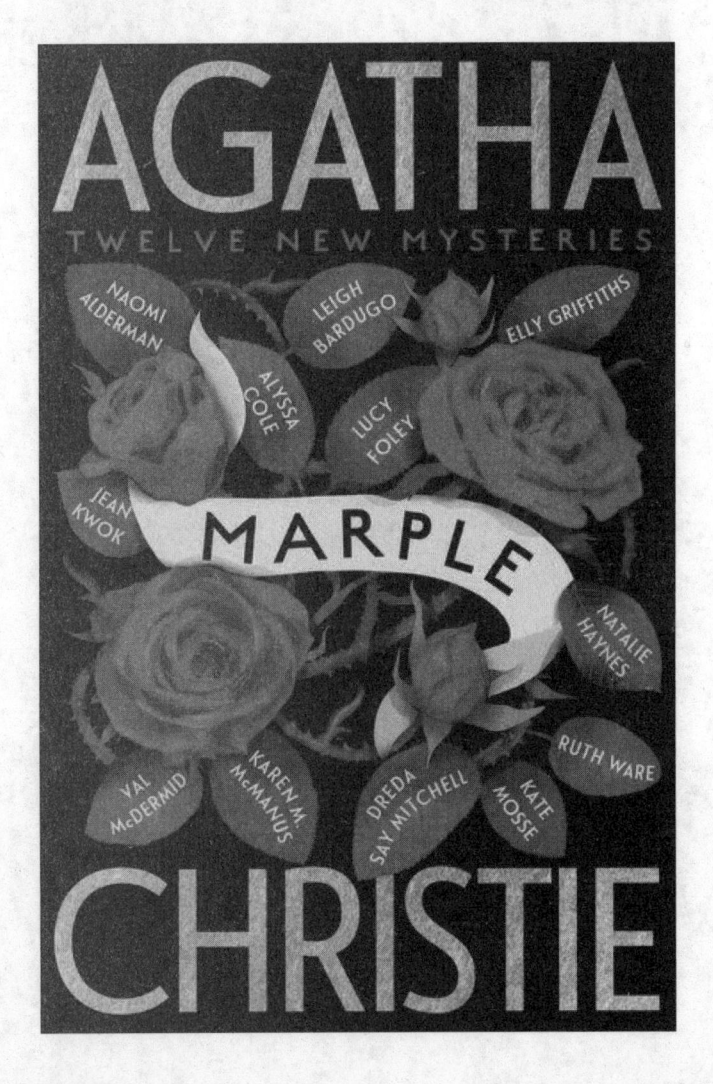

Agatha Christie's legendary sleuth, Jane Marple, returns to solve twelve baffling cases in this all-new collection, penned by a host of acclaimed authors skilled in the fine art of mystery and murder.